THE BRIDGE

CAN A SHARED DESTINY TRAVEL ACROSS TIME?

NIKKI BROADWELL

The Bridge

Nikki Broadwell

ISBN: 978-0-9979941-3-1

Cover by www.stunningbookcovers.com

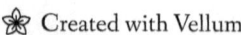 Created with Vellum

OTHER BOOKS BY NIKKI:

Time Gap

A Witch in Time Saves Nine

The moon in Her Eyes

The Last Keeper of the Light

Rosemary for Remembrance

Burning Night

Raven and Hummingbird series

Siobhan's Secret

Dagda's Daughter

Kat's Conundrum

Raven's Runes

~You have to know what is lost in order to find it again~

ONE

Fell, 2468

Fehin loosened his hold on the dragon's neck and slid off, landing with a soft thud on the damp ground. Judging from the dense tropical forest surrounding him the dragon had brought them close to the former village of Fell. The land of Far Isle hadn't changed much in the eight years since Fehin had been gone. Why the dragon had brought him here to this particular spot was a mystery, but Aki was smart and always had reasons for what he did.

He left Aki to forage and moved through the thick underbrush wondering what he might find. But nothing could have prepared him for the sight of his half-brother, Wolf, sitting cross-legged in the middle of a flat rock.

"Hello," Wolf said, his lips rising in his version of a smile.

Fehin had a moment of panic. Wolf was younger and yet twice as big. Dark stubble accentuated his jutting chin and the malevolent expression in his eyes was one Fehin would never share. The only features they had in common were pale skin and black hair, which came from their Scottish heritage on their father's side. The last time he'd seen Wolf was right before his half-brother was stripped of his powers and banished to the Norse world of Svartalfheim, a cold and barren world where dark dwarves worked beneath the ground mining and crafting swords. They were dangerous creatures and wouldn't hesitate to kill a human being. He hadn't thought of Wolf for years, assuming he was dead along with their father and Wolf's mother, Ella. And yet here he was.

Fehin and Wolf shared a sorcerer father, Brandubh, but Ella was a sorceress as well, and because of this Wolf had inherited too much magic—and, unfortunately, a psychopathic nature to go along with it.

"How did you get here?" Fehin asked, forcing himself to step forward.

Wolf waved his hand dismissively. "That stupid Norn should have known I couldn't be contained forever."

Fehin breathed deeply to slow his racing heart before lowering himself onto the rock next to his brother. He deflected the waves of negativity coming from Wolf and then put up a shield of white light. "How'd you know I was coming?"

Wolf looked down and then raked his heavy hair off his forehead, a habit he'd picked up from their father. "It doesn't matter how far apart we are, Fehin, I can always read your thoughts. And by the way, I know all about Thule."

Fehin paled. Thule was secret. No one knew anything about the island he'd conjured except the Norse gods and those who lived there. They'd been living in peace for eight years now. This had to be a bluff and so he decided not to respond.

Several moments went by before Wolf finally admitted, "Well, I know the name, but I don't know where it is."

Fehin closed out any thoughts of Thule. Reading minds was a gift they'd both inherited from their father, and right now

Wolf was probing his. Even the thought of Wolf finding the island made Fehin's blood run cold.

"I need your help."

Wolf's beseeching expression was very out of character and Fehin raised his eyebrows. Was it possible Wolf had escaped his prison without sorcery?

"I want to go to the Otherworld but I can't get there without your boat."

"*Skidbladnir* doesn't belong to me."

"But you can sail her, right?"

Skidbladnir was a magical Viking long ship belonging to Fehin's mother, Gertrude. The boat had originally been a smaller sailboat named *Gypsy,* but Wolf had burned that one to the ground trying to kill Ella and Brandubh who were on board at the time. *Skidbladnir* could travel through time just as *Gypsy* had, but Fehin had never considered sailing her alone. "Why do you want to go to the Otherworld? It's in the past."

"I know *when* it is," Wolf snapped. "I have business there. Are you such a momma's boy that you can't take her on a sail by yourself?"

Fehin didn't rise to the bait even though his cheeks grew hot. "I could, but I won't."

Wolf's narrowed eyes grew dark as he stared at Fehin and a moment later he got up and walked away. Fehin watched him disappear into the forest, and then let out his held breath. Wolf made him more nervous than anyone he'd ever encountered. And why Wolf would want to go to the Otherworld was a complete mystery.

Fehin had heard tales of the mystical Otherworld from his mother. People she knew had pulled the place back from the brink of destruction. It was Fehin's father who had instigated the war to begin with. But then again Fehin wouldn't be on the earth if his mother and Brandubh hadn't met during that terrible time.

Peace had prevailed there ever since. Was something happening that he should know about? With that question an image arrived in his mind: a shimmering sun-drenched meadow full of wildflowers, a wide rushing river lined with rushes and cattails and on the hill behind it, a rustic cottage. A girl stood at the front door, a bright halo of hair surrounding her heart-shaped face, and her wide eyes were focused on him. The thought of Wolf anywhere near her gave him a very bad feeling. Who was she?

TWO

Fell 2468

After Wolf had gone, Fehin wandered aimlessly through the forest. His brother's abrupt appearance had shaken him. Far Isle had gone through a terrible time due to Wolf and his evil. Wolf had challenged all the deities with his insatiable need to be in control and thousands had died at his half-brother's hand. No wonder Loki had ordered his punishment.

When he felt a presence he turned, his gaze meeting the green-gold eyes of the dragon. Aki seemed restless. "Are you trying to tell me it's time to go?" Fehin grabbed hold of the bony protuberance on the dragon's back and pulled himself up. But when the dragon took off it was not in the direction of Thule.

When they landed in the bailey of Loki's castle Fehin wasn't surprised. Aki's parents and sister lived here. His glance toward the entrance to the castle revealed a scowling bigger than life god heading quickly toward him. Meanwhile Aki had disappeared and there was the sound of dragons bellowing in the distance.

"Are you aware that Wolf has escaped?" Loki shouted. It

took him another long stride to reach Fehin and then he was glowering down on him.

Fehin had lived here with this god from the time he was two until nearly seven years old and was not cowed by the bulging eyes and the wiry

red hair that stood away from his head like angry tangled snakes. "I just ran into him in Fell."

Loki let out a sound between a grunt and a roar. "That exile was supposed to be permanent."

"If it makes you feel any better, I don't think he has powers."

"Then how did he get out?"

Loki's voice boomed like a cannon going off. Fehin resisted the impulse to plug his ears. "He didn't tell me. Do you have any idea why he'd want to travel to the Otherworld?"

Loki's wide eyes widened even further. "The Otherworld is four-hundred years in the past!"

"Wolf asked me to sail him there on *Skidbladnir*."

"I trust you said no."

"I told him it isn't my boat."

Loki pushed his massive hands through his hair. "He must expect to regain his powers there. But how he figured that out and what he hopes to accomplish is something for the Norns to decide. I would like to get my hands on whoever let him out."

"Do you want me to go there and speak with my father? He might know."

Loki shook his head. "Too dangerous and Brandubh is probably dead by now."

A pang of sadness moved through Fehin at the thought of his father being no more. Despite his past deeds Brandubh still held a place in his heart. "The Norns are seers?" he asked, trying to put his mind on something else.

"The Norns control the destinies of gods and men, Fehin.

It was, Skuld, one of their own, who meted out his punishment and it is she I must call upon now."

Fehin had a slightly ill feeling as he thought about the past. Far Isle had been free of Wolf for many years and the idea of the terror and killing returning was something he didn't want to contemplate. He and many of the former residents were now safe on Thule but anyone who had come here since would be prey to Wolf's evil if he were to regain his powers. "If his powers can be restored in the Otherworld, will he have them when he comes back here?"

"Not if I can help it." Loki turned away and headed toward the castle, his right hand held up in a cursory wave of farewell. Fehin watched him go, his gaze taking in the dark exterior walls of the enormous castle that housed the god and all his servants and guards as well as a few goddesses now and then. Loki was not one to go without female company for long.

You would never know from the stark exterior the opulence of what lay inside. Somehow the deep gold and brilliant reds of the furnishings against the pale marble floors and walls brought light into a space that should have been dark. Fehin thought of the goddesses who moved freely along those halls dressed in gossamer clothing that barely hid what lay beneath the transparent layers of silk. He was fascinated with them when he lived here and tried hard to hear and understand their whispered conversations. Freyja, the goddess of love and beauty, had taken the place of his mother during those years of exile and when Gertrude reappeared and took him away he remembered feeling sad for a time. But those were the memories of a seven-year-old boy and hardly worth thinking about now.

Fehin turned away and called for Aki in his dragon-master voice and when the dragon appeared he climbed on his back and mentally gave the order to return to Thule. The dragon ran, his huge wings displacing air with a swooshing sound before lifting straight up. As they banked over Fell's beach Fehin caught sight of Wolf standing alone. His half-brother looked up as they flew by and the anger and hostility in his dark eyes gave Fehin a chill. The dragon flew from there out to sea, making a few evasive maneuvers in case Wolf was watching.

Once they reached open water another vision of the mysterious girl came into Fehin's mind and this time it felt like she was calling to him.

"What do you really think Wolf is up to?" Fehin's mother asked as they walked along the trail into the mountains. It was herb-gathering day and the two of them were seeking out the wild yarrow, mountain mint and arnica that grew along the cliffs.

"He didn't say and I couldn't pick up anything when we were together. Mostly I was trying to keep thoughts of Thule out of my mind. If he found this place..."

Gertrude stopped and turned, her dark eyes meeting his. "He won't find it."

Fehin hoped she was right as he scanned across the expanse of palms and tropical fruit trees, the strange pink feathery trees that Fehin made up when he was seven that grew odd-shaped delicious fruits, and the wooden houses nestled beneath them here and there. The sound of children's laughter could be heard echoing in the distance and then the deeper richer lilt of adult voices as they went about their daily business. It was his magic that had created this safe haven. Since the time of the conjuring the island had taken on a life of its own, producing everything they needed for a full and abundant life.

Many of the residents were in their sixties and seventies but had appeared to age backward. It was rare for someone to get sick and when it happened it was nearly always due to a mental process that had gone unchecked. A woman had come down with what at first had been deemed a terrible infection but when she entered the sacred space built for such things and sweated in the heat from the fire she was shown the real reason behind her malaise. She was jealous of another woman in the community and had shut herself off from this person, even hiding her feelings from herself.

It was the way of things here to talk things out, to sweat things out and to keep minds clear through meditation and exercise. If they didn't do so the island manifested whatever they suppressed. Fehin thought back to the spear-wielding, half-naked men who had attacked the village causing mass pandemonium and actually killing a few people before someone realized why it was happening. After setting up weekly meetings to discuss grievances and let go of emotions that would otherwise fester, there had been no more sign of them.

His mother seemed pensive on the way home and when Kafir, his surrogate father, joined them by the fire with a pot of tea, Fehin sensed that something was up.

After passing Fehin a cup, Gertrude glanced briefly at Kafir whose slight nod gave Fehin a distinct prickly feeling along his arms. Whatever was coming had been discussed without him.

"Fehin," Gertrude began, "Kafir and I have been talking about your future. You're sixteen now and this is the only place you've ever lived."

"I lived with Loki for a few years."

"Yes, that's true, but it hardly qualifies. Kafir and I think you need some time away from Thule, away from Far Isle and also away from Loki. It's time for you to be with people your own age." She waved her hand around indicating the island. "The children here are all younger than you are."

"I know. They were all born after we came here."

Kafir leveled his unusual turquoise eyes on Fehin, rubbing a hand across his rough beard. "Your mother and I have been discussing sending you to college."

Fehin instinctively knew they weren't being honest and wondered why not. "College? Where?"

"In Milltown where I lived," his mother answered. "You've been there and met my friend Carla. She can help you get settled."

Fehin remembered Carla from his one trip to Milltown when he was seven years old. She was nice enough but many years had gone by since then. He'd heard about colleges from listening to conversations between his mother and Kafir as well as discussions from others living on the island, but had never considered going to one. "Don't you need to take a test?"

"Gunnar can get you in."

That name set up a red flag. Gunnar was a time-traveling druid who moved from one era to another with ease. If he was involved there was magic afoot for sure. "I've read tons of books. Why do I need college? You told me a year ago that I seemed brighter than many adults you've known."

"You are extremely bright but that doesn't mean you're educated. You've read all the books I brought with me so at least you've experienced the classics. But there's so much more." Gertrude moved closer and put her hand on his arm. "I have no way of getting more books for you, Fehin. We don't have electricity here, so we have no cars, no computers, no cell phones, no electronics of any kind. You haven't studied math or science, you've never been in an airplane, and you haven't even ridden in a car. There are so many things in the world you know nothing about."

"I'm sorry I couldn't include all that when I set this place up. I could only conjure what I could imagine."

"Sweetheart, I'm not complaining, I'm just saying that it would be good for you to understand more of life."

"I like things simple."

Gertrude scoffed. "You can't know that unless you've experienced another way. Computers are a part of everyday life in Milltown. It's like having a library at your fingertips. You're smart, Fehin. Who knows what you could accomplish with a little education?"

"Have you actually spoken to Gunnar?"

"Yes, they have," Gunnar said, appearing out of the ether like a resurrected ghost. "And as you know, neither your mother nor Kafir are able to travel into the past."

"So, the decision has been made without me." Fehin turned away to hide his sudden tears. Wasn't conjuring an island and everything on it enough? Did they want him to go away and learn about electronics so he could add those to the island? And what good would a car do here? He shook his head and wiped his face with his sleeve.

"We had lives before we came here," his mother continued. "We traveled and had careers. For all of us Thule is a dream come true. But that's because we have something to compare it with." Gertrude watched him worriedly. "What is it, Fehin? You look upset."

"What's the real reason you're sending me away?"

Gertrude slanted a glance at Kafir. "College will give you a broader understanding of the world, Fehin. It might even increase your magic."

"I don't care about any of that. Where did you get the idea that I did?"

His mother looked flustered for a moment. "I...I thought you'd be pleased."

There was uncomfortable silence before Gunnar chimed in. "I spoke to your mother and Kafir about this several days ago. You're sixteen now, Fehin. There are no girls, or for that matter, boys, in your age group here."

"So this is your way of finding me a mate?"

"No, Fehin," his mother answered. "This is about opening your eyes to a wider world. You'll understand once you see it."

Fehin stared from one to the other and then rose from the log and headed to the deserted part of the beach where he could think all this through. Why had college suddenly come up? It felt like Wolf's appearance in Fell had been a bad omen all around.

THREE

Otherworld

"Airy, please! This is for your own good!"

"But what if I don't want to leave? What can I possibly get out of going to college that MacCuill can't teach me?"

"MacCuill can't teach you about the outside world or what it's like to have friends."

"I have lots of friends here, Mama."

Maeve frowned and then looked away. Her voice when she spoke again had taken on a decidedly superior tone that Airy didn't like at all. "You need to meet people more like yourself, Airy."

When Harold walked into the room Airy turned to him. "What do you think, Papa? Do I need to be sent away from here?"

Her father looked dumbfounded for a moment, his confused gaze going to Maeve. "I thought we were going to discuss this issue before you mentioned it to her."

"I'm sorry Harold, it just came out. We can't go on

pretending about Airy's future. Today is her sixteenth birthday."

"Thank you so much for this horrible present!" Airy yelled, trying not to cry. "Do you think the people here are beneath us or do you just want to get rid of me?"

When Maeve took a step toward her Airy backed away.

"I'm not trying to get rid of you, sweetheart, I want you to have the education you deserve. Your father and I didn't come into the Otherworld until we were in our twenties. We had both gone to college and worked for several years before that. We decided to remain here because we loved it, not because we hadn't seen the rest of the world. You've lived here all your sixteen years with only a couple of trips to visit your grandparents in Massachusetts. You need to experience another way of life."

Airy hated the expression on her mother's face, the look that said she knew best. "I hate you both right now!" she screamed before turning to run through the open door. She ran down the hill toward the copse of beech and oak trees on the far side of the meadow. Once she reached the comforting shadows beneath the trees, she stopped to catch her breath. She wiped her tears away and then sat down next to an ancient beech. "What should I do?" she wailed, looking up into the wide branches.

"Do about what?" a boy's voice answered, eclipsing the tree's response.

Airy turned to see Evan, a friend of hers, walking toward her from under the canopy. He had a smile on his open face, freckles standing out against his pale skin.

"Oh, Evan, they want to send me away. They think I'm too good for the likes of you or any of my other friends. I hate them right now, especially my mother."

Evan crouched down next her. "You *are* too good for us,

Airy. Your Ma saved this place. She's a legend in her own time. Everyone here whispers her name. And your Da...well, he's the reincarnated first king of Scotland! You're lucky to have such fine parents."

"But I'm not her, Evan. I'm just a girl with no powers."

Evan put his hand on her shoulder. "Not for long."

"You don't know that."

"I'll miss you, Airy, but I think you should do what your Ma thinks best. You should respect her and your Da like the rest of us do."

Airy shook her head and wiped at the tears that refused to stop. A voice called and for a moment Airy thought it was her mother but then Evan stood up.

"I have to go. Hope to see you before you leave but if I don't, know that I'll be wishin' ye all the best."

"Thanks, Ev," Airy mumbled, feeling suddenly bereft. "Bye!" she called as he disappeared from view.

Maybe it would do her good to get out of here for a while. Following in her mother's footsteps was an impossible task and she was sick of feeling like she couldn't live up to Maeve's accomplishments. She was tired of everyone talking about her mother as though she was some kind of goddess.

When she came up the path, she heard her parents raised voices and paused to listen.

"MacCuill thinks Airy has a destiny that's already been written."

"Where does he get these ideas?" Harold answered, chuckling.

"Don't make fun, Harold. Think about what happened to the two of us. And besides, he's a druid. He knows things that we aren't privy to. And also, the goddess of prophecy said that Airy's future is mixed up with someone who lives there."

Harold laughed again. "Mixed up? That doesn't sound very goddess-like."

"Stop it, Harold! Those weren't her exact words. If you don't believe me you should talk with MacCuill before we go. And there was something else—something about Airy and this other person being a bridge...do you realize what that could mean? MacCuill told me just the other day about..."

"Aren't you making more of this than you should? Are you really serious?" Harold interrupted.

"Yes, I'm serious. What did you think? School starts in a little over a month and she needs to be prepped. She's never even seen a computer."

Airy heard her father sigh. "I didn't want to lose her so soon."

"We're not losing her. We can visit whenever we want. This is what she's meant to do and where she's meant to be."

"You know what I mean." A long silence followed this statement and when Airy walked through the door her parents were holding each other tightly.

"So, when do I go?"

Airy tried to listen to what her mother was saying but her mind kept wandering. She couldn't believe she would be leaving here in less than a week. So far, she'd had a crash course on what her mother referred to as 'electronic gadgets', none of which made much sense, and warnings about the many cars and buses, trains and planes, not to mention a ton of other things she couldn't remember. Her few short trips to her grandparent's house had not prepared her for the culture of this modern world.

"I can't take in any more information," she finally said, holding her hands over her ears. "I don't get anything you're telling me."

Her mother glanced over at her father who was sitting in the chair across from them reading a book. "Can't you help, Harold?"

"What do you want me to do? She won't understand until she sees what you're talking about. She's a fast learner and if we get there early, we can try and give her the computer basics. I'm sure they've had other kids who were computer illiterate."

"In this day and age? I highly doubt it."

"We'll just have to tell them she was raised by wolves."

"God, Harold, you're no help at all!"

"Maeve, you're taking this too seriously. And you're scaring her," he added, glancing at Airy.

Airy realized that she must have looked like a frightened rabbit because that's exactly how she felt. How she could fit into this alien world they described was beyond her. "Is MacCuill coming with us?"

"Absolutely! He's going to work the magic to get you in. People going to college have transcripts and they've been accepted. You, on the other hand, have neither."

"This is sounding worse and worse," Airy muttered.

"If it's anything like my college days you're going to love it!" her mother said in a false cheery voice. "And you'll get to spend time with your grandparents. They're very excited."

When Airy glanced toward her father he grimaced and went back to his book.

Why was this suddenly happening? What had she done to deserve being separated from everything she loved? She thought of her herb garden, the tinctures and potions she'd learned how to produce. Would she be able to continue what she'd begun at this college? The potions were her calling; she'd hoped to become a healer, not like her mother but in her own way.

FOUR

Fell, 2468

Early the next morning Gunnar came to Fehin while he was feeding the chickens and the sheep. "By my calculations this is the right time to leave," the druid announced solemnly.

Fehin turned and tried to probe his mind but Gunnar had locked him out. He was definitely hiding something. "I thought I'd have more time to say good-bye."

"You can come back right after you left if you want. No one will even miss you."

Fehin tried to smile but failed miserably. "I'll feel the distance even if they don't. And how will I get back?"

"We'll stay in touch through the ether. You can call on me anytime."

"I still don't get what calculations you're making," Fehin muttered before heading away to gather his things and say goodbye to his menagerie. He might not see them for a very long time.

He found Aki huddled under the trees half asleep, his shoulders hunched. The dragon knew what was coming and there was nothing Fehin could say to console him. Aki had been with him since Fehin was seven years old and they'd formed a very strong bond. They could communicate telepathically which was not something he could do with his other animals. Kafir might take him out occasionally but mostly the dragon would be stuck here on the island. "You should think about your mate," Fehin told him, nodding to the female dragon twenty feet away. "You could raise babies while I'm gone." The mournful look Aki gave him tore at Fehin's heart.

On his way back to gather his things he overheard Gertrude and Kafir talking with Gunnar and hid behind a tree to listen.

"He doesn't suspect any of it," Gunnar said.

"And what if you get the timelines mixed up?" Kafir asked.

"What do you take me for?" the druid answered in an irritated tone. "This has all been pre-ordained."

"But my baby! He's been through so much!"

"He's not a baby, Gertrude. He's nearly a grown man. This is his destiny and we can't ignore it."

"But..."

"None of us know what's in his future. We only know that he is to be enrolled in the college in Milltown in the year 2021."

"Will he come back here when he graduates?"

"We don't even know if he *will* graduate, Gertrude. The only information I've received is to make sure he's where he's supposed to be on a certain date."

Fehin could hear muffled sobs and realized that his mother was crying. His first thought was to comfort her but then anger rose inside him. He was merely a pawn in a game he knew nothing about.

· · ·

GUNNAR WAS ALREADY on board *Skidbladnir* when Fehin climbed on deck. He'd said a cursory goodbye to his mother and Kafir, ignoring the pained looks on their faces as he turned his back to head to the dock. He hated to leave so coldly but he couldn't get over what they'd done. He should have confronted them but he knew if he opened his mouth, he'd end up shouting.

"I'll navigate since I know where we're going," Gunnar said after stowing his things. "While we travel I'll give you a crash course about the world you'll be living in."

Fehin helped the druid ready the boat and lift the sails and then came to stand next to him at the helm. He felt rigid with anger but he wasn't ready to talk about it yet.

"What questions do you have?" Gunnar asked as they began to sail away from the only real home Fehin had ever known.

It was just the opening Fehin needed. "I overheard you talking about my future, Gunnar. I'd like you to tell me what's really going on."

Gunnar turned. "If you overheard then you know as much as I do. All I can tell you is that the message came through loud and clear. You are to be in Milltown, Massachusetts on September sixteenth, 2026. And that's where I plan to take you."

"What was all that about pre-ordained and my destiny then?"

A rare smile came across the druid's face. "How else could I describe it? I'm not privy to where these messages come from or even what they mean. I do my part to fulfill them and I don't question the gods."

"The gods? What gods?"

"Shall I call it a higher power, Fehin? I don't know what gods sent this particular message."

"Loki?"

Gunnar shook his head. "This did not come from Loki."

Loki and Odin were the only gods Fehin had come into contact with other than Freyja and her handmaidens. He knew the pantheon of Norse gods and a few Celtic gods and goddesses from what his mother had taught him, but other than that he was at a loss. "Are there gods where we're going?"

"The gods aren't recognized as such. There's only one god the people worship."

"Which one is it?"

Gunnar shook his head. "You wouldn't know him."

Fehin stared at the druid, willing him to go on, but Gunnar had nothing more to say on the subject. "Maybe once we get there you can stick around for a while," Fehin muttered. "I'm sure I'll need you."

Gunnar gazed into the dense fog that indicated the beginning of the timeline distortions. "That won't be possible. I'll try to fill you in on what you need to know while we travel but after I see you settled, I must leave."

When the first time shift hit, Fehin lost his footing and fell heavily to the deck, bruising his knees. He'd been so caught up with his inner thoughts that he hadn't prepared. He hung on and stayed where he was as the boat twisted and turned. By the time the boat settled again he was too enervated to even think. When Gunnar began to talk, he heard the words as if from a distance.

This world you are about to enter is filled with stimulation. There are lights and noise and people everywhere. I've already explained the various vehicles that rumble up and down the streets. You've seen them before but you may not remember. All of this will make it hard for you to concentrate. But concentrate you must. The classes you will be attending will be especially difficult since you have no knowledge to fall back on. You must rely on your intuition. If you take in what I have to offer, you'll be better prepared. After a few weeks you'll become accustomed to it all. But under no circumstances are you to reveal who you are and where you come from.

Fehin listened to the druid's droning voice as though hypnotized. He could feel the information pouring from the druid's mind into his own, making him dizzy. He fell asleep to the sounds and didn't wake up again until the boat had come to a stop. "Where are we?" he asked, sitting up and rubbing his eyes.

"We're in Boston Harbor."

"Did you talk all night?"

The druid nodded and then moved toward the companionway.

Fehin shook his head, trying to remember anything the druid had placed in his mind. He hoped he'd taken it in because when he looked outside, the sight of the busy chaotic harbor, the noise level and the disturbed thoughts he was picking up telepathically made him want to cover his ears and hide.

FIVE

Otherworld

"Wake up, sweet one."

Airy opened her eyes to see her father's smiling clean-shaven face bending over her.

"Today's the day."

Airy groaned and rolled over, pulling the covers over her head. It was barely light out. But a moment later she heard her mother's impatient voice calling up the stairs. "Harold, is she up? We need to be out of here in less than an hour to make the plane!"

"Come on, Airy. This will be great. And you haven't seen your grandparents for a couple of years now. Just think what fun you'll have with all your cousins. We'll stay until you're settled."

Airy sat up and looked at her father. Despite his positive speech he didn't look very happy. "At least I know you'll miss me." When her father's arms came around her, she leaned into him, trying hard to stop the tears that threatened to spill over.

He let her go too soon and stood up. "I hope you packed last night."

"I did." Airy climbed out of bed and headed for the bathroom to wash her face. Despite her feelings yesterday about this being a good thing she felt heavy and uncertain. When she looked in the mirror there were dark smudges under her eyes and she didn't recognize the combined expression of terror and sadness in them.

MacCuill was in the lower hall when Airy dragged her bag behind her down the stairs.

"The boatman is waiting," he said, grabbing her bag.

"But I haven't had breakfast!" Airy felt whiney and small but she couldn't stop herself.

"That's your own fault, Airy. We woke you in plenty of time. Honestly, what have you been doing up there?"

Maeve's impatience was getting on Airy's nerves. She wished her mother would stay home and let her go with her father and MacCuill. Anger rose up and a second later she was screaming at the top of her lungs. "Why are you treating me like this? I hate you!"

"Don't talk to your mother that way!" her father yelled as she streaked through the door. She ran toward the horse pen and when Facet came to the fence, she buried her face in his mane letting her tears fall onto his fur.

A hand came onto her shoulder and she looked up to see MacCuill's deep blue eyes gazing into her own. "It's time to go," he said, taking her hand and leading the way down the hill.

"Why is Mama being so mean?"

"Maeve loves you, Airy. I don't think she's excited about having you so far away."

"But this entire thing was her idea."

MacCuill shook his head. "This isn't her idea. It came from the goddess of prophecy."

"What? But my parents…"

"They've been making the best of things. It's been very hard on both of them."

"I don't understand."

"No one does, Airy. That's how destiny's work."

At the bottom of the hill the river came into view, tendrils of pale mist obscuring the water. The boatman waited, oar in his hand. He'd been here longer than anyone, even the druids, his boat moving up and down this river for as long as time itself. He was blind and Airy had never grown used to his milky eyes and right now he seemed to be staring directly at her. She always had the impression that the boatman could see in another way, maybe from a sense that only he had. She smiled in the hopes that she was right.

"Come along, Airy," her mother coaxed, holding out her hand. Airy took hold of her fingers and stepped into the coracle and settled next to her mother on the narrow wooden seat. MacCuill and her father sat in the other end and without a word the boatman put his oar into the water and they moved swiftly forward into the swirling fog.

Airy spent the entire plane trip in a state of panic. This was the beginning of something she had no control over and hadn't wanted to do in the first place. And underlying all that was the idea of an unknown destiny that was already laid out for her.

She finally fell asleep, her dreams taking her to a light-filled land with gods and goddesses, dragons and other strange creatures. There was someone there with her but she could never catch a glimpse of who it was. She knew this couldn't be the United States and it certainly wasn't the Otherworld. When she woke the images scattered like snowflakes in wind and she was back on the plane. Her hand went to the middle of her stomach. She felt heat under her fingers as though it had something to tell her. But when she asked, she got no response.

SIX

Boston Harbor, 2026

"*GET YOUR THINGS TOGETHER*, Fehin. Time to head to Milltown."

Fehin looked out the porthole at the massive array of enormous ships, registering the heavy sounds that beat like drums in his ears--banging, crashing, people yelling, the drone of something in the air he couldn't see. "I don't like it here," he muttered, turning to pack up his clothes.

"You don't have to like it," Gunnar said. "Milltown will be better."

"I was there. I remember it. But I was little then and thought it was exciting to be in another place. I don't feel that way now."

"I'm not going to apologize for this, Fehin. Nor am I going to sugar coat what your life will be like. Things have changed since the last time you visited and not for the better. But this is what is required and this is what you will do."

Fehin stared hard at the druid who had always been kind to him. This was not a kind speech and the tone was less than soothing. "I don't know what I'm supposed to do."

"First thing is to get you enrolled and settled. After that you'll have a crash course in anything you can't remember."

"Remember?"

Gunnar's gray eyes narrowed. "Yes. Everything I told you on the way."

Fehin tried to remember details but the lump in his throat kept him from accessing anything. He couldn't understand why Gunnar was treating him like this. And when he tried to probe the druid's mind, he came up against something solid. He grabbed his bag and followed Gunnar off the boat and into the chaos of the modern world. He wanted to plug his ears and shut his eyes but instead he gritted his teeth and climbed into the waiting taxi Gunnar flagged down.

Fehin felt as though his head was about to explode. Sensory overload. His eyes were drawn to billboards advertising everything from electronic devices, to insurance, whatever that was, to hospitals, to companies with names that meant nothing to him and luxurious places to stay with sumptuous rooms and huge pools to swim in. Ads were on every available surface, including cars. There were too many thought forms floating around in the atmosphere and mostly they were dark and negative. The place diminished his spirit.

Once they left the city limits, he searched for trees, green grass, anything that resembled home, but instead, muddy pens came into view crowded with cattle, the stench making him gag. "What's going on there?" he asked.

Gunnar glanced over and then made a face. "Holding pens before they're slaughtered."

Fehin tried to stop the tears that sprang into his eyes. The animals on Thule were well cared for until the day they were killed and the way it was done prevented them from knowing what was coming. Fehin had handpicked the people for this job. Meat was not the mainstay of their diet, but they did eat a lot of eggs and cheese. Mostly they consumed the fruits and vegetables they grew, seasoning them with herbs.

He saw other similar pens as they moved down the highway, each one worse than the one before. "What types of wildlife live here?"

"Not much of anything anymore. Most of the animals and birds have died out from pesticides and over hunting. There are still some zoos around but I doubt you'd want to see creatures behind bars."

"You're right about that," Fehin said, thinking about books he'd read. Thule was filled with Fehin's creations—strange creatures that his seven-year-old mind had conjured. Since then, others had arrived, birds that landed from far off places, animals that appeared on their own. Wild pigs roamed through the mountains as well as sheep and all sorts of ground squirrels and rabbits. The place was teeming with wildlife.

Somehow Gunnar managed to enroll Fehin, even picking out several classes for him. These included history of the world, political science, ancient history, physics and a college math class for non-math majors. His major was history.

The dorm room proved to be more difficult since all of them had been spoken for, but with some magic Gunnar was able to free one up. Fehin didn't question how he did it.

He shared a room with a boy around his own age who barely looked up from the device in his hand when Fehin arrived.

"We need to get you a phone," Gunnar said, watching him.

"Is that what that is?"

Gunnar nodded. "Good thing I have a lot of the local tender on me," he said.

~

THREE DAYS later Fehin had a computer, a credit card, a bank account, several new sets of clothing and shoes, and a handbook Gunnar produced called, 'Everything You Need to Know About the Twenty-first Century'. When Fehin asked him where he got it he just grinned, the first real smile Fehin has seen on his face since before their departure. He leafed through it, noticing that the second half of the book was blank.

"I have to go now, Fehin. School starts the day after tomorrow. Until then I suggest you read up. You don't want to stand out here. Undo attention could foil your plans."

"What plans? My only plan is to attend the classes you set out and try to put up with this place. So far I hate it."

"The plan will come clear," Gunnar said enigmatically.

"You seem in a very good mood. What happened?"

"I'm leaving, that's what happened. You're young, I'm sure you'll grow to like it once you make some friends."

Fehin shook his head. "I don't think so. What if I get confused?"

"Call me, but don't do it frivolously. I have important things going on."

"I'm sure you do," Fehin said. "I wish I was doing them with you."

When Gunnar grabbed him and pulled him close Fehin let out a gasp of surprise. This man never hugged anyone.

Once he released him Gunnar took hold of his shoulders. "Just remember why you're here," he said. "And know that you are sorely missed back home. Once you get used to things I know you'll enjoy being around others your own age. Remember who you are."

"Who am I?"

"You're a boy who conjured an island and everything on it,

that's who you are. Never forget that." Gunnar watched him for a moment and then added. "And don't let anyone see what you can do, Fehin. It would be very dangerous."

Fehin stared at him, willing him to stay, but already the druid was walking away. "Good-bye, Gunnar," he called out. The disturbed and jumbled thoughts of people walking by him paraded through his mind, making him feel ill.

Gunnar raised his hand but didn't turn around and a second later he wasn't there. *He does magic right out in the open*, Fehin thought, wondering why it was so important for him to keep his skills a secret. He had to figure out how to block out the disturbed thoughts of others. Otherwise, he might go insane.

Before attending his first class he read most of the book Gunnar had given him. It had a smattering of everything, including a list of the ongoing wars around the globe and why they continued. Since the United States was so far away from the conflicts, they managed to keep clear of it, but that didn't mean the government didn't have their fingers in every pie. The U.S. had an enormous military, the biggest in the world, and sent their young men and women to die for causes that had no meaning. They armed whatever side might benefit them with no thought to how many were being killed.

Climate change had been encroaching for two decades due to man-made pollution and had hit a peak around 2015. Many denied its existence, but when water began to run out it was officially confirmed. After that pivotal year, water became a precious commodity controlled by a very few.

The larger conflicts in other parts of the world raged on over water, oil, religion and hostilities dating back thousands of years and could continue indefinitely. A large faction of people were made rich from these wars. The divide between rich and poor, at least in this country, had grown and was still growing.

The more he read the more he wished he were back on Thule. When he examined the faces of students and the people in the streets and probed their minds, most were oblivious about anything beyond their own lives. It was like they'd been brainwashed. He felt the fears they'd suppressed, the frustrations that had them walking a tight wire that could and did break with alarming regularity.

In 2017 a trade agreement had been enacted that extended corporate power into several other countries, bypassing existing environmental laws and forming a new world order. Following the 2020 presidential election an amendment to the constitution had been quietly ratified that gave corporations the right to appoint members of congress, changing what had been in place for over two-hundred years. This action led to a few feeble demonstrations, but the militarized police put a stop to it pretty quickly.

With wounded soldiers coming back from war, and all the computerized systems that had taken the place of humans, the number of out of work people began to grow. This resulted in massive poverty and a populace too disenfranchised to have the energy to rise up against it. The systems set up to help workers were gone, as well as the social safety nets that had been in place since 1935. College was astronomically expensive so that only the very wealthy could attend.

Fehin had a moment of shame thinking about the magic that brought him here. His mother had been so positive about Milltown, so excited for him. He wished she could see what had happened in such a short time. He wiped away his tears and read on.

Electronics was the salve that soothed a populace without a voice. Computers, so-called smart phones, cd players, I-pads, I-Pods were cheap and plentiful and nearly everyone had at least one or two of these. Listening to music, watching TV shows, and surfing the Internet were just part of the entertainment package provided by corporations who profited from a distracted populace. There were cars that drove themselves, robotics that cleaned houses and did other menial tasks, human DNA enhancement and testing to prevent disease in the people who could afford such things. Medicines were plentiful but only to those who could pay the exorbitant prices. And all of it lined the pockets of those aligned with the corporations.

The natural world had been driven to the point of extinction by greed and lack of anything resembling stewardship. As far as understanding any of it, Fehin figured he'd have to study for the rest of his life just to get the basics. All he knew was what he had read and what his mother had explained before he left Thule. A pandemic had swept through the world a few years before, killing off millions. The government in the U.S. was a supposed democracy, a wonderful egalitarian system run by the people. How would she feel seeing how things had deteriorated?

He skipped to the end of the written part and stared at the blank pages. Of course, it hadn't been written yet. Would these fill in as time went on? Did he have something to do with what would fill these pages?

By the time he closed the book he felt weighted down. How could one person have any influence on this out-of-control world? He thought of the word, *Koyaanisqatsi*, mentioned in the text. It was a Hopi Indian term meaning 'world out of balance'. Maybe he could visit these peoples he'd read about. They lived in different areas of the country on what was known as reservations, placed there by the early settlers who arrived from other countries. But the Native Americans were here first and it struck him to the core of his being how unfair this was.

He added Native American studies to his list of classes

SEVEN

Milltown, Massachusetts, 2026

"I don't want to share a room."

"Airy, there are no single rooms here. This is what students do." Maeve smoothed Airy's hair back from her forehead with a look of concern.

"That girl in there scares me," Airy confessed, her eyes filling. "Why is she dressed like that and why does she have a ring pierced through her lip? It's creepy."

Maeve sighed heavily. "Things have changed drastically since I attended this school, although there were a few girls with tattoos and piercings then as well. Don't judge her too harshly. There are always reasons why people do these things. It doesn't mean anything about who they are."

"She didn't even answer when I said hello. Can't I get another room?"

"I'm afraid not. MacCuill arranged for this one ahead of time and the dorms are full now. School starts the day after tomorrow." Maeve turned to Harold, her whispered words barely loud enough for Airy to hear. "What's happened?" she asked him, her gaze going toward the street where men and women pushed shopping baskets full of belongings. Tents were set up between high-rises and on any small patch of grass. Police roamed through them, rousting some and leaving others, their voices full of menace. "There are so many more homeless now. And the police...." Her eyes widened as they met his. "I worry about leaving her here."

Airy's father shook his head, frowning. "Corporate take-over as far as I can tell. Did you read about the last elections? I don't like leaving her either, but maybe it's her mission to correct it. It's definitely not a place I want to live."

"She'll be safe on campus," MacCuill added in a hoarse whisper.

Maeve plastered a smile on her face before she turned to Airy. "We need to buy you some new clothes and a computer and several other things. You don't fit in dressed as you are."

Airy looked down at her bright woven tunic, her hand-made leather sandals. Observing the other girls' attire made her realize how far from fitting in she was. Her hair was wrong, her clothes were wrong and worse than that, she had a Scottish accent.

"You can play that one up," MacCuill said, reading her mind. "Being from somewhere exotic will give you an allure."

"I don't want an allure! I want to go home with you. Please don't make me stay here!" Airy was openly crying now.

"Sweetheart, don't cry." Harold's arms came around her. "It's going to be all right, you'll see."

Feeling her father's arms only made Airy cry harder. Everything made her nervous. And the classes they'd enrolled her in sounded boring and awful. The only one she had any interest in was the drawing class. How could she possibly sit in airless rooms for hours on end without butter-flies, grass, flowers and trees around her? At home they were her friends. So far she'd heard no birds, and hadn't seen one rabbit or even a squirrel. And where were the butterflies, the bees?

"Airy, you have to pull yourself together," Maeve said, turning suddenly stern. "We're leaving this afternoon and by then I expect you to be smiling and talking with other students. This behavior is attracting attention and that's the last thing you need. I had a wonderful time at this college. The professors are great; the classes we enrolled you in will surely be interesting if you give them a chance."

When Harold released her, Airy wiped her face. Her tears disappeared as anger took over. "Why don't you just go?" she asked, frowning at her mother.

Maeve's eyes went wide. "You are really pushing it, Airy. My patience is just about worn through."

By the time they got back from the mall Airy had forgotten her anger. Laden with bags of new clothes and shoes had given her a lift. Maybe being here wouldn't be so bad after all. But when she faced her parents and MacCuill in the courtyard to say good-bye panic came rushing back. "What am I supposed to be doing while I'm here?" she asked wildly.

"Just enjoy yourself, Airy. Whatever destiny lies before you will reveal itself in its own time. I know mine did." Maeve took hold of her hand and then pulled her in for a hug. "We love you so much. And don't forget to call your grandparents. Do you think you can work that smart phone we got you?"

Airy pulled away and reached into the pocket of her new skirt. "I think so," she said, handing it to her father. "If not I'm sure there's someone who can help me. Everybody has phones."

MacCuill smiled. "A beautiful and sweet-natured girl like

you will have no problem finding friends--don't be afraid to ask for help."

"And that goes for the computer, dealing with the credit card, your bank account and all the other trappings of this world. There's a lot to remember," her father added. "I just inputted all the numbers you might need," he continued, showing her where they were stored. "Your Halston grandparents and Finna and Alex are in here. If you need to reach us call them. And," he added, glancing down the street, "try and stay on campus as much as you can. There are a lot of rough-looking characters out there." He handed back the phone and then pulled her close. "And don't take your mother's mood seriously, Airy. She loves you very much," he whispered.

Airy wasn't prepared for the rush of emotion that hit her when the three of them walked away. She wanted to call after them but stopped herself. Her mother was right. It was time to pull herself together.

In her room she tried again to talk with her new roommate, realizing that the reason she wasn't responding was because of the ear buds in her ears. She must be listening to music.

Airy put her clothes away and then set up her computer on the desk next to her bed, hoping she would remember everything her parents had told her about how to operate the thing. It looked innocent sitting there, all silvery and new, but her intuition told her that she would be screaming at it soon enough.

"You want to get something to eat?"

Airy turned to see her new roommate staring at her out of eyes thickly lined in black. "Sure," she said awkwardly and then stood and reached for her backpack that held her wallet. "My name's Airy," she said holding out her hand.

"Storm," the other girl said, taking hold of Airy's fingers.

"Before we go could you show me how to turn this thing on?"

Storm walked over and pressed a button on the side. "Your first computer?"

Airy nodded.

By the time they'd found the student union Maeve had learned that Storm came from California, a state in the western part of the country, and that she'd grown up on a commune, a word that Airy didn't fully understand. But after Storm explained she got the gist of it right away. It was very similar to life in the Otherworld. Airy's cover story developed by MacCuill was that she had lived abroad for a good portion of her younger life. The true part was that she had relatives who lived in Halston, a town not far from Milltown. The two girls found out they were sharing at least one class together since Storm's major was art.

Airy's major, chosen for her by her mother, was English, with classes in writing in her future as well as modern literature and one history class. Her mother had explained that it was a well-rounded liberal arts degree. MacCuill had added Comparative Religions to the list, saying that it might help her better understand the world she was living in.

At the end of their meal Airy had decided that she liked Storm despite her spiky hair, ripped black jeans, and the indigo tattoos of snakes and other unidentified creatures twining up and down her arms. Underneath the veneer was an interesting and intelligent girl who had chosen to make a certain fashion statement. Airy hoped she would find a style too, looking down at her pleated skirt and knee-high socks. Maybe she should have waited to go shopping.

When the dark-haired boy entered the cafeteria and stared at her she tried not to pay attention. It was only after feeling his gaze on her for the fifth or sixth time that she turned to look at him, and in that split second something inside her chest turned over. She'd seen lots of boys before, even had a sort of boyfriend back home. But this was different. It wasn't about his looks, although he had a thick shock of dark hair that fell down over his forehead and dark eyes that seemed to hold secrets she longed to know. She shook herself, turning her attention back to Storm, but the feeling in the pit of her stomach was back and this time it refused to be ignored. Her moonstone ring seemed to glow for a second but when she examined it more closely it was the usual innocuous gray.

"He seems to like you," Storm said, watching him. "But I think I'd steer clear. He looks straight off the farm." Airy didn't ask what she meant.

EIGHT

Fehin unpacked his gear trying not to be intimidated by the bulked-out guy sitting on the bed across from him talking on his phone. *I've dealt with gods a lot more fearsome than this guy,* he told himself. They had introduced themselves but other than that they had yet to say another word. Brent was his name. Gunnar had assured Fehin that roommates rarely became close friends. That was fine with Fehin, since he felt a need to hunker down and concentrate. Classes began tomorrow and he had no idea what he was doing.

In the student union he found a seat, unloading his tray on the table as he'd seen others do. His gaze was drawn to the two girls sitting across from him, an unlikely pair. One of them looked like a pirate and the other...well, simply put, she was gorgeous, with masses of red hair and pale freckled skin. He probed her mind finding a confusing array of emotions and thoughts that skittered away as soon as he grabbed onto them. He felt embarrassed when their eyes met; Gunnar had warned him more than once about using his 'skills', as he'd put it, for his own gain. He wondered for a moment if she was the girl in his visions but dismissed it.

He could barely eat, his ears attuned to the conversation going on between the two girls. He knew now that the red-haired girl was Airy and that her major was English. They probably wouldn't have any classes together. This was the first time in his life he'd had nervous tremors in his stomach at the mere idea of approaching her. But then again, how many girls his own age had he met? The answer was exactly none. He finally gave up the eating idea, threw his food in the garbage can and left the union. He had to pick up his books before four o'clock.

Living according to a schedule was an alien concept, he thought, taking his phone out of his pocket to check the time. In his world things were done according to when the sun rose and when it set. Meals came regularly but weren't set in stone like they were here.

He looked down at the rectangle in his hand. Apparently, this little device did just about everything, from e-mail, some-thing Gunnar had explained in great detail, to keeping time, to taking pictures, or photos, as they were called. He could also record things on it and dictate ideas that might come to him when he was away from his computer. He could also use it to look things up on the Internet. There was even an alarm to wake him in the morning as well as apps he could download, whatever that meant, and games and other things he could buy; tiny pictures of them came up whenever he opened his phone. But if he didn't charge it up every night it would go dead and be useless to him. So many things to remember.

Airy stayed in his mind on the short walk to the bookstore. He knew nothing about her—they hadn't even exchanged words. Was this what it was like to be around girls his own age?

If so, he was going to have a tough time of it. The feeling in his stomach was back, a pulling sensation that must be nerves.

He could barely carry the pile of tomes to the checkout desk. After paying with his credit card, he stuffed them into his backpack and then heaved it onto his back. Good thing he didn't have far to go. The credit card thing had been easier than he thought; all he had to do was remember to pay his bill every month. Gunnar had shown him a way to set up automatic billing but it was too complicated for his mind to grasp.

On his walk back to the dorm he saw her again. He tried to ignore the weird feeling in his stomach, the uneven beat of his heart. As he moved into the stair-well he realized that she lived in the same dorm as he did—on the girl's floor just above his. He listened to her lilting chatter as she and the other girl moved up the stairs and then he heard the sound of the door closing and she was gone.

When he entered his room, Brent was bent over his computer looking at pictures of naked women. In Fehin's world people often went without clothes. Was it a novelty here? He opened his own computer and pressed the button to turn it on. He had to be up to speed on this thing soon or he'd drop behind. This piece of metal was his lifeline with its program for writing papers and endless supply of information. It was like the libraries he'd heard about from his mother. The school had a large library of its own and he planned to spend a lot of time there. According to Gunnar there was only so much you could research online.

In the e-mail program Gunnar had set up he found one from the druid. *Read the book and good luck* was all it said. When he tried to send one back, he got a message saying it was undeliverable. His gaze was drawn to the window and when he looked out, he saw the girl again. She was standing beneath a large oak tree on the far side of the courtyard with her arms outstretched. Butterflies circled around her head and it looked like she was talking to the tree.

NINE

Airy stared out the window of the classroom, her chin in her hand. A breeze had come up and some of the leaves were drifting to the ground while others circled in whirlwinds of color before floating away. It was fall and they weren't making food anymore, the chlorophyll breaking down and revealing the brilliant gold and oranges and reds that had been obscured by the green pigment. MacCuill had explained all this years ago.

The trees here were slower to respond when she spoke to them but she had managed to converse with a few—mostly the older ones with thick trunks and wisdom in their branches. Something was going on with the butterflies and the bees. They'd been agitated when they came around. She hadn't had time to find out why.

"And what do you think, Airmid?"

Airy turned to see the professor staring at her from behind horn rimmed glasses. "I...what was the question?"

"The question is why aren't you paying attention? You'll need to know this on the test."

There was a titter of laughter around the room. Heat rose into her cheeks.

"We were discussing Chaucer and his influences on later writing. I suggest you keep your focus on what's going on *inside* the room rather than out."

Once class was over Airy gathered her books together and left the room. The other students scattered in small groups leaving her to walk down the long hallway alone. Classes had begun two weeks before and it was becoming harder and harder to concentrate. She hoped fervently that she wouldn't flunk out. MacCuill's lessons had never been this boring.

Outside she headed to her new friend—an enormous oak with wide branches that spread like a canopy. She wanted to climb it, but knew this would attract attention. Better to enjoy the tree from the ground. The leaves had turned scarlet and many lay under her feet, crunching as she drew close. "Why can't I pay attention?" she whispered, looking up.

There was a rumble that Airy felt inside her body, an indication of an answer, but before it reached her someone behind her said, "What are you doing?"

Airy turned to see the boy with the raven-colored hair standing behind her. The question was innocent enough, but a flush crept up her neck. "I was asking the tree a question."

"The trees speak to you?"

Airy frowned. "Of course. Don't they speak to you?"

"Uh, um…I'd have to say no, but then again I haven't really tried."

"I thought everyone could talk to trees. You search for the place inside you that's like them. There's no separation."

"Really?"

When Airy's eyes met his she was unable to breathe, much less speak. She swallowed and looked away. "Think of a spider-web, that's what everything is, including us."

"The web of life, I get it."

"I don't think you really do. Nothing is separate, including humans. If you can't talk to trees then something is off inside you."

The boy shook his head and then looked around as though checking for other people close by. "I wouldn't mention this to others if I were you. My name's Fehin, by the way."

"Airy."

"I know."

Airy stared at him quizzically. "How do you know?"

Fehin looked away for a moment. "I eavesdropped," he finally said with a sheepish grin.

"Oh, in the cafeteria."

He nodded and then moved closer. "You live on the floor above me."

Airy didn't know what to say to this. She was tongue-tied again and had a very strange feeling in the pit of her stomach. "I...I have to get to my history class."

"World history?"

She nodded.

"I'm in that class. We can walk together if you like. Can't believe I haven't noticed you before."

"I may have skipped it a few times," Airy admitted, blushing.

As they headed into the building together Airy stole a glance at his profile. He had a straight nose, high cheekbones and a chin that was neither too small nor too large. Long eyelashes rimmed his dark eyes. He seemed like someone she would like to know but he also made her nervous for some reason.

She looked down, watching the ants moving single file across the walkway. When she took a long step and then jumped sideways, Fehin looked over at her. "What are you doing?"

"Trying to keep from stepping on the ants."

Fehin glanced down. "I didn't even notice them."

"They have a right to their lives. They work really hard." When she turned he was watching her with an intent look.

"Where do you come from?" he asked just before they entered the building.

Airy waved her hand around vaguely. "Oh, I lived in Europe for a while. My paternal grandparents live in Halston-- not too far from here." Her answer seemed to satisfy him. At the entrance to the classroom, he stopped to let her go ahead. Once she found a seat, he found one next to her, settling in and placing his backpack on the floor beside him. She snuck another look at him, noticing the new-looking jeans and plaid shirt, the way he pushed his dark hair back before reaching into his bag for paper and pencil.

This class was even harder for her to fathom, especially in close proximity to this boy. By the time the hour ended she had no idea what the professor had said or what their assignment was.

"What did you think?" he asked as they walked together down the steps toward the student union. It was lunchtime and both had a break until their next class.

"I...I was confused. I haven't ever studied this kind of history and this seemed way too much to understand."

"It should be easier since you've lived in Europe. My mother told me all about the different countries there." He suddenly blushed. "I mean I knew about them, but I..."

"That's okay. You're way ahead of me. I may have lived there, but I was too young to learn their history."

Fehin laughed. "Looks like we'll both be struggling. Maybe we can help each other."

By now they'd reached the student union and Fehin led the way to a table. Airy met his gaze as they sat down. His unusual eye color was a mix of green and brown that reminded her of moss or a shaded forest pool. "I'd like that," she managed to murmur, looking away.

"Your eyes are amazing," he said.

She turned back, smiling. "I was thinking the same about yours."

They bought their lunch, bringing it back to the table, but in the end neither one of them ate much of anything.

"THAT GUY'S KIND OF A DORK," Storm said. "Not sure why you'd want to hang around him."

Airy and Storm were in their dorm room and Airy had just finished explaining her day, including lunch with Fehin. "What kind of an animal is a dork?"

Storm stared at her. "It's not an animal, Airy. Dork refers to someone who's out of the loop—completely uncool--like a geek or a nerd. He must cut his hair with nail scissors, and the way he dresses—who the hell wears plaid?"

"And you with your nose ring, spiked hair and ripped clothes feel you can judge him?"

Storm frowned. "Hey, that was uncalled for. At least I have a style. Look at you, Miss prim and proper with your knee socks and loafers." She made a sound in the back of her throat. "Yeah, on second thought maybe you two are made for each other."

Airy felt something boiling inside her. It was anger but also a feeling of protection. Maybe part of why she liked him was because he didn't fit in. "He's really nice, Storm. I don't judge people by how they look; I judge them by how they behave.

And I'm sorry if my appearance doesn't please you. What exactly would you suggest?"

"Well, for one thing I'd cut that hair—there's too much of it." Storm stepped back to look her over. "You need some jewelry other than that ring—maybe some earrings. But you need to get your ears pierced to do that. And I'd get rid of the knee socks and cutesy little blouses and skirts and wear T-shirts. They're just hipper, you know?"

"Actually, I don't even know what that word means."

Storm laughed. "I rest my case."

Airy turned to look in the mirror. "Can you cut my hair?"

WHEN AIRY PASSED a group of girls on her way to class, one of them called out, "What are you, a witch?" The other girls looked fearful, moving off the walkway.

"What do you mean?" she asked, confused.

"What do you think I mean?" the girl answered pointing to the butterflies circling around Airy's head, the bees that had landed on her hands and arms. A line of chirping tree frogs followed behind her.

Airy laughed. "They've been trying to tell me something but I've been too distracted to get their message. Can you understand them?"

The blonde girl gawked at her and then turned to her companions. "What did I tell you? She's definitely a freak." She rejoined her friends and then they all hurried away.

"I'm sorry, slow down," she muttered as a butterfly landed on her nose. "You're being poisoned? Is that what you're trying to tell me? What can I do?"

TEN

Rain poured down, heavy storm clouds piling up, one on top of the other. Fehin wondered if this was a normal storm or had something to do with all the fear and anger the people carried. On Thule out-of-control emotions caused hurricanes. If it was the same here this place should be having torrential downpours and tornadoes on a daily basis.

He tried to respect what Gunnar had told him, but he couldn't stop the crowd of disturbing thoughts that assaulted him from nearly every person he passed. It was as though his filtering system didn't work here. He felt like screaming half the time. He chuckled at the image of yelling nonstop to keep thoughts from coming into his mind and what might happen as a result. He'd probably be dragged off campus and stuck in prison or somewhere worse. He shook his head. There was no escaping it.

He had yet to get one of the devices that most listened to. He'd thought at first it was music, but from what he overheard it sounded like cats being strangled. Sometimes he could hear a deep rhythmic boom in the background. Drums were ancient instruments, used in times of war to rally people. The steady sounds connected to man's primal instincts. Was that why all the guys were teetering on the edge of self-restraint? He'd already seen two brawls begun over race differences that ended with no resolution. Nerves were like bows strung too tight. He decided he would have to borrow a disc from Brent to get the full gist of it. But the idea of even talking to the guy gave him a bad feeling. Brent reminded him of Wolf.

FEHIN WATCHED the sheet of silver pouring off the roof, his thoughts turning to Airy. He'd seen her in class this morning but hardly recognized her. She'd cut her hair, which now stood up in spiky tufts. Silver hoops hung from her ears, and her clothes—well, let's just say they revealed a lot more of her, with low cut T-shirts and jeans that hugged her slender body. She'd also taken to wearing shoes with heels that made her wobble when she walked. And now her eyes were lined in the same way as her roommate.

He'd planned to talk with her after class but her appearance scared him away. He couldn't imagine what this girl and he had in common. But when he saw her again beneath the oak tree, he changed his mind. He hurried across the courtyard. "Talking to trees again?" he asked, coming up beside her. The rain was lighter here, stopped by the wide boughs and leaves still clinging to the branches.

She started and turned to face him, the green of her eyes even more dramatic with the dark lines she'd drawn around them. "They're wise beings, Fehin. I asked about the poisons the butterflies and bees told me about. Pesticides are killing them. There aren't many left. Why do people do this?" Her eyes filled with tears before she turned back to the tree.

"There's a lot about this place I don't get," he said,

responding to her question. "It's so crowded everywhere and everyone's so upset all the time. I don't really know what pesticides are, but I can guess. We don't use them where I come from. Did the tree have an answer?"

"They don't answer in English, silly. I have to decipher the particular aromas they send out—chemical messages I guess you'd say. It doesn't always work since they're so old and what they want me to know doesn't resonate because I'm another species. They didn't respond at all about the poisons, and my other question about failing my history class is not a concept they understand. Why did those girls call me a witch?" she asked suddenly, her eyes wide.

"What girls?" Fehin asked, looking around.

"They're not here now. The butterflies were asking questions but I couldn't decipher them. I know they want me to do something about it. The girls wouldn't help."

Fehin smiled. "You're different from them. That's why I said you should keep these things to yourself."

"But why?"

The look on her face was so open. This girl was either crazy or like him. "Airy, you may be the only one who can do these things."

She sighed and her shoulders drooped. "I was afraid of that. Now I really want to go home."

"Where is home? And don't tell me Europe, because I know that isn't true."

"You won't believe me."

"Try me," he said, moving closer and picking up the scent of her lemony perfume. At least she hadn't changed that.

"My mother is a seer and I think I am too."

"A seer. You mean you can look into the future?"

"Something like that."

"Where did you get that ring?"

Airy looked down at her hand. "It's a moonstone that belonged to my grandmother. It was magical way back when."

"Magical? In what way?" Fehin asked, bending to examine it. The stone was oval and smooth, the surface opaque, but when he touched it, it gave off a little spark and began to glow.

Airy seemed unconcerned as she waved her hand around. "Back when my Nana first had it, it showed her how to get to Caer Sidi. She gave it to my mother and now I have it. It's a family heirloom."

Fehin frowned. "The Care City?"

"It's a place." When she noticed the expression on his face, she looked stricken. "I shouldn't have told you. I'm not supposed to share any of this."

"It's okay. I won't tell anyone as long as you don't share what I'm about to show you." The rain had finally stopped, and the clouds were drifting away. The air had turned cool and breezy. Fehin grabbed her arm. "It might help with the history test. Is that the class you're worried about?"

Airy nodded. "I don't get any of it."

"Follow me," he said, leading the way across campus and into a park on the other side of the football field. After walking single file down a narrow path in the woods, he came to a stop in the middle of a clearing. Fehin glanced at her and then began moving his hands in patterns.

When a tiny perfect medieval village appeared on the ground in front of him, she clapped her hands in delight. "I knew it!" she said, smiling. "You're like me."

Fehin grinned. "This is a typical European town from the mid 1200's, the time period on the test. I thought it might help to visualize it."

Airy stared in fascination at life going on below her. Carts filled with produce were being pulled along by miniscule horses. A high-pitched shout drew her attention to a small boy running away after stealing an apple. A man ran after him brandishing a club. There were soldiers marching across the drawbridge, their helmets shining in the sun. She turned, her eyes bright. "You must be the boy I was supposed to meet. Corra said our destinies were connected."

Fehin pushed his hair back with both hands, trying to focus on the over-excited girl. Gunnar would be furious that he'd revealed his magic. "I don't know any Corra," was all he could think to say as the tiny village disappeared in a puff of smoke. What he showed her was only the beginning of what he'd planned. He muttered a few words under his breath and then Airy lowered herself onto the ground and closed her eyes.

Fehin hurried away. He'd been a fool to trust her with this. What she'd said about destinies disturbed him, considering the conversation he'd overheard between Gunnar and his parents before he left. Was she right about the two of them? Something was definitely drawing them together. And what about the butterflies and bees? This was no normal girl.

By the time he got back to campus he was late for his math class, slinking in to find a seat in the back. The professor ignored him, continuing to write numbers and undecipherable symbols on the blackboard. This was Fehin's most confusing class. And today, with his mind on the girl asleep under that tree, he was even more distracted than usual. He'd probably caused her to miss her next class. He had to steer clear of her until he could determine who she really was.

ELEVEN

Airy opened her eyes and gazed around, wondering why she was here. Where was Fehin? She looked down at the wristwatch her mother had forced on her and jumped up.

By the time she reached campus and looked at her watch again she decided to skip the class. There was no point in arriving five minutes before it ended. Turning her mind back to how she'd come to be in the woods made her light-headed. Fehin wouldn't have just left her there. She must have imagined it. Was talking to trees and animals so unusual? Maybe she'd had her 'powers' all along and didn't know it. The medieval village appeared in her mind, complete with cows and sheep and carts pulled by teensy horses. It *did* help to visualize it, but she needed a lot more if she was to pass the test. And she knew in that moment that it wasn't a dream.

She waited for Fehin outside the student union but he didn't show up. Maybe he didn't like her new look. Storm had assured her it was very 'now', especially with her newly pierced ears and the earrings she'd borrowed. But was it wise to take advice from a girl who dressed all in black day in and day out?

She frowned. If this change in her appearance ruined her relationship with Fehin he was shallower than she thought. But then again, some of this new look didn't even fit for her. Even so, she had to try it out.

When she reached into her back pocket her fingers curled around the small envelope from her grandparents. They had invited her to Halston for Thanksgiving and had even offered to come down and pick her up. She wondered if Fehin had any place to go for the holiday.

IT WAS the week before Thanksgiving before she saw Fehin again. He'd skipped the World History class they shared and hadn't shown up at the student union for several days. The only reason she noticed him this time was because of his plaid shirt. The bright reds and blues caught her eye as he hurried away from her. She took off after him, nearly falling in her haste to catch up. Heels were not meant for running.

"Are you avoiding me?" she asked, trying to catch her breath as she grabbed hold of his shirt.

When Fehin turned he stared right through her. "No. I'm just busy," he answered.

"Fehin, what's wrong? Is it my hair? It'll grow back."

"It's not your hair, Airy. I just have to buckle down and study. I can't spend my extra time talking to trees."

Airy blanched. "The way you said that sounded like you don't believe me."

"Maybe I don't."

Airy frowned. "I thought you were my friend."

"Do friends have to believe every crazy thing the other one says?" He moved away from her, continuing on his former route across campus.

"You are a horrible person!" she yelled. How could she have trusted such a jerk? A moment later clouds massed and roiled in the sky, and a jagged streak of lightning struck a pine tree less than two hundred yards away.

Fehin stopped in mid-stride and turned back, his eyes wide. A second later he was by her side, his fingers digging into her flesh. "What did you just do?"

"I...I didn't do anything," she said, wrenching away from him. "Why don't you leave me alone!" she screamed. Above them the dark clouds opened, sending torrents of rain down and within seconds they were both drenched.

Fehin dragged her across the slippery flagstones and under an overhang. "You caused this storm," he said, watching her. "What else can you do?"

Airy stared at him angrily. "I certainly did not cause this storm. The only thing I can do is talk to trees, oh, and animals and birds and insects and frogs and snakes. Other than that, I'm perfectly normal. Every single thing on the earth has a spirit, you know."

"You are anything but normal, Airy. Maybe you were right about the destiny thing."

"You mean on the day you pretended you weren't even there?"

Fehin's face turned beet red and he couldn't meet her eyes. "I'm sorry about that. I thought you were..."

"You thought I was like any other girl here. Well, I'm not. I come from a long line of seers and apparently, I have skills that I didn't think of as skills. I lied when I said I lived in Europe. The truth is I come from a place called Otherworld. I thought everybody could do what I do."

"Otherworld? That's where you live?" Fehin looked about to cry as he reached out and touched her cheek. "I'm so sorry, Airy." A second later she was folded into his arms. It felt so good until he pulled away. When she looked at him, he seemed worried, his eyes clouded as he gazed at her.

"What does this mean?" he asked. "Are we supposed to be doing something together—some destiny that I don't know anything about?"

She reached for his hand, not wanting to lose the connection. "I don't know," she said, twining her fingers through his. "All I know is that my destiny is linked with a boy from an island that only I can see, and that somehow we are supposed to be a bridge—but a bridge to what I have no idea."

"A bridge." Fehin stared over her shoulder into the distance. He shook his head. "I come from the future. I live on an island that I conjured. And even though I haven't been there, I know all about Otherworld. I can do a lot of magical things. I can read minds. But building a bridge? I have no idea how to do that."

Airy shushed him with her hand and then leaned close, placing her lips on his. She'd never kissed a boy before and when he kissed her back with his arms tight around her, she trembled. Once the kiss was over they stared into each other's eyes. Finally Airy broke the silence. "At least we like each other again. Tell me about this island you made. What year do you come from?"

"2468," he answered.

"2468? How is that possible?"

"How is talking to trees possible? My mother lived here in Milltown before I was born. If we look in the newspaper archives in the library, I bet I can find an article about her."

"Is she a witch?"

Fehin shook his head. "She's psychic and she used to do readings at the Crystal Guide here in town."

"Let's look her up," Airy said, pulling him by the hand. "And later maybe we can go to the Crystal Guide. I bet they have a book on herbal lore. There aren't any classes and it's what I'm most interested in."

"You mean like healing herbs or teas?" he asked, hurrying behind her.

"Mostly I make tinctures and potions. But I have a lot more to learn." She pulled open the door of the library and led the way inside.

It took an hour to find the Milltown Gazette article dated June 13, 2011. It said: **Gertrude Besnick's disappearance and presumed death at sea in the fall of 2010 has sparked the re-release of her last book, published after she vanished. The Tower has since become an international best seller and been at the top of the list for months.**

Airy stared at Fehin. "The Tower is on the reading list for my Modern Lit class!"

Fehin looked surprised. "Wow. I haven't even read it. She wrote another one earlier. It's called The Hanged Man. Are you familiar with the Tarot?"

"Not really."

At Airy's puzzled expression, he continued. "I was born in the future but I was kidnapped by a sorceress when I was a year old. My mother searched for me and then gave up because she thought I was dead. That's when she came back here. But in reality, I was living with Loki."

Airy's confusion deepened. "Loki is...?"

"The Norse God of fire. He's also known as the trickster god. He raised me until I was six."

Airy watched Fehin's eyes darken with the past. "You didn't see your mother for five years?"

"Someone got a message into the past that gave her the idea

that I might be alive. Mothers and their cubs." He threw his hands into the air and then laughed.

"It's not funny, Fehin. It sounds terrible for you and for her. How old were you when she came back?"

"I was six when she worked out a deal with Loki."

"And when you conjured the island?"

"Seven. I've lived there ever since."

"Only seven years old? Wow. I wasn't supposed to come into my powers until this year."

"But you told me you've been able to do these things your entire life."

"I didn't know they were special. I just had my sixteenth birthday, so maybe I'll discover other things I can do."

"I did too."

Airy heard Fehin say something, but when she looked at him his mouth was closed. "Telepathic communication?" she asked, surprised.

Fehin smiled and looked down. "Just thought I'd try it out. And I thought you should know that my mother spent time in Otherworld. It's where she met my father and where I was conceived."

Airy heard a noise behind them and glanced toward the door. Someone had just entered the darkened room where they'd been perusing the microfiche archives. A second later something smashed into the back of her head. She heard Fehin's scream just before she blacked out.

TWELVE

It was dark as pitch now that the machine had been hurled to the ground. Fehin was trying to locate Airy when he caught sight of the person who hit her. Unbelievably it was Wolf. "How in hell did you get here?" he asked his brother.

Wolf smiled, showing teeth that had a distinctively canine look to them. "Hell, indeed," he said. "It was easy—I followed you."

"But I was with Gunnar on the boat."

"I guess you could say I stowed away."

Fehin moved to Airy and picked up her limp hand. "Why in Loki's name did you hit her?"

"She was getting on my nerves and I wanted to talk to you."

Fehin put his fingers on Airy's wrist feeling for a pulse. It was steady. "So, what is it?" he asked, lifting Airy into a seated position.

"I need your help to get my powers back. My mother had good luck here in Milltown, so I thought that I..."

"I can't help you," Fehin interrupted, pulling Airy closer.

"Oh, I think you can. I've seen your handiwork." Wolf

stared at him, his eyes narrowing. "And if you don't, I'll really hurt this girl you seem so fond of—maybe not today, but soon. You know I'm telling the truth."

Fehin tried not to let the creeping revulsion overtake him. Yes, he did believe him, but he wasn't about to admit it. "Get out of here," he said,

focusing on Airy. He knew his brother was gone when the putrid air in the room cleared. A moment later Airy opened her eyes. "What happened?" she asked, rubbing the back of her head.

Fehin helped her up and the two of them headed out of the library and then slowly made their way across campus toward the dorms. On the way he explained about his brother, trying to ignore the look of horror that came across her face as he talked about their common father and the past. He tried to make it as succinct as possible, but who wouldn't react badly to hearing about the man who orchestrated a war in Otherworld? Airy's mother knew Brandubh as well as anyone, and if the woman had any idea that Fehin was involved with her daughter she'd be horrified.

By the time they reached the stairwell, Airy's face was as white as the walls. "What are you going to do?" she asked in a small voice.

"I don't know. All I know is I have to keep you safe."

The plan they came up with was risky and required Storm's cooperation. "How will you get her to agree?" he asked after they'd gone over all their options.

"I'll think of something. But if you get caught in my room you'll be expelled."

"Being expelled is the least of my problems. You and I are supposed to be on some sort of mission that neither of us can figure out, and now my vile brother has come on the scene. If you get hurt, I'll never forgive myself."

"It wouldn't be your fault," she said, laying a hand on his cheek.

"Yes, it would." He pointed up the stairs. "Go talk it over with the pirate and let me know what she says."

"The pirate?" Airy laughed. "That's good, Fehin. I won't tell you what she calls you."

Back in his dorm room Fehin stared at the floor. Brent was out for the moment, probably in a bar downtown drinking with his buddies. He'd invited Fehin along a couple of times, but the idea of spending a minute longer than he had to with the guy did not appeal. Fehin was tired of listening to his ear-splitting music and watching him masturbate to pictures of naked women on the Internet. Yes, he knew all about masturbation now, had even tried it a few times. But he didn't do it in front of Brent or anyone else. The guy was a disgusting beast.

But Wolf was worse than that and dangerous as well. He would kill Airy without any remorse whatsoever. Thank the gods Wolf didn't have powers. He had to figure out how to get rid of him. But after an hour of coming up with nothing he decided it was time to call on Gunnar.

FEHIN WAS in the woods where he'd taken Airy, trying, unsuccessfully, to call on the druid. The forest stood silent around him, an aura of waiting permeating the atmosphere. He'd been at it for twenty minutes before he felt a change in pressure, signaling the druid's arrival. "What took you so long?" he demanded.

"I'm not at your beck and call, Fehin. And I sincerely hope this is something important."

"Is the appearance of Wolf in Milltown important enough for you?"

Gunnar narrowed his eyes. "I suppose that comes under the category of compelling. When did this happen?"

"He told me he stowed away, so he's been here as long as I have—doing what, I have no idea."

"Scoping things out, probably. What did he say he wanted?"

Fehin scoffed. "What do you think? He wants his powers back. But the worst of it is he's threatened Airy."

Gunnar raised his eyebrows. "Ah, so you've met."

Fehin pressed his lips together. "If you know anything about whatever this is we're supposed to be doing, you'd better tell me. I'm really pissed that you didn't say anything before."

"Pissed? That's a new word for you, isn't it? I guess you're learning the modern lingo."

"Don't change the subject. I mean it, Gunnar. If Wolf hurts her, I'll..."

"You have powers and he doesn't. How is he going to hurt her?"

"Have you seen him lately? He's a fucking brute."

"More language. You seem to be picking up all sorts of new words while you're here."

Fehin watched him without speaking and then probed his mind, getting a glimpse of something he hadn't seen before. Gunnar knew Wolf was on that boat. But a second later the druid shut him out.

"Why didn't you tell me?" he yelled.

Gunnar grew serious. "He's part of it, Fehin. Wolf is part of it."

"And what is *it*, exactly?"

"I don't know. If I did, I'd tell you."

"I'm supposed to put up with Wolf and at the same time complete some destiny I don't understand?"

"You can manage it. I've seen what you can do."

"What about Airy? She's at risk as long as my brother's around."

Gunnar sighed. "She's not some sniveling weak-willed girl. She's the daughter and great granddaughter of two very powerful women and coming into her own. Who knows what she can do?"

"She's scared and so am I."

"That's the proper response to danger, Fehin. You two make a good team."

"You're not going to help me."

"There's nothing I can do." The druid stared at him for a moment and then softened. "Have faith in yourself and the girl. I do."

And with that statement the druid disappeared.

THIRTEEN

"It would only be for a short time, Storm. Did you hear what I said about Wolf? We need to time to come up with a plan."

Airy's roommate appeared very put out, her frown drilling into Airy from where Storm paced. Outside the sun was shining and Airy longed to be out in it. The small room felt claustrophobic. Why didn't any of these rooms have windows that opened?

"How do I know this isn't some ploy for the two of you to have sex?" her roommate demanded. Storm pressed her lips together. "I can't understand why you're attracted to the little geek."

Airy ignored the geek comment, focusing on the sex part, which she found embarrassing and uncalled for. "There's no way we're going to have sex here or anywhere else!"

"Really? I saw you two kissing."

Airy frowned. This could be one of two things: either Storm was a lesbian or she didn't have a boyfriend and was jealous that Airy did. She was betting on the latter but it wouldn't surprise her if her roommate were gay. She knew all about this after listening in on several conversations in the lunchroom. It seemed a popular topic of conversation. It was the same where she came from, but mostly what others chose to do or not do was ignored unless it turned into some kind of a problem. And then the druids would be called to settle differences. "We like each other. I admit I'm attracted to him. But sex? If it ever happens it will be somewhere private, believe me."

Storm let out a long sigh. "You do know that if you're caught, both of you could be expelled."

"We know. But I'm telling you, that brother of his is a monster."

Storm raised her eyebrows and then smiled wickedly. "Do you think I'd like him? I could take him off your hands if he's as burly as you say. Is he cute?"

Airy shook her head in frustration. "I couldn't see him since he was behind me when he knocked me out. But please, don't let me stop you from dating a psychopath."

"According to Fehin. Maybe that description is just a bunch of bullshit."

"Fehin wouldn't lie about this. I trust him. Now what is your answer?"

"Just at night?"

Airy nodded. "He'll have to come in and out before the hall monitor comes by."

"Okay, but if I don't like the arrangement, I want it to stop immediately."

"Thanks, Storm." Airy threw her arms around the other girl, nearly knocking her down. S

"Good god, girl. Take it easy!" Storm yelled, pulling away. "I'm not a hugger as you might have guessed had you been paying attention."

"Sorry. I'm just so grateful."

"You won't be if I decide to kick him out. Remember your promise."

Airy gave her a quick wave before hurrying out the door and down the stairwell to where Fehin was waiting. "She said yes!"

Fehin grinned. "Let's take a walk in the park now that your tempests are gone."

"They weren't my storms, Fehin. I…"

"Calm down, Airy. I'm just teasing, although I do think you were responsible for most of it. The same thing happened on the island before we figured out what was going on."

"I have a class."

"So do I," Fehin answered, gazing at her. "But we also have important things to discuss."

"You mean like how not to get caught and thrown out?"

A sheepish grin moved across Fehin's face. "That and a few other things that occurred to me while I was waiting."

"If I flunk out, I'm blaming you."

By now they were walking by the windows of the classroom Airy was supposed to be in. "They can see me!" she whispered, hunching down.

Fehin glanced at the window. "No one's looking. They're watching the professor. Now come on." He tugged her hand and began to jog.

"WITH ALL THE excitement I forgot to invite you to my grandparents' house for Thanksgiving. Do you have plans?"

They had taken shelter under a massive pine tree and were huddled on a bed of pine needles that were still somewhat damp from the recent rain. The pungent smell of resin permeated the cold air and the drip of rain droplets that never reached them made it seem like they were enclosed inside a cathedral of trees. Airy breathed deeply, mentally sending out thanks to these ancient beings. Way better than sitting in a stuffy classroom.

Fehin fiddled with a twig he'd picked up and a moment later there was a tiny figure walking across the needles. Before Airy could comment, the figure disappeared, leaving behind a puff of smoke. He looked up. "I don't have any plans except maybe catching up on all the homework I've neglected since I met you. But I'm still worried about Wolf."

Airy sucked in her breath. "He won't follow us up there?"

"Don't underestimate him. He's been keeping out of sight until recently; I have no idea what he's up to. I've tried probing his mind but he's cut himself off."

"Would you consider doing what he asked? If you did, he'd leave us alone."

Fehin's eyes widened. "Are you kidding? The guy is seriously crazy. If I told you all the creepy stuff he's done..."

"Please don't. I'm scared enough already."

Fehin turned away. "Gunnar thinks we make a good team."

"Who's Gunnar?"

"He's the druid who brought me here. He travels through time."

"I have a druid too." Airy giggled. "If anyone overheard our conversations, they'd put us in one of those places I've been reading about—insane asylum, I think they're called."

Fehin grinned. "They're called mental hospitals now. At least they don't burn witches at the stake anymore. That was shocking to read about. It happened not far from here."

"Salem witch trials. I read about it too. Just think--I could have been one of them. Creepy. How can people live like they do here? They don't even notice what's all around—it's like they're locked inside their heads."

"They're lost in the parallel universe of electronics."

Airy tried to smile but the reality of this statement wasn't funny. "Is

that what we're supposed to change? Because if it is, I don't feel up it."

"I don't know. I agree it sounds pretty much impossible."

A bird began to trill in the tree across from them, the complex song moving up and down octaves as it flitted from branch to branch. "The bird thinks we can do it," Airy announced, looking up. "It says its species is being wiped out by pesticides."

Fehin looked skeptical as he watched the bird fly away. "When you say, 'it says', what do you mean?"

"I told you before, it's not in words. Maybe it's more like when you communicated telepathically. It just comes into my head and I know."

Fehin grabbed hold of Airy's hand. "I'm glad we met."

"I don't think we had much of a choice," she answered, gazing into his moss-green eyes. "Now if we could only figure out the bridge thing."

"Gunnar says we'll know when it's time."

"Isn't that what all of them say?" Airy shook her head. "I'm pretty sure MacCuill said something similar. Do you think they know each other?"

Fehin turned from conjuring a tiny horse and rider. "I know Gunnar travels to Otherworld. Pretty good chance they've met."

"All of this is so strange." She stared into space for a moment, and then slanted a look his way. "You never answered about Thanksgiving. Will you come?"

Fehin nodded and then pulled her to her feet. "I've got another class in fifteen minutes and I can't miss this one. It's prep for a test."

"Do you want to go to church with me on Sunday?" Airy asked. "It's homework for my comparative religions class."

"Sure. What time?"

"The service starts at ten. It's only a couple of blocks down the road from school."

FOURTEEN

On Sunday Fehin dutifully accompanied Airy to the Pres-byterian Church. They sat in a pew in the back whispering as the minister droned on about goodness and evil.

"He seems so *separate*," Airy hissed into Fehin's ear. "And everything he's talking about is self-evident."

"Maybe to you," Fehin whispered back. "Remember you come from a place where people recognize the web of life."

"But what he's saying doesn't have anything to do with the web of life. Remind me to tell you about the Crion," she whis-pered back.

A woman in the row in front of them turned and frowned, shushing them with a finger on her lips.

"Who are the Crion?" Fehin asked once the service was over and they were outside the church.

"They consider themselves the keepers of the wisdom in Otherworld. They keep the energy in balance. You would love them, Fehin. They're only four-feet tall. Their eyes are this amazing shade of amber. They look sort of like what a fox would look like if it was human."

"What they're doing sounds similar to the Hopi. They're a Native American tribe who consider it their job to keep the balance of the world."

"Where are they? I'd love to meet them."

"They live in the southwest of the United States, but they keep to themselves. I think you have to have special permission to go to their villages."

"I'm glad to hear about them. It makes me feel better about this country."

"You wouldn't believe what was done to the local tribes when the Europeans arrived. It's sickening."

"Could the bridge be about them? Maybe they'd help us."

Fehin laughed. "We'd have to know what we were doing first."

"Seriously, I'd love to visit that part of the country."

"Maybe we could take a backpacking trip over summer break."

"It's a long way from here, isn't it?"

Fehin nodded. "It's on the other side of the country. We could take a bus or a train."

Airy watched him, her eyes bright. "That sounds fun. I wonder if my grandparents would mind? I'm sure they expect me to come up there for the summer."

"You wouldn't go home to Otherworld?"

Airy shook her head. "I haven't heard a word from my parents and I'm pretty sure they want me to stay here, since it's my destiny and all." She pursed her lips.

"Our destiny," Fehin amended, chuckling. "I'll look into the Hopi thing and see if it's even feasible. My Native American Studies professor might have some ideas."

∽

FEHIN FELT VERY close to this girl he barely knew. The strength of the feelings surprised him since he'd never experienced anything remotely like it before. Maybe it was partially because they were both odd ducks in this place, or maybe because of the shared destiny. Was this a normal girl boy thing? And then he laughed. There was nothing normal about either one of them, how could they have a normal relationship?

But there were topics they couldn't discuss, like his father. The last time he'd brought him up Airy had asked him to stop; she'd heard too many creepy stories about Brandubh from her parents. Fehin couldn't blame her since the man had very nearly destroyed Otherworld. He assured her his father had been banished, sent to a place he could never escape. But somehow Wolf had escaped from the same place. He was pondering this when he heard a voice.

"Are you coming to class today?"

He turned to see a boy in his math class staring at him. Gary was nice enough, but for some reason Fehin didn't feel comfortable around him. "I have to since we're having a test."

Gary laughed. "You missed the last one."

"I did?"

"Yeah, you did. I saw you with that girl—the one with the red hair? Don't say I blame you for skipping out."

Fehin didn't know he'd missed a test that day and hoped Gary was mistaken. Every test counted 25% of the grade. "I guess I'd better talk with the TA. I'll have to make it up."

It was sometime later in the afternoon that Fehin saw Wolf and Gary walking across the quad together. What the hell?

～

"CAN YOU TWO PLEASE SHUT UP?"

Fehin glanced at the pirate. "Sorry," he said, sliding closer to Airy.

"We probably should go to sleep now," Airy whispered in his ear.

"How can I when I'm lying next to you?"

"If we can't sleep then we can't do this, Fehin. I'll never make it on no sleep."

"I'm looking forward to Thanksgiving," Fehin whispered. The bed was narrow and too small for two people, but when he suggested sleeping on the floor, she'd said no. He was trying to relax but her proximity and the scent of her was driving him mad.

He finally fell into a fitful sleep with dreams of Wolf barging through the door and his feeble attempts to stave off the larger boy. When he woke in the morning Airy was not in bed. He turned to see her pulling on her jeans.

"I thought you were still asleep," she said, flushing.

"Where's the pirate?"

"She's gone to breakfast. You better be careful. If she hears you call her that you'll be out of here in a second."

"Maybe she'd appreciate the name," he muttered, swinging his legs off the bed. At Airy's insistence he'd slept in his jeans. He reached for his shirt where he'd hung it over a chair and pulled it on. "Only two more days until break."

Airy had turned her back to button her blouse. "I hope you can behave yourself while we're up there."

"Whatever do you mean?" he asked innocently, pulling on his socks and shoes.

"My grandparents are free thinkers, but I doubt they'll let us share a room."

Fehin chuckled. "I'd be most surprised if they did, Airy. After all, we're only sixteen."

Airy laughed. "They'll like you."

"Who's in there?" a voice called out. Fehin dove under the bed just before the door opened revealing the older girl who monitored the dorm. "Who were you talking to?" she demanded.

"Hi Sandy. I was talking to myself. I do it a lot," Airy answered.

"If there's a boy in here, you're in major trouble. You know it's against the rules."

"There's no one in here but me."

Under the bed Fehin waved his hands, deflecting the monitor's attention and putting something else in her head.

"Are you getting along with Storm?" Sandy asked, as though that was the entire reason she came in.

"Storm and I get along great," Airy answered.

"Well, good then. See you later," she said before backing out the door and closing it.

Fehin slid out from under the bed and stood up, brushing the dust off his shirt and jeans.

"What did you do?" Airy whispered.

"Just a little magic trick."

Airy shook her head and then hugged him. "We've got to get to class. Wait here until I tell you," she said, opening the door and stepping out. A second later she popped her head through the doorway. "I think she's gone, but hurry. "

Fehin grabbed his pack and handed Airy hers before the two of them hurried down the hall and then snuck down the stairwell. "Meet for lunch?" Fehin asked.

"Not today. I've got to study for a test I'm taking this afternoon. I don't get why they make us do this right before a vacation."

"Would you rather do it when you get back? That would mean worrying about it for the entire break."

Airy grimaced and then headed off in the direction of the English building.

All the distractions of the night had kept Fehin from thinking about Wolf and Gary, but now the entire scene came rushing back. Was Wolf enrolled here? How did he know Gary? He sent his thoughts out, searching for his half-brother, but there was no sign of him. Either that or he was completely locked out of his brother's headspace. Not a good sign.

FIFTEEN

"Fehin, the car's downstairs!" Airy called. Fehin was in his own dorm room packing and she hoped he would hurry because she hated to keep her grandfather waiting. She heard a clatter on the metal stairs and then he was there, his bulging pack on his back.

There had been snow the night before, leaving the flag-stones slick and treacherous. "Follow me," she said, heading across the quad as quickly as she dared.

Fehin trudged behind her and she could hear him muttering what sounded like curses. But he didn't curse, did he? When she looked back, he was looking down, his eyebrows scrunched. "What's wrong?"

He started and then stared into the distance. "Stuff with Wolf. I'll tell you later."

A shiver of apprehension went up Airy's spine. What now? But she couldn't focus on it since her grandfather was standing next to the car with his arms held out.

"Sweetheart! It's been too long!" He hugged her and then pulled back. "Look at you, all grown up!"

Airy turned as Fehin approached. "Grandpa, this is my friend Fehin I told you about."

He held out his hand. "Hello, young man. Just call me Hank."

They piled into the Volvo station wagon, Airy in the front and Fehin in back. "Your Dad just called me, sweetheart. Said he'd call again tomorrow when the family is all there. He's concerned about you because of the changes since he and your mother moved away. There's more poverty now, but I don't think it's as bad as he imagines. Your grandmother and I are lucky because we have the farm and our savings invested in the stock market. It's higher than it's ever been."

Airy glanced at her grandfather, noticing that his hair had turned gray since the last time she'd seen him. Her Dad had some gray too, and she noticed the resemblance between them. "I haven't spoken with them since I've been here."

"You haven't?"

"I can't call them in Otherworld."

"Why haven't they called you? Finna and Alex have phones."

"I don't know, Grandpa. Maybe they think it's better for me to be on my own."

Hank shook his head. "I'll have to have a talk with that son of mine. Sometimes I think those two live in a fairy world."

"Otherworld is like a fairy world."

Her grandfather frowned. "They should keep in touch, Airy. It's not right to drop an innocent girl like you off in this crazy place and not check in once in a while." He glanced in the rearview mirror as though he'd said something wrong.

"It's okay, Grandpa. Fehin knows all about it. He's from 2366."

"2468," Fehin corrected.

"From the future, eh? Your mother wouldn't be Gertrude, by any chance?"

"How did you...?" Airy began.

"That's right," Fehin answered. "She used to live here. Did you meet her?"

"Indeed I did, young man, and her friend Carla as well. Have you seen Carla since you've been here?"

"I didn't want to disturb her. My mother can never come back. It's a pact she made with Loki."

"You didn't tell me that," Airy said, turning.

"It didn't come up. I'm sure there's lots of stuff we don't know about each other."

Hank turned in his seat. "I'm sorry to hear I won't see your mother again. She's an author, isn't she?"

"She wrote two books to change the future. I doubt she'll write another."

"And was she successful?"

Fehin shrugged. "The future is always reshaping itself. At least the corrupt people who were ruining things were banished."

"Except for your brother," Airy said before clapping a hand over her mouth. They didn't need to divulge all this to her grandfather.

"You have a brother?"

"Half-brother," Fehin said, waving his hands in the air.

Hank seemed lost in thought for a moment and then he said, "Your grandmother can't wait to see you, Airy. Did you know we have three dogs now? The old Irish wolfhounds and now a mutt that looks like a hound dog. His name is Mutt." Hank let out a guffaw. "And all your uncles and aunts and cousins will be at the house tomorrow. It should be wild."

Airy turned, her thankful gaze meeting Fehin's across the

seatback. He smiled and stuck his thumb in the air, a gesture she didn't understand.

She watched the familiar scenery go by as they grew closer to the farmhouse, excitement making it hard to sit still. Houses were further apart up here, forests more plentiful. Wide fields were empty now, harrowed and ready for planting in the spring. Silos dotted the landscape, silver towers glinting in the winter sunshine. But then she noticed the lack of cows and sheep that were normally grazing in the fields. And when she looked closer, she noticed that the bare trees were actually dead and most of the houses were empty and falling down.

A few minutes later her grandfather pulled the vintage station wagon into the driveway and cut the motor. "One thing I have to tell you, Airy. The foxes and the rabbits and a lot of the bird population are gone."

"Why?"

"Hard to say. Could be pesticides from the farms around here, could be they've moved on. Monsanto bought Charlie's place across the way and planted some kind of seeds that have to be replaced every year. I heard they have the insecticide right inside the seed. Saves on pesticides, I suppose. I've also seen them spraying from the air. Could be that's killed off some wildlife. We used to collect our seeds but now everything's changed. And there isn't much good water anymore after the fracking that's polluted a lot of wells. Good thing we got rid of our sheep and horses before all this happened. Your grandmother and I don't talk about it much since it upsets her. Try not to mention it, okay?"

Airy nodded, memories of the cavorting baby foxes and rabbits running through her mind. They'd been her friends as much as the trees. Tears filled her eyes but then she saw her grandmother appear on the porch. She jumped out of the car and ran up the porch steps feeling six years old again.

"Airy! You've grown so! You look like a young woman now. But what's happened to your beautiful long hair?"

Airy smiled as her grandmother's arms came round her. "This style is more modern," she answered.

"And who is this?" her grandmother asked as Fehin came up the steps carrying their packs.

Fehin held out his hand. "I'm Fehin."

"You can call me Grace," she said pulling him into a hug.

"So where are we sleeping?" Airy asked, heading inside.

"I've put you in the blue room where you normally stay. Fehin's in the room at the end of the hall. Do you need some help?"

"No, thanks, we've got it." Airy pulled her pack behind her as she climbed the stairs. "C'mon Fehin. I'll show you where your room is."

Airy put her pack down on the bench at the foot of the mahogany four-poster bed and turned to Fehin. "Aren't they great?"

"Pretty cool for grandparents," he answered.

"I love this room," she said, gazing at the blue flowered wallpaper, the matching curtains on either side of the dormer windows and the fireplace in the corner. An eighteenth-century desk sat against the wall, one that she had used many times in the past. She pulled open the top draw, examining her scribbling that no one had thought to throw away.

When she turned, Fehin was staring out the window. "Follow me. I'll show you where you're sleeping."

In the hall they heard scrabbling and whining and in the next second two enormous dogs bounded in, one of them jumping up on Airy to lick her face. "Oh, look at you, Lorna Doone! You got a bath! And Rufus, you sweetie." Airy bent down to greet the dogs, burying her face in their fur.

"They say they like you," she said, peering up at Fehin.

"Did they really or did you just make that up?"

Airy laughed and stood up. "No, they really did communicate something like that. Maybe it was a little less exuberant."

"You mean like, 'who is this dufus?'"

Airy frowned. "What's a dufus?"

"It means someone who is sort of stupid or out of touch. Haven't you learned anything at school?"

Airy giggled. "Is it like dork or geek?"

"Somewhat. Where did you hear those words?"

"Never mind. Let's go to your room. It has a great view over the meadow."

The Fitzhugh family owned several acres of land, most of which was visible from the room Fehin was staying in. Airy pointed out the woods where she played when she was little, the meadow where she rode her pony and the tree house that was now in disrepair. In the distance there was a sheen indicating a pond. "I love it here!" she cried, dancing around the room, her gaze going to all the familiar pieces of furniture as she breathed in the smells of lemony furniture polish and old wood. "I have to go talk to my favorite tree. I'll introduce you. He was my first one. And tomorrow you'll get to meet all seven of my cousins," she added, laughing. Their eyes met and then before she could stop herself, she kissed him.

And they were still kissing when Grace walked through the door.

SIXTEEN

Fehin pulled away first, his embarrassed gaze going to Airy's grandmother. "I...we...I'm sorry...."

Grace waved her hand in the air. "Don't apologize Fehin. I was young once, believe it or not."

Fehin had no trouble believing it since he could still see the girl in her bright blue eyes and slight form. Aside from the color of her long hair she hardly looked old enough to have a sixteen-year-old granddaughter.

"Grandma, Fehin and I like each other."

Grace laughed, a tinkling sound. "That is glaringly obvious, sweet one. Now what I came to say was that there are extra boots, hats, gloves and coats downstairs. You two don't seem at all prepared for the weather up here. Didn't your parents send you with proper clothing for the cold weather? There's a forecast for snow this weekend."

"I guess they thought we'd buy these things on our own. Weather in Otherworld is fairly temperate."

"The island never gets cold, unless..." Fehin noticed Airy's subtle head shake and broke off in mid-sentence.

"Well, maybe while you're here we can go into Halston to the general store and buy you some proper winter clothes and shoes," Grace said with a glance toward the flimsy sneakers on Airy's feet. "Come down when you're settled," she said, turning to go. "I need some help with the pies," she added, winking.

Once the door closed Airy let out a long sigh. "That was awkward," she said.

Fehin noticed the flush that even now infused her cheeks with bright color. For his part he was still in the throes of what he'd felt when she pressed against him. "Your grandmother seemed okay with it."

Airy looked worried. "But if she tells Grandpa, he'll tell my parents. I don't want them to know about this, Fehin. You're Brandubh's son. They'll never approve."

"Didn't you tell me that the goddess of prophecy mentioned me and the island? How can they disapprove if this is our destiny?"

Airy shook her head. "She didn't mention you by name and my parents have so much animosity toward your father. We're like Romeo and Juliet."

"Who are they?"

Airy smiled. "You need to take a literature class. They're characters from a play of the same name by Shakespeare--two lovers from warring families. It's a tragic story."

"I don't think I'd like it." Fehin's gaze went to the window where a swirl of white blinded him for a moment. The snow reminded him of Wolf and the freezing cold weather his brother had brought down on Far Isle before Fehin moved everyone to the island. It had been a bleak time with many deaths. A second later he saw himself lying ill in a hospital bed. A feeling of helplessness washed over him. This was not a premonition he cared to share.

In the meantime, Airy was also staring out the window. "Things have changed since I was here last. What if my tree is dead like the ones we passed?"

"Is that what you were trying to say in the car?"

"The farms are gone. I remember the families that lived in those houses that are all falling down. You heard what Grandpa said about water and pesticides and what's happened to the animals. I know this is connected to our destiny."

"I'm sorry, Airy. I know how hard it is to see things change for the worse. I went through the same thing in Fell after Wolf destroyed it all."

"And what did you do?"

Fehin grimaced. "I created an island and moved everybody."

Airy stared at him. "Can you move everyone from here?"

"I don't think it's possible."

"What are we going to do?"

"Right now we're going to drop off my backpack in my room, go downstairs and have a pleasant conversation with your grandparents."

SEVENTEEN

"Now listen to me, Airy! You can't involve yourself with this boy!"

Airy's heart sank. Her grandmother had told her grandfather and now her parents knew about Fehin. She pressed the phone to her ear trying not to cry. "But Mum, he's..."

"Not another word. Now promise me."

"I don't think I can." She heard her mother say something about talking sense into her and then her father's voice came on the line.

"Airy, the entire reason you're there is to learn about the world outside Otherworld and discover your destiny. This does not include hanging around with someone who can't be trusted. Please take this to heart and think about it. Your mother and I are worried."

"If you're so worried, why haven't you called or come to see me?" Airy cried, wiping away tears. She glanced toward Fehin sitting at the dining room table.

There was silence for a moment and then her father said, "We've had some things going on here..."

"Obviously more important than me. Goodbye, Dad." Airy handed the phone to her grandmother who looked concerned as she took it.

"Harold? What did you say to the girl?"

But Airy didn't hear the rest of the conversation as she fled from the room. She flung the front door open and ran outside, slamming it hard behind her. It was Thanksgiving morning and all her excitement about seeing her relatives had disappeared with a single phone call.

She ran through the snow in her sneakers, hardly feeling the wet cold that seeped through the light canvas as she crossed the meadow. Once she reached the ancient oak tree she climbed up as she'd done so many times in the past, huddling in the crook of perfectly placed branches.

The tears were warm where they tracked down her cheeks and for a moment or two, she concentrated on the warmth and the comfort that came from the tree. The oak was sending her a message but in her distraught state it took a moment to tune in. And then it was clear. It wasn't in words but the gist of it resonated inside her and she knew she was right about Fehin and that her parents were wrong.

"Airy!"

Airy reluctantly climbed down when she heard her grand-mother's lilting call. She didn't know what to expect now that her grandparents knew about Fehin's father and every other horrible detail of the past. If she lost their support too, she wasn't sure how she would manage.

At the house she climbed the steps slowly and then shed her soaked shoes and jacket before opening the door. But instead of stern faces, her grandparents and Fehin were sitting together at the breakfast table calmly talking.

"Come have breakfast, darling," her grandmother invited,

pointing to the empty chair beside hers. "Fehin's been filling us in on his history. He's a special boy, this friend of yours."

When Airy's gaze met Fehin's she breathed a sigh of relief and sank into her chair.

ONCE THE REST of the family arrived the day turned into a blur of joyful greetings, wet dogs tracking in mud, snowball fights and snowman building, followed by a turkey dinner with all the trimmings. When it was time for dinner the younger generation trooped in, shedding wet gloves, hats, boots and coats in a pile at the front door. They found seats at the long trestle-style table, all of them red-faced from the cold.

Fehin got along well with Airy's relatives, fitting in as though he'd known them his entire life. Airy watched in fascination as he conversed with them on varied subjects. His knowledge of building, growing vegetables and animal husbandry were the most surprising.

He'd be the perfect person to be stranded with on a desert island, she thought, her mind going to the television shows like Survivor and The Bachelor she'd watched since arriving at the college in Milltown. The student union had a wide-screened one of these devices and some nights were devoted to the student's favorite shows. Airy had picked up a lot of slang from watching, as well as some swear words that she tried hard not to use.

A stab of pure happiness went through her as she gazed around at her cousins. With four sets of aunts and uncles the children ranged in age from six to twenty-two years old. The only people missing were her parents, making her wonder why they weren't here. It would have been the perfect time for them to see everyone. And then she thought about the phone conversation and had a sick feeling in the pit of her stomach. They didn't trust her. She'd never thought she would have such negative feelings about her parents. At this moment she didn't care if she ever saw them again.

EIGHTEEN

Something woke him—a sound or a smell or maybe the dream that drifted away as he opened his eyes. Airy had been in it as well as Wolf, but the only thing that remained was a deep foreboding about the future.

He heard a soft knock on the door and then Airy whispered, "Fehin, are you awake?"

He jumped out of bed and hurried to the door, registering how cold the wood was beneath his feet and how warm he'd been under his down comforter. When he opened it Airy was standing there shivering in her thin nightgown, her eyes wide and frightened. "Can I come in?"

He nodded and then closed the door after her. "What time is it?"

"I think about five. I had a terrible dream."

"Climb in here," Fehin said, holding the covers back. "It's warmer."

Airy moved in beside him and pulled the covers over her bent knees. "I'm scared," she said.

Fehin pulled her close. "Maybe you're just cold," he said rubbing her hands between his.

"The dream was so real—it was some future disaster we'll be faced with."

"So, like a premonition?"

She nodded. "It was you and me and Wolf. We were doing something that neither of us wanted to do, but Wolf was making us. I felt so helpless. What does it mean?"

Fehin wrapped his arms around her shivering body. "Do you know where we were?"

Airy shook her head and began to cry. "I don't know," she said, pressing her head against his neck.

He felt her tears on his skin, her breath in his ear and it was all he could do not to scream. He had an overwhelming urge to kiss her, but held himself back. He'd vowed to respect where they were. The idea of her grandparents seeing them engaged in anything more than holding hands made him shudder. He had to concentrate on the dream and his brother and try to ignore what was going on in his body.

"I'm sorry he's invading your mind. I thought he'd lost all his powers. Was it a dream or did it seem like more?"

"This was more than a dream. I *felt* him, Fehin. And what about the bridge? So far all I've come up with is a bridge from Otherworld to your island."

"That can't be it. I think it's between this world and what we consider magical—the bridge would change how people see things."

"How can two teenagers get the entire world to believe in things they're sure don't exist?"

"What about God? Think about the service at the church. They believe in a gray-haired old man up in the sky who runs everything."

"Those same people would think we were linked to the devil."

Fehin sighed. "You're probably right. There's a big difference between that and the spirit world."

"They'd never believe it," Airy said in a tone of resignation. "Demonizing another is only a projection—we all need to own our shadow sides."

Fehin frowned. "Where did that come from?"

"I've been reading Jung in my psych class. He was an amazing man and able to put what we're talking about into layman's terms."

"Don't get discouraged. We'll figure it out. But I think you'd better get back to your own room before somebody notices."

"ARE you two up for some shopping today?" Grace asked at the breakfast table.

Fehin looked over at Airy who seemed lost in her own thoughts. "What do you think?" he asked.

"Huh? What? Oh, shopping. Sounds fine to me."

Grace rose from the table and began clearing the plates. "Say in an hour?"

Fehin nodded, and then kicked Airy under the table. She jumped and looked up.

"An hour? Sounds fine," she said.

Once Grace was out of earshot Fehin grabbed her shoulder. "You're acting weird, and if you don't get it together your grandmother will start asking questions."

"I can't help it. I can't stop thinking about Wolf. I need to talk to the oak. He'll know what to do."

"Why don't you do it before we leave and then maybe you can enjoy picking out winter clothes."

When Airy left the house Fehin went up to his room. He reached out to his brother and this time there was an answer. "I'm watching you," Wolf said.

Fehin tried to keep the connection, tried to see what nasty thoughts were roaming around in Wolf's head, but he'd severed the contact. "Damn," he muttered, pressing his lips together in frustration. He stared out the window, watching Airy move across the meadow with her head down. A few minutes later he lost sight of her as she entered the woods.

He raced from the room, took the stairs two at a time and tore out of the house, his bare feet sinking deep into the snow. "Airy!" he yelled, cupping his hands around his mouth. Wolf was waiting for her—he knew it like he knew his own mind.

NINETEEN

Just as Airy entered the woods she heard Fehin call her name. She ignored him and kept walking, her mind on the questions to ask her old friend and the beauty of the snow-laden trees all around her. It was so quiet and peaceful here. The only thing missing were her bird friends and all the animals that had taken shelter here. Sadness moved through her as she saw them in her mind's eye.

The ancient oak had helped in the past—he would help her again; he could explain what had happened to the foxes and the rabbits. But then again, the questions she asked him when she was small, like where she left her doll, and had Lorna Doone chewed up her stuffed animal, were nothing compared to what was going on now. This felt like a matter of life or death. It was then that she heard the whispering all around her. The trees were all talking at once and she couldn't figure out what they were saying. "Slow down," she said. "One at a time."

But she never got to hear their message because someone looped a thick rope around her neck and dragged her away. Choking, her hands went to her neck, struggling to keep the rope from cutting off her breath. Her shoes pulled off and the rough ground dug into her bare heels. But the pain was nothing compared to the utter terror that moved through every cell of her body.

It wasn't long before they were in an area she'd never been before. Her tormentor grunted but she couldn't get a look at him. Where was he taking her? It became clear when he hauled her into an abandoned house that had obviously stood derelict for many years. The roof shingles were mostly gone, the joists open and a few missing; the windows were cracked and glass shards sparkled across the floor. The inside of the house stunk like mouse droppings and rot.

He tied her hands behind her back before he pulled the rope from around her neck. It was then that she caught a glimpse of his face, her gasp dying in her throat as he turned his malevolent gaze on hers. He was enormous with a bull neck, his hands swollen and disfigured as though from frostbite. His eyes were so like Fehin's, except they contained no light, and his mouth, also recognizable, was pulled up in a sneer. Wolf was the monster depiction of his brother.

"You walked right into my trap," he said in a gravelly voice before letting out a terrible laugh that scared her even more than his appearance.

"What trap was that?" she asked, trying to breathe deeply.

"The dream. I planted the dream. And you followed just as I wanted you to."

"What did the dream have to do with me talking to my tree?"

"Don't fuck with me," he said, and then dragged her by the arms toward a gaping hole in the floor.

Airy glanced around wildly, trying to think of some way to escape. "Surely you're not planning to just leave me in here."

"Until I get what I want."

"And what is it you want?"

"You know what I want and so does my brother. Now let's see how smart he is," he said, stuffing a filthy rag into her mouth. She gagged and tried to spit it out but it stayed where it was. He pushed her, sending her tumbling painfully into the pit below. She couldn't move, her legs twisted beneath her, her arms bent back and secured, and now she couldn't scream either. She watched in horror as he nailed boards over her prison, blocking out all light.

AIRY HAD no idea how much time had gone by. The only sounds she heard were the scuffling of rats and mice. She reached out to the creatures that occupied her prison, but her mind was so full of fear that she couldn't make a connection.

Her arms ached and she was sure that one of the bones in her right leg was broken. The pain of it made her eyes water. When she tried to shift it felt like knives were stabbing into her. Where was Fehin? She'd sent message after message his way. And then she thought about how far Wolf had dragged her. It had taken what seemed like an hour to get to this abandoned house. Surely there were gouges and tracks in the mud. But this property did not belong to her grandparents. And she doubted that Wolf was stupid enough to leave his tracks in the snow. He was smart—as smart as his brother and a lot more devious.

She must have fallen asleep because she came awake with a start, unable to remember where she was for a moment. But then the horror of her situation came back. She tried hard not to cry but the tears came, sobs racking her body. And following the tears came a terror so deep she thought she might die from it. Her heart pounded as though it would fly out of her chest. This could end up being her grave.

It was a long time later, maybe even the next day, when thirst began to plague her. At first it was a mild sensation in the back of her throat but then it was all consuming. If only she could get this stinking rag out of her mouth. But even rolling her head against the ground didn't do it and finally she gave up.

Sometime after that she realized she was about to black out. She was dizzy and disoriented, colors flashing across her vision. She had no reference for night or day, no sense of how much time had passed. She fought against it, trying to keep awake; she knew all about hypothermia, had read about it in one of her books. But it took her anyway.

TWENTY

Fehin was frantic. He'd searched every inch of the Fitzhugh property and had found no sign of her anywhere. He'd tried over and over to contact Wolf but had come up against a blank wall.

"Where did you say you saw her last?" Grace asked again, her tear-streaked face making Fehin want to cry himself.

"She was heading into the woods to talk with her tree. You must know the one."

"And we couldn't find a footprint anywhere around there. Are you positive this is your brother's work? It could be some lunatic serial killer. There's a prison thirty miles up the road."

Fehin tried to be patient with her. They'd had this same conversation earlier today and yesterday as well. "I'm sure of it."

"Hank will be back with the police soon—I wish we'd called them sooner."

"How could you with the power out?"

It was Monday morning and Airy had been missing since

early on Friday. Around noon on that day a storm had raged across the area, taking down power lines and dropping branches from trees like they were toothpicks. It seemed like a tornado, a type of storm unheard of in these parts. Fehin had a feeling he knew where it came from. But now all was still, as though Airy's energy had been depleted. Even the snow had stopped. When he went outside the stillness felt like an absence.

Fehin hadn't slept, his nights filled with images of Airy being tortured. He felt responsible for what had happened, apologizing over and over to her grandparents. They waved them off, but he knew they held him at least partially account-able. It was his brother who had done this. They asked him several times how Wolf had known they were here, as though Fehin had led him up here on purpose.

Why would Wolf do this and not contact him? And then the realization hit that Wolf might simply have killed her just to be rid of her. He saw her then, eyes closed, face pale as death. And when he reached out there was nothing. He doubled over in pain. And then the tears came. It was way past time to call on Gunnar.

THAT STUPID IDIOT, Wolf thought. *He's going to let that girl die rather than to tap into our birthright—telepathic commu-nication. Fehin doesn't have the power to do anything for me, but won't it be nice to see him blamed for this? And with the dark thoughts I'm sending his way on a daily basis he'll soon be unable to function at all.* Wolf chuckled to himself, hurrying to catch the bus back to Milltown. He and Gary had a gig going that would bring him some good money. With any luck the rest of his powers would soon return on their own.

"SO, what you're telling me is that Airy has been gone for three days and you've done nothing about it?" Gunnar glared at Fehin. "You do know she could be dead by now."

"That isn't helping, Gunnar," Fehin said, trying not to grab him by the neck and squeeze. "I searched the entire property. I thought Wolf would contact me."

"And you're positive it was Wolf?"

"Of course, I am."

At that moment Hank and the police arrived and Grace rushed out of the kitchen, her focus on the front door. The dogs began to bark and, in the commotion, Gunnar slipped away, taking Fehin with him. Once they were outside, the druid said, "This entire scenario seems very strange. Have you tried to reach Airy telepathically?"

"I've tried over and over."

Gunnar grunted in obvious disgust. "Center yourself, boy! Do you want her to die?" With that statement the druid disappeared.

Fehin turned to see several policemen with dogs on leashes working their way across the meadow. He hoped fervently they would find her. In his room he meditated, saying no to the thoughts that kept intruding. It took a long while but finally he was calm enough to send his thoughts out to her. Airy, *tell me how to find you.* She was unconscious, her mind barely able to track. She was somewhere very dark. When he heard the word 'hurry', he grew weak with fear. She was very near death.

THE POLICE and the dogs were back, their dour expressions saying it all. Fehin felt his heart drop, and when he glanced at

Grace, she burst into tears. In the midst of this he heard Gunnar in his mind asking to meet him outside the house. He hurried through the front door and then around to the back to the privet hedge.

Gunnar was waiting there, his expression dark. "I can't find Wolf."

Fehin opened his mouth and closed it. "He has to be here! Why would he leave without getting what he wanted?"

"Did you ever consider that Wolf's motives may not be what you think?" Gunnar had no sympathy, the expression on his face as serious as Fehin had ever seen. "This is up to you now, Fehin. You know your brother's methods. You need to put yourself inside his head. Where would he take her?"

Fehin was wild, his mind splintering off in several directions at once. "I can't. I don't know how he thinks! And I've never been here before—how would I know where he'd take her?" In truth he could tap into his brother's mind, but the sucking darkness he found there pulled him down, tempting him with the idea of unlimited power.

"Fehin, listen to me," Gunnar said, grabbing his arm. "You conjured an island and you saved a thousand people from your brother's evil. You know how to read minds. You can do this."

"Why can't *you* find her?"

"It's isn't up to me to find her. I've helped as much as I'm allowed."

"Allowed by who?"

"Stop trying to wheedle out of this. You're related to Wolf, you're Brandubh's son. Now tap into that part of you. It may be painful to look at the darker side of yourself, but in this case it just may save Airy."

"You think she's still alive."

Gunnar narrowed his eyes and then disappeared.

Fehin stared into the spot where the druid had been. He

loved Airy. If she died, he didn't want to live. Maybe this would turn out like Romeo and Juliet after all. Without thinking he found himself wandering across the meadow and into the forest on the other side. When he came to the oak tree Airy had shown him, he stopped and looked up. "I've never spoken to a tree before but I would be most grateful if you could help me. I know you love her as much as I do. I have to find her, but I don't know where to look."

The forest stood silent around him. He sat down in the mud and put his head in his hands and then looked deeply into his own psyche, searching the part of him that could kill another human being without a second thought. But if he entered that tangled morass, he might never find his way out. He was a sorcerer's son as much as Wolf was.

It was the vision of Airy's pale face that made the decision for him, sending a jolt of adrenaline through every cell of his body. He sent his thoughts out through the ether searching for Wolf, and when he found him, he wormed his way into Wolf's thoughts, seeking the ones he needed. He could feel his half-brother's depravity, his utter lack of compassion, mercy, or sympathy. As soon as he found what he needed he fought his way out of the rotting weeds, the mire and filth, bursting free and slamming a wall down between his mind and Wolf's. He took a deep breath, filling his lungs with the life-giving oxygen coming from the trees. He knew what to do.

A fence ran around the Fitzhugh property with gates that mostly stood open; the sheep and other animals they'd kept were long gone. Fehin headed south from the woods, walking through one of these gates and following some inner voice that directed him that way. In the distance another copse of trees loomed dark and in the meadow in front was a derelict house. It was the perfect place to hide someone.

"Airy?" he called out. There was no answer. It was then he

noticed the footprint and the gouges in the mud leading to the entrance. He hurtled through the doorway, coming to a stop in the dim interior. "Airy?" he called again, louder this time.

He could smell fresh sawdust. And then he saw it--the boards that had recently been nailed into place. He tore at them, cutting his hands as he tried to rip them loose. Finally, he got another board and pried them up, one by one. He couldn't see a thing but he could feel Airy down there in the dark. He switched on his small flashlight before lowering himself down.

When he found her, she was twisted into a shape that could only mean broken bones. "My gods, what has he done to you?" Tears ran down his cheeks as he moved her gently into a sitting position and took the rag out of her mouth. Her face was pale as death, purple shadows under her closed eyes. Her head lolled to the side, and when he felt for a pulse, it was thready and weak.

He untied her arms and picked her up, hoisting her partially out before climbing out himself. He put his arms gently around her shoulders and legs, cradling her body against his chest and began the trip back to the farmhouse. His tears fell onto her face as he moved through the snow. There was no sign of life from her aside from the slight rise and fall of her chest.

∾

"WE'RE FOREVER INDEBTED TO YOU," Hank told Fehin, glancing at Grace beside him. She smiled weakly, her pale face registering the extreme stress she was under.

The three of them were standing together outside Airy's hospital room. She was back from surgery, but hadn't yet come out of the anesthesia. Fehin gazed into the older man's eyes, noticing the shadow of untruth that lay behind that statement. He sensed distrust and when he probed further, he saw that Hank believed that Fehin was involved in his granddaughter's abduction. Both Hank and Grace believed that he and Wolf had conspired together. How else could Fehin have found her so easily?

WHEN FEHIN REACHED the farmhouse hours before, he'd been met with confused hysteria and frantic calls to the hospital and the ambulance company. It hadn't been long before the shrill sound of sirens blared, and then the MT's were placing Airy's limp body on the stretcher and carrying her out to the waiting vehicle. Fehin watched them leave, a feeling of utter futility washing over him. No one had said a word, but he knew there was a good chance she wouldn't make it. Airy's parents and grandparents had been on the phone for a long time after the ambulance whisked Airy away. And when Fehin left the room to go back upstairs he'd heard Hank mention Brandubh. Harold and Maeve were now on their way to Halston from Otherworld, due to arrive at Boston airport this evening. He dreaded meeting them.

It was another hour before the doctor allowed them into Airy's room. "She's very weak," he told them. "It was a compound break, and with her severe dehydration and blood loss we were lucky we didn't lose her. Please keep it short—she needs to rest."

When they entered the room Airy was propped up on pillows, her eyes red-rimmed and shadowed. Her gaze went to Fehin first and she held out her hand. But when Fehin moved forward, Hank muscled by him, taking her outstretched fingers in his. "Sweetheart, I can't tell you how worried we've been. What a terrible ordeal you've been through."

Airy tried to smile and then winced. Her leg was in traction waiting for the swelling to go down. Once it did the doctors would put on a cast. "I owe it all to Fehin," she said, gazing at him over her grandfather's shoulder.

"Yes, well..." Hank turned to his wife. "Grace and I love you very much, sweetheart. We feel terrible that this happened on our watch. Your parents are on their way. They should be in to see you tonight."

Grace moved to the other side of the bed, taking Airy's other hand in hers. "My dear, sweet Airy. You look so pale. I'm so glad you're in one piece."

"Time to go now," the nurse called out from the doorway. "She needs her rest."

"Of course, she does," Hank said, moving toward the door and gesturing to his wife.

When Fehin took a step toward the bed Hank grabbed his shoulder. "You heard what the nurse said."

"Fehin," Airy called out, but Fehin had already been dragged from the room.

"Don't you need to get back to school?" Hank asked once they were in the car.

"I don't want to leave her."

"You can't expect to stay with us while Harold and Maeve are here," Grace added. "It would be better for all concerned if you go back before they arrive."

Fehin was barely able to control his anger. He hadn't had a chance to talk to Airy yet, and apparently, he would not be granted that privilege.

"There's a bus leaving in an hour. I think you should be on

it," Hank muttered as they drove into the driveway. "I'll give you a lift down to Halston."

"Thank you, sir," Fehin answered through gritted teeth. In the house he went upstairs to collect his things.

TWENTY-ONE

"Where's Fehin?" Airy asked, looking around.

Harold shook his head and then glanced at Maeve. "We haven't seen him since we got here. He must have gone back to school."

"But he didn't even say goodbye!"

"I'm sure he was anxious to get back to Milltown and classes, Airy."

Airy stared at her father's impassive face. "He's not like that. Do you realize that I'd be dead if it wasn't for him?"

"About that," Maeve began, darting a glance at Harold. "Your grandparents and we agree that there's something very fishy about what happened to you. It wouldn't surprise me if Fehin were involved. You do understand who his father is."

"What?" When Airy leaned forward, pain shot through her calf and thigh. She fell back against the pillows trying to catch her breath. "There's no way Fehin was involved in this. I told Grandma all about Wolf and what Fehin told me. Wolf hoped to get his powers back."

"So why did he kidnap you and then not contact Fehin?

We both think your trust in Fehin is commendable, sweetheart, but the facts are there. He found you when no one else could. Wolf doesn't exist. You have to understand that this boy's father is a sorcerer."

"I don't care who his father is. Wolf is the one who dragged me there and threw me in that pit. I saw him. I already told you that!"

"Maybe you were hallucinating after all the trauma. You said there was a resemblance."

Airy shook her head and turned to stare out the window. Fehin was gone and she was stuck here until the cast came off-- a good three months. And the doc had said she might need physical therapy after that. "When can I go home?"

Harold looked surprised. "You mean to Otherworld? We aren't taking you back with us, if that's what you mean."

Airy sighed heavily. "I meant to Grams."

"The doc said in a couple of days."

After her parents left Airy tried to contact Fehin telepathically, surprised when he answered her.

Are you all right? he asked.

I'm fine but I miss you. Can you come back up?

There was a long pause and she thought she'd lost the connection, but then she heard: *I can't, Airy. Everyone thinks I did this to you.*

Airy wanted to tell him that wasn't true, but he was right. *I'm sorry,* she finally answered. There was no response after that.

Harold and Maeve spent three days in Halston before saying they had to get back. "I want you to promise that you will have nothing to do with this boy ever again," her father said sternly. "I don't want to worry about you when we get home."

Airy had always trusted her father, had known that in a

pinch he would take her side. What she saw on his face was a resoluteness that refused to be budged. "But, Da, he..."

"Airy, I'm serious. Your mother and I have been through a war caused by this boy's father. You cannot expect to continue with this friendship."

Airy nodded and looked down.

CHRISTMAS HAD COME AND GONE, the New Year as well, and Airy was still lying around the farmhouse in Halston and bored to tears. Her grandparents had set up a bed for her on the first floor so she could avoid the long climb upstairs. The cast was due to come off in another month, but until then she had to find a way to catch up on homework. Now she needed to speak with her professors and find out what to do. The entire ordeal in the pit seemed fuzzy in her mind, as though she'd made it all up.

Over the course of these past months, she'd heard nothing from Fehin, even though she'd reached out to him many times. On the phone her parents had gone on and on about Brandubh's sorcery, relaying in graphic detail the horrible things he'd done in Otherworld. He'd killed many and hurt many others with no remorse whatsoever. Her grandparents had backed up their position, rehashing her ordeal and how strange it all was. Fehin was not who he pretended to be.

What she remembered of that November day had softened around the edges, making her wonder if in her shock it really had been Fehin who put her in that pit. What did she really know about him other than what he'd shared, which was not much at all? Maybe there wasn't a Wolf; maybe in her panic she'd made Fehin into a monster in her mind. The only other time she'd supposedly come into contact with him had been in the library where she hadn't seen his face. In the darkness it could have been Fehin who hit her on the back of the head. Having someone you trust do such horrible things was enough to cause hallucinations. She'd read about this sort of scenario in her psych class.

~

"YOU'VE MISSED so much school now there's probably no reason to go back," her grandfather said in early February when she brought it up.

"I'm going back, Grandpa. I'll repeat the classes if I have to. I can't stay here forever."

"Your grandmother and I have enjoyed having you here so much, Airy. We both worry about Fehin being there. We don't want you getting involved with him again, and neither do your parents."

Airy looked up. "I get it, Grandpa. You and Mum and Dad have finally convinced me. I plan to stay away from him."

Her grandfather smiled. "I'm so glad to hear that, sweetheart."

When he bent to kiss her, she smelled his distinctive after-shave, basking in the familiar comfort of his arms around her.

FOR THE NEXT month she concentrated on the work her professors had provided her with, hoping she could pass the tests they gave her when she returned. The time went by more quickly now that she had studying to do, her grandfather's computer allowing her to get the lengthy e-mails the college sent. Most of the textbooks and reading material for her litera-ture and psychology classes she could access online. There were only two classes she knew she would fail. Math was one of them and the World History she shared with Fehin was another.

But at night alone in her bed her mind wandered down twisting paths that didn't lead neatly to the conclusions she'd made. Many nights she woke with tears on her face. If Fehin wasn't the boy she was linked with, then who was it?

~

"JESUS, Mary and Joseph, it's good to see you!" Storm cried when Airy walked into the dorm room in March. A second later Airy was crushed in her friend's arms.

"I thought you didn't hug," she laughed when Storm released her.

Storm made a funny face, her mouth quirking. "Special circumstances," she said. "I wondered if you'd be back at all. Fehin said…"

Airy stared. "You talked to him?"

"Yeah. When he got back, he filled me in on the broken leg and all. The snow up there must have been treacherous for you to fall hard enough to do so much damage."

Airy stared at her dorm mate. "Fehin was lying, Storm. It didn't happen like that."

"So how did it happen?"

"He tried to kill me."

TWENTY-TWO

Fehin had tried several times to contact Airy since their one telepathic conversation, but she had not responded. He didn't know what to think. It was March now and he was sure the cast was off. She must be coming back to school soon. When he walked across campus, he could hear birds singing for the first time in several months. The trees had catkins now. The down jacket he'd bought was too warm and he pulled it off and stuffed it into his pack. Without Airy his world had narrowed and dulled. He felt heavy and listless and his grades had suffered from his inability to concentrate.

Out of the corner of his eye he saw a flash of red and turned to see a willowy girl disappearing around the corner of the building ahead of him. Although the hair was longer now, he was positive it was Airy. No one else he'd ever met had hair that particular shade between red and gold. He took off running, slipping in the mud as he rounded the corner. She was not far ahead and he noticed the uneven gait, a reminder of what he'd allowed to happen.

When he felt the magnetic pull, he was positive. "Airy!" he called out.

She turned, her eyes going wide when she saw him. And then she limped away as though he was a leper.

"Wait!" he called, but she'd already slipped inside the building. When he opened the door, she'd disappeared.

Fehin was unable to move for at least a full minute, his heart contracting painfully. Had she decided to avoid him without even telling him why? Her parents must have finally convinced her that he couldn't be trusted. When tears welled, he angrily wiped them away. At this moment he wished he'd never met her.

It was later in the afternoon when he saw Storm coming out of a classroom next to his. As she walked by, he stepped out in front her, nearly tripping her in the process.

"Jesus, Fehin. What do *you* want?"

"I need to talk to you."

Storm shook her head and then looked around. "I can guess why," she said. "If I were you, I'd give up on her. She seems convinced that you're a bad dude."

"Do you agree?"

Storm seemed surprised by the question. "I...well, if you must know I think she's wrong."

"Did you tell her that?"

Storm laughed. "I told her you were too much of a goober to do anything like that."

"Not sure what that word means, but I have a good idea," Fehin said, looking down. "I have to talk to her."

Storm stared at him, her thickly lined eyes narrowing as she thought. "I don't know what to tell you," she finally said. "She's stubborn."

"I could sneak into your room. It's the only place she can't run away from me."

"Don't tell her I told you, but she'll be in the library tonight between six and seven. Good luck," she added before heading away down the hall.

Fehin walked into his next class feeling slightly more hopeful. He spent the rest of the day practicing what to say to her.

IT WAS 6:30 when Fehin found Airy in a cubby, her head bent over a thick book she'd pulled from the shelves. He'd wandered through the library for nearly twenty minutes before discovering where she was. When he touched her shoulder she started, and when she saw who it was, she pressed her body away from him as though he was about to hit her.

"Are you afraid of me?" He didn't need to ask; he could see it in her eyes.

"Go away," she hissed.

"Airy, at least have the courtesy to explain. The last time we were together we loved each other. How could things change so fast?"

"I never loved you, Fehin. I just thought I did. It was silly and childish. Now I know who you are."

"And who am I?" he whispered.

Airy stared at him for a moment and then turned away. "You know who you are. Now please leave me alone."

"I like your hair," he said. "It's grown."

Airy ran her fingers through the chin length curls and for a moment he could see the hint of a smile, but then she stiffened, her eyes going dark. "I don't trust you, Fehin. We can't be together. I seriously want you to stay away from me. If you don't, I'll contact the school authorities and tell them you're stalking me."

The cold look she gave him after the harsh words was like an ice pick stabbing into his chest. He watched her for another moment and then turned and walked away. He fought the tears that welled as he headed toward the entrance, but by the time he was outside he had to stop to wipe them away. He shook his head, furious at his own weakness and also the expectations that had now been dashed for good.

TWENTY-THREE

Airy tried to stop the tears but there was nothing she could do. Her gaze followed Fehin as he walked toward the front of the library and then she put her head on the desk and gave over to her grief.

His face had been so full of pain, his eyes filling with tears when she told him she didn't trust him. And while she was saying the hurtful words her insides were telling her something very different. She could feel the connection between them in her belly, as though there was a bungee cord stretching more and more the further he moved away. Soon it would break altogether. The words in the book blurred when she tried to continue reading and so she gave up and replaced it on the shelf where she'd found it. She gathered her materials together and left the library.

"Did you tell him I'd be there?" she demanded, once she was back in her dorm room.

Surprised, Storm turned from her computer. "I might have. So what? You need to at least explain your position, Airy. It isn't fair to just cut him loose like that."

"He's the one who hurt me, Storm! He nearly killed me!" Airy sat down heavily on her bed and pressed her fingers into her temples.

"And you think this, why?"

Airy wanted to scream but she held it back. She couldn't reveal the true horror of what had happened and the background that went along with it. *Wolf was a figment of my imagination,* she told herself, rubbing her temples. "Because...because..."

"Because your parents and grandparents said so? I have a hard time seeing Fehin in this role. He's a lot of things, but cruel is definitely not one of them."

The feeling was back in the pit of her stomach, the one that demanded attention. Her insides were not in agreement with her mind. "But he...he..."

Storm rose and sat down on the bed next to Airy. "When I first talked to you on the phone after the incident you said it was some other creepy dude who kidnapped you. You even described him, and what you described bore no resemblance to Fehin. What happened between that conversation and when you got back to college?"

Airy barely remembered talking to Storm. She must have still been under anesthesia. The question was a good one because right now she wasn't sure of anything. "I don't know," she finally answered.

AIRY SLEPT BADLY THAT NIGHT, waking to the claustrophobia and abject terror of being gagged and stuck in that lightless pit. She remembered in detail the voice of her attacker, the grunts he made. His laugh. There was no way Fehin could duplicate that voice. She should have trusted herself. Her parents and grandparents were wrong.

Before her first class the next morning Airy called her grandparents in Scotland. When Finna answered she began to cry. "Nana, can you talk to my parents about Fehin? They think he's some kind of monster."

"Airy, we don't see Harold and Maeve very often now. I can try and talk with them, but the last time we spoke they seemed very convinced that he was not who he pretends to be. They mentioned what happened to you up in Halston. It sounded quite horrific. I can understand their worry."

"It wasn't him, Nana. It was his half-brother, Wolf. Ask MacCuill to talk to them. Corra told me that Fehin and I are linked. Well, she said a boy, but I know the boy is Fehin because of how I feel inside when I'm around him. I feel terrible because I believed them, and now I've hurt him really badly, and...."

"Slow down, sweetheart. If you want me to speak with MacCuill I'll do so, but you know how stubborn your mother can be."

"Thanks, Nana. I love him."

"Airy, you're only sixteen. Loves will come and go."

"You're wrong. Fehin and I have a destiny together. Corra will tell you."

"I'll do what I can, but I don't promise anything."

Airy hung up the phone feeling a tiny bit better. Now she had to talk with Fehin, and that would not be so easy.

In her dorm room Airy put on her favorite blouse and a clean pair of jeans and then fluffed out her hair. She didn't wear any make-up because she knew Fehin didn't like it. Her hands were shaking as she practiced what to say. She didn't know where to find him. Their paths rarely crossed now that she'd dropped World History.

Just as she was about to leave the room her cell phone rang. It was her Halston grandparents' number and for a moment she didn't answer. But then she swiped across the screen and said hello.

"Sweetheart, we miss you," Grace said. "How are things going?"

"Good," she answered warily.

"Airy, your mother called me today from Scotland. She said you're considering...."

Already? It was only an hour since she spoke to Finna. They sure didn't waste any time. "I know what she said," Airy interrupted. "Grandma, I don't mean to be disrespectful, but you're wrong about Fehin. I should never have listened to you in the first place. Sorry, but I have to go. I need to apologize to him." Airy hit the 'end call' button, her heart pounding. She'd never hung up on her grandmother before. She hurried down the hall, and then limped carefully down the stairwell, her mind on Fehin. Her Modern Literature class began in ten minutes and when it was over, she planned to search until she found him.

TWENTY-FOUR

Fehin packed his backpack with all his clothing and a few favorite books before he headed to the bank. He closed out his account and stuck the money into a belt he wrapped around his waist underneath his shirt.

At a gas station he purchased a map of the country and headed west along the road leading to the main thoroughfare. There was no reason to stay at college. Without Airy's friendship he felt like an empty shell, scooped out and hollow. He'd never felt this kind of pain in his life and he didn't understand what to do with it. Would it go away?

The decision to leave had been made the night in the library, the look on Airy's face giving him all the information he needed. She didn't trust him or care about him anymore. That night he'd been in so much pain he thought he might die from it, lying in his bed curled into a tight ball and trying to keep Brent from hearing him cry. By morning he'd made up his mind.

He'd considered contacting Gunnar and arranging with the druid to sail him back home to the future, but the thought of

Thule and his life there held nothing for him anymore. He had to discover who he was and what destiny he could possibly have without Airy. And besides, he dreaded the druid's wrath. The depths of his hurt could not tolerate another nasty word or look from Gunnar.

After asking around, he found out what he needed to know about hitchhiking. It was simple enough to stick his thumb out as he walked. When a car stopped Fehin looked up in surprise. It had been nearly an hour of walking in the rain with cars whizzing by him. He'd pretty much given up hope.

"Where ya goin'?" the middle-aged man asked, pulling his Honda Civic over to the side of the road. He had a friendly roundish face, brown hair and blue eyes.

"West," Fehin replied.

"Hop in. I'm heading to Interstate 90. How far ya goin'?"

Fehin shook his head. "Not sure. I'll know when I see it."

"Are you a student at the college?"

"I was."

"Flunk out or just decide to call it quits?"

"Called it quits."

The man said his name was Jim and that he was a traveling salesman. "Not much call for us anymore," he confided with a grin. "I guess I'm due to become obsolete. Everyone buys from the Internet now."

As he chattered on Fehin tuned out, his gaze going to the rural scenery flying by. Even this far out he saw tents set up, people of all ages and colors hitching rides or begging along the road--so many children without parents and so many people out of work.

By the time they'd driven through New York and into Pennsylvania Fehin couldn't take the chatter another second. When they stopped for gas, he thanked Jim, got out and pulled his pack after him.

He walked into the closest town and found a place to eat and then asked about a cheap motel someplace within walking distance. After that he made his way to the motel and booked a room. In the room he took a shower and switched on the TV and then quickly switched if off--too much noise and confusion. What he wanted now was the peace that came from walking along the beach, taking care of his animals and staring out at the dark water that went on forever. But Thule itself and having to talk about all this with his parents was a burden he couldn't tolerate right now.

He fell into a restless sleep, dreaming about Thule and later dreaming that Airy was in the bed next to him. He could feel her warmth and hear her soft breathing. But when he turned to kiss her, he woke himself up. It was the middle of the night but he got up anyway. He picked up his pack and left the room. Constant movement was the only way he knew to keep the pain at bay.

TWENTY-FIVE

"But where is he?" Airy asked.

The blonde-haired boy coming out of the World History classroom frowned. "How would I know?" he asked. "I know who he is but we're not friends. He keeps to himself."

Airy searched out other familiar faces but nearly everyone had gone. Finally, she approached the professor. "Have you seen Fehin this week?" she asked him as he was gathering his papers together.

He looked up. "Fehin?" He gazed into the distance for a moment. "He hasn't been here for the last two classes," he answered. "If you see him, you better warn him about the upcoming test. It counts 20% of the grade."

Airy walked down the hall wondering where else to look. She'd checked the lunchroom and the library and had even gone to the woods behind campus. She'd been searching for two days now. Where was he? The bungee cord in her stomach was stretched as far as it could go. She could feel it straining inside her.

The only thing left to do was to ask his roommate. Brent would surely know.

It was late when she snuck into the dorm and knocked on Fehin's door. She hoped it would be Fehin who opened it, but instead she was faced with Brent, who looked her over in a way that made her very nervous. "Um...Brent...I was wondering if you've seen Fehin?" she asked, trying to avoid his avid gaze.

"Why don't you come in and we can talk about it?" He leered at her suggestively and held the door open.

"Uh...no thanks. I'm just looking for Fehin."

Brent made a face. "That little dweeb? What do you see in him?"

"Is he here or not?"

"Haven't seen him in a few days. He must have gone walk-a-bout."

"What does that mean?"

"It's an Australian term that means going to find yourself. His clothes and pack are gone."

"He's gone?" Airy's stomach did a little flip. She'd tried to contact him telepathically and had no luck. She'd thought at the time that he was mad at her, but now...now she didn't know what to think.

"Yeah, and good riddance, I say. I heard him crying the night before he left—what a little fairy."

Airy stepped back and had to steady herself against the wall. This was all her fault. She turned and hurried away, hearing the door close behind her.

In her room again she let the tears fall. "He's gone, Storm. He's not at college anymore. And I chased him away. What am I going to do?" Airy threw herself face down on the bed.

"I'm not that surprised after what you said to him. He must have felt really shitty."

Airy twisted around to look up at her dorm mate. "Thanks

for making me feel even worse," she said, wiping at her face. "Where could he have gone?"

"Home?"

"You don't understand. Home for him is...oh never mind. What should I do?"

The expression on Storm's face might have been sympathetic if it hadn't been for the kohl around her eyes, her black lipstick and the ring in her lip.

"Not much you can do. If he's gone, he's gone. Unless you communicate telepathically you may as well give it up."

Airy pushed herself up. "Why did you say that?"

"Say what?"

"The thing about telepathic communication."

Storm shrugged. "Just mentioning the impossible. You don't, do you?" She grinned and then sat on her bed across from Airy.

"No, of course not," Airy answered.

The next morning Airy stayed in bed. She had a horrible headache and felt sick to her stomach. She hadn't slept all night. Maybe she'd eaten something bad the day before or maybe she was coming down with something.

When Storm left for classes, Airy got on the computer and typed in 'telepathic communication' and then sat back as Google loaded. She clicked on an article entitled, '10 Steps to Master Telepathic Communication' and then read what it said. Following the directions, she breathed deeply and cleared her thoughts and then relaxed before picturing Fehin in her mind as though he was standing right in front of her. She kept the transmission short as the article had suggested. *Where are you?*

She waited a long time for an answer and then lay back on the bed and dozed.

I'm in Pennsylvania.

Airy woke with a start. *Why?*

No answer and then a very faint one. *I couldn't stay there without you in my life.*

Airy's mind filled with hope and longing. *Fehin, come back. I love you.*

But there was no more response from him. Where was Pennsylvania?

∾

AIRY COULD BARELY CONCENTRATE on her classes. Fehin was gone because of her and there was no way to reach him. She'd stopped answering her phone when her grandparents called, sure that they would only go on about the same subject—the one she didn't want to talk about.

"Airy, you're a good student. Why are you skipping classes and not turning in homework?"

Airy gazed at her professor. The woman, who was also her advisor, looked sincerely concerned. "I haven't been feeling well, Professor Hartman. I may have mono." Airy had heard about this disease that afflicted so many students. It was an easy out.

"If you have mono, you should go home. The only cure is rest. Shall I contact your grandparents? They're responsible for you, aren't they?"

"No, don't call them. Let me figure it out. Maybe it isn't mono and I'm just exhausted for some reason."

"Perhaps it's seasonal allergies. There are over-the-counter drugs for that, you know."

Airy didn't know but she nodded anyway. "I'll try to keep up," she said before picking up her books.

Outside in the sunshine her thoughts turned, as they always did, to Fehin. She'd had no more luck in her efforts to contact him through the ether and wondered if maybe she'd dreamed the last conversation. Today she planned to consult the trees, something she hadn't done since her ordeal. Her oak hadn't helped her at all that day. Why hadn't the trees warned her?

It was May now and most of the trees around the courtyard had leafed out. Maybe with the uplifting spring energy they would be easier to contact. She wandered here and there looking for the right one, and when she found it, she realized it was the pine where Fehin had conjured the medieval village. The memory brought tears to her eyes.

A light wind moved the top branches, sending a few dried needles down to land at her feet. She picked one up remembering Fehin fiddling with a twig and then the little figure that came alive. He'd never talked much about what he could do, and now she wished she knew. In all honesty they didn't know each other that well. But their hearts were linked—she was sure of that. She stilled her mind and looked up where sky jig sawed through the patchwork of branches. "What should I do?" she asked out loud.

The answer came though her senses and had no connection to words. But she understood nonetheless. She had to focus on why she was here. Her destiny.

"What about Fehin?"

All she heard after that was wind moving through the branches and the groan as limbs swayed and rubbed together. She waited for a long time and then finally gave up and headed back to campus.

∼

"DARLING, will you come up for the summer?" her grandmother asked.

Airy pressed the phone to her ear trying not to cry. The

spring semester was nearly over and she still hadn't had any communication from Fehin. "I don't know what I'm going to do yet."

"Your parents will be here in July, you know. We're all thrilled that things have turned out the way they have. We were so worried."

During their recent conversations Airy had finally divulged that she hadn't seen or heard from Fehin since March. The glee with which they received this news made her blood boil.

"I hope you can get your grades up before the end of the year, dear. Let me know your plans as soon as you can."

Airy hung up the phone and turned toward her last class of the day. It was unseasonably warm and she had on a sleeveless T-shirt and shorts, her hair pinned up off her neck. Her left leg was still smaller than the other one, but at least she was walking without a limp now—a definite improvement.

As she entered the building an official-looking person was heading into the classroom. A second later the professor glanced out the door and gestured to her. "Airy, there's someone in the office who would like to speak with you."

Airy followed the woman down the hall, wondering if she was being expelled. Her grades had dropped and she'd flunked at least one class.

When she walked into the office a blonde woman with kind eyes who looked to be in her fifties held out her hand. "I'm Carla, Airy. I'm a friend of Fehin's mother. Gertrude sent a message through Gunnar asking me to reach out to you. Do you know Gunnar?"

"I know who he is," Airy answered, her heartbeat speeding up.

Carla smiled. "Sit down, won't you?" She patted the chair next to her.

Airy sat and then tugged at her T-shirt, trying to cover the skin between where it ended and her shorts began. She finally folded her hands in her lap to keep them quiet.

"I knew Fehin when he was small. He came to stay with me for a few days. I don't know if you know the truth about his mother and what happened—why she can never come back here."

"He told me a little bit about it."

Carla let a moment go by before she continued. "Gertrude and I were best friends. I was also her publicist. Did you know she's an author?"

"I did know that. Fehin and I looked her up on microfiche."

Carla looked away and sighed and then turned to face Airy again. She picked up one of Airy's hands and held it between hers. "To get to the point, Airy, Fehin contacted his mother through Gunnar. The message he sent mentioned you and whatever destiny may lie between you. He said there'd been a terrible misunderstanding and he hoped that someone could clear it up. You see, he's dying."

"Dying?" Airy felt the blood leave her face. Her stomach gave a heave and she thought she might be sick.

Carla squeezed her hand. "I'm so sorry to be the one to tell you all this."

Airy tried to breathe but there was tightness in her chest that pressed against her lungs. The bungee had finally snapped. "What happened to him?"

"He contracted some kind of bacterial infection that the doctors can't seem to get hold of. He's in a hospital in Colorado. I could take you there if you want to go."

"Of course, I want to go." Airy wiped the tears from her cheek and tried

to concentrate on the wall in front of her. It was a sickly shade of green. Why would anyone paint a wall that color?

"I thought you'd say that. I've booked us on a flight that

leaves tonight, if that works for you. He may not have much time."

"NO!" Airy shrieked, her hand going to her mouth. A vision of him the last time she'd seen him rose up in her mind. He was sick because of her.

Carla reached out with both arms and pulled Airy close. "It's all right to be sad, Airy."

Airy sobbed for several long moments before she managed to get herself under control. She pulled away and wiped her face with the back of her hand. "When and where should I meet you?"

"Why don't you go get packed and then we can have a bite to eat before the flight leaves. I'll meet you on the other side of the quad in say, thirty minutes?"

Airy barely knew what she was doing as she raced to her room and began throwing clothes into her bag.

"What's happening?" Storm asked, walking in.

"Fehin's dying, Storm. I have to go say goodbye."

TWENTY-SIX

Fehin lay on his back in the hospital bed, his mind going over what had brought him to this point. It hadn't been his intention to kill himself, although there had been moments during the past months when he wished he were dead. Maybe that's why it happened. He knew the power of the mind, but for some reason could no longer control his own. His thoughts were as dark as night and had been for quite some time.

"How are we today?" the chipper nurse asked, walking in. She picked up the chart and checked something off before coming by him to adjust the tube in his arm. "The doctor will be in later," she said before leaving him alone again.

Fehin wondered if summoning Gunnar had been the best idea. The druid had assured him he would talk with Fehin's mother and Kafir and explain the situation. As to his concern about the girl, the druid wasn't sure how that could be solved. Maybe it was better this way, Fehin thought to himself. The last time he'd heard from Airy was right before he'd begun to feel sick. They sent a couple of messages through the ether, but he'd been unable to do it again. It seemed the sickness had taken away all his magical abilities. He was barely able to lift his hand now, his body wasted and his stomach unable to keep anything down. Without the drip line he'd have been dead a month ago.

He turned his head to stare at the trees outside his window. Wind was whipping though the branches and they moved as though they were beings that might decide to pull up their roots and walk away. Their swaying branches took on a dance of joy and he could almost see faces within them. And then he thought of Airy and how she communicated with trees. He didn't have the strength to cry anymore. Pains racked his body from time to time, but mostly he could feel the life energy slowly ebbing away. It wouldn't be long now.

In his dreams he was always with Airy, their arms looped around each other or their hands clasped with fingers intertwined. The smile on her face lit up her eyes and made him feel happy. Waking from these was the worst time for him, the knowledge of where he was and what he'd lost. Sometimes the nurses gave him morphine and he would slip into a place where he couldn't feel. It was a good drug.

IT WAS deep night when he awakened from one of these, jerking from sleep to let out a yelp of pain. He could see her standing next to his bed, a cruel hallucination. He closed his eyes.

"Fehin?"

His eyes popped open and then a light turned on.

"Fehin, I'm here." Her fingers took hold of his and he could feel her heartbeat in them. His stomach contracted as the magnetic pull of her closeness worked inside him. "Airy?" he croaked.

"What happened to you?"

She was crying now and he could feel each tear as it landed on him. They were warm. He tried to sit up but it was impossible. "I don't know," he said, falling back.

"Fehin, you do know. You made this happen," she whispered. "You made yourself sick. You can heal it."

"I can't heal it. I can't control anything."

"Don't say that."

When Fehin let out a loud groan the nurse came running. "He needs to rest now.

"I'm all right," he told her, trying to focus on Airy. Her hair was longer and framed her face and she seemed more filled out, as though she'd grown since they'd been together. Her eyes were so green. "You're beautiful."

"Fehin, I love you. I'm so sorry. Did I do this?"

He shook his head and turned away. "We were apart. I hurt so much. I wanted to die, Airy," he continued, turning to focus on her face again. He closed his eyes and felt himself slipping into the place where nothing mattered. Must be morphine in the drip line.

"I won't let you leave me," he heard her say, and then he was gone, drifting in a narcotic sea.

TWENTY-SEVEN

Airy was very alarmed by Fehin's emaciated body, his deathly pallor, and his inability to even sit up. The way he fell asleep in mid-sentence was not right. If only she had known sooner what he was going through. This was completely her fault. If he died, she would never forgive herself. It was time to go, but instead of leaving she took her shoes off, pulled the covers back and crawled into the bed beside him. She pressed close and wrapped her arms around him as her mind sought his, telling him over and over how much she loved him.

"You can't be in here!" the nurse cried, entering the room.

"Please," Airy begged, tears streaming down her face. "He could be dead by morning."

The nurse watched her for a moment and then relented. "Okay, but don't disrupt the drip. I'll check back in a few hours. And by the way, your friend is staying at the Motel 6 just down the street. She asked me to let you know and to tell you she'll be back in the morning."

Airy encased them both in golden light. She pressed both hands to his chest, infusing him with the energy from her body.

She could feel the light enter him, his sigh as he received it. "You have to help me, Fehin," she whispered. "Your thoughts are as much a part of this as anything. Send them to me."

She felt rather than heard the overwhelming sadness that encased the love he felt for her. It was as though his feelings had been buried deep inside an impenetrable tangled wood. "I'm here now and I'm not going anywhere. There's no need to carry this sadness. But in order to heal, you have to let it go."

She felt him shift, his mind struggling with the emotions that had ground him down. But a moment later he let go of their connection and she couldn't reach him at all.

Airy woke from the dream with an intake of breath. Beside her Fehin had moved onto his side, his body as close to hers as it could get. Their right hands were clasped together and he held them against his heart. His eyes were closed and when she touched his face, she felt the wetness of tears. "Fehin?"

But he was far away in a place she couldn't reach.

Airy carefully pulled her hand out of his and moved off the bed. It was time to talk with the doctor. A second later the door opened and the nurse entered the room.

"Oh, you moved him," she observed, heading over to adjust the drip.

"I didn't move him."

The nurse turned. "He hasn't been able to move at all for at least a month now," she said, surprised. She looked down. "He has a different expression on his face, more peaceful. Perhaps with the morphine his death will be without pain after all."

Airy blanched. "He's not going to die if I have anything to do with it."

The nurse smiled sadly. "I'm afraid you don't have much choice, dear. All the tests point to imminent organ failure."

"Is there a place where I can shower?" she asked, trying to avoid the oh- so-sympathetic gaze.

"Right there," the nurse said, pointing to the back of the room.

Airy grabbed her pack and entered the antiseptic smelling space. She locked the door before staring at her face in the mirror. Her eyes were red-rimmed from lack of sleep, purple shadows in the hollows beneath them. "I will save him," she whispered. "He will not die."

"AIRY, you shouldn't get your hopes up," Carla said. "The doctors informed me yesterday that there is nothing more they can do besides making sure he's as comfortable as possible."

It was early morning and Airy had run into Carla in the waiting room on her way to get some tea, her unguarded comments arousing Carla's belief in traditional medicine. "They need to stop the drugs," Airy told her. "I'm not sure what they are, but they're making him worse."

Carla's eyes widened. "He's on morphine to ease the pain! It would be cruel to take it away."

Airy assessed Carla, wondering if she should confide in the woman. Being friends with Gertrude, Carla must know all about Otherworld and the magic that was part of everyday life. "I can't reach him, Carla. He's gone into some kind of drug-induced dream world. I need him to help me."

Carla frowned. "Help you what?"

Airy gazed at the wall and then made a decision before turning to face her. "His emotions did this. His emotions can get him out, but I have to be able to reach him telepathically. Without that, nothing can change."

Carla stared at her for several long moments. "I know how special Fehin is and how terrible it will be to lose him, but..."

"I guess I'll have to talk with the doctor," Airy interrupted before heading away. In the cafeteria she thought through her options. She knew the doctor would not agree, and neither would the nurse. She had to come up with another way to stop the drugs.

When Airy entered Fehin's hospital room sometime later a lanky man dressed in many shades of green was standing next to the bed. His gray gaze settled on her with a look that reminded her of MacCuill. "Are you Gunnar?" she asked, hoping she was correct.

When he nodded, she let out a long sigh of relief. "I'm so happy you're here."

TWENTY-EIGHT

Fehin was dreaming his usual dream but this time it was slightly different. It was as though he'd brought Airy into his current situation. She was curled up next to him and bringing him warmth—so much warmth. He'd been cold for as long as he could remember. In his dream he was able to move and rolled onto his side to move closer to her. He took hold of her hand and pressed it against his heart. He felt her talking to him in his mind, urging him to do something, but there seemed to be a fog between his mind and hers—he couldn't understand her words even though he knew they were important.

A golden light entered his body bringing energy with it and he took it deep inside. If only this dream was real, he thought to himself, falling back into the void that was morphine.

"Fehin, are you awake?"

Fehin opened his eyes, blearily trying to focus on where the voice was coming from. His gaze took in two people, one of them female and one of them male. He closed his eyes against the light. It was too bright.

"Fehin!"

This time the voice was male and seemed determined "What is it?" he asked without opening his eyes.

A moment later someone was shaking him by the shoulder in an irritating way. Why wouldn't they leave him alone and let him die?

"Open your eyes, Fehin," the voice demanded.

Fehin attempted to focus. "Gunnar?"

"That's right and Airy's here too. It's important that you listen to what we have to say."

Fehin turned his head away, but fingers grabbed his chin, turning it back. "We are about to stop the drip," the druid announced. "Be prepared."

Fehin frowned. "Why would you do that? It's the only thing keeping me from the pain."

"Fehin," he heard Airy say. "It's the only way to reach you. I can't do it otherwise."

"So don't do it. Just leave me alone."

Airy's face loomed over his. "I told you I won't let you die, but I need your help."

Fehin stared into her green eyes noticing they were filled with tears. He had a second of hope before something clamped down around his heart.

"Don't you dare go away again," she said, shaking his shoulder. "Now listen to me. Gunnar is going to take the needle out of your vein and then you're going to listen in your mind to what I have to say. Do you understand?" she hissed, turning to look toward the door. "We don't have much time before the nurse comes back."

Fehin watched her and then lowered his gaze to his wrist as something tugged there. He watched the needle pull out, feeling a twinge for a moment and then it was done, but he knew that shortly the agony would be back with nothing to stop it. "Why are you torturing me?"

Neither person answered, and then Airy climbed into the bed and took

his hand in hers. He felt her warmth as she lay down next to him. She was like a sun, the light surrounding her radiating into his body. It was his dream, but this time his eyes were open. "Airy..."

"Don't waste your energy talking, Fehin. I want you to listen to my

thoughts and do what I tell you."

At that moment the nurse walked in, followed by the doctor. "What's going on in here?" the doctor asked, his gaze going from Gunnar to Fehin and then to the drip. "Why did you stop the drip? What are you people doing to my patient?" He moved quickly forward and grabbed Fehin's arm to reconnect the drip, but before he could manage it a white fog filled the room, obliterating everything from sight.

Fehin heard raised voices and scuffling and then there was utter silence, followed by a voice inside his head saying, *I love you, please forgive me.* He felt the words as though they were luminescent cobwebs, delicate lacework that moved inside him.

"I love you too, Airy," he answered out loud. "But..."

"If you love me you will focus on that feeling. Let everything go, including the pain. Remember who you are, Fehin— the man who can conjure an island—a man who knows all about how darkness can take over the mind. Go back before this started to when we first met. Concentrate on how you felt then."

Fehin groaned. He didn't know if the sudden pain that ratcheted through every part of him was from lack of morphine or what Airy was saying. He pulled his hand out of hers and tried to turn away, but she wouldn't let him.

"We have a destiny together-- did you forget that? We're

linked by a lot more than what we feel for each other. You can't leave me alone to face this on my own."

Fehin grappled with the barriers he'd erected. How could he pull them down? It was the only thing keeping him from agony. "It's dense, Airy. It has a life of its own."

"You're the one who put it there. Think about the island, the people and what they faced. You're like them now. You have to tell me everything—all of it."

Tears rolled down his cheeks as he sent the terrible thoughts into her mind. "I hated you, I hated my life. I've wanted to die since that day in the library. You hurt me, Airy. You did this."

"Keep going."

"Why did you listen to them? Why didn't you believe in me?"

"I was a fool, Fehin. I didn't trust myself. I do now."

A scuffle by the bed took Fehin's attention and through the fog that still lingered he saw the druid carry an unconscious doctor from the room.

Airy put her hand on his heart. "Get it all out, Fehin. You have to clear the negative so that the positive can come in."

Fehin reached out to touch her face and when his eyes met hers it was as though a wave crashed over him. For a long harrowing moment, he felt like he was drowning. He slumped back against the bed and closed his eyes.

"Time to let him rest," the druid said.

"I'll stay with him," he heard Airy say, and then he was asleep, and this time he looked forward to waking.

TWENTY-NINE

Airy woke when she felt him stir. When she opened her eyes, he was gazing at her face.

"I feel better," he said, reaching for her hand. "You did something."

"I helped *you* do something," she replied. After that she rolled away and out of bed. "Are you hungry?"

Fehin pushed himself up and looked around the room as though seeing it for the first time. "I think I am," he said, surprised.

"I'll get us something to eat and then I'm taking you out of here."

"Did I dream Gunnar or was he really here?"

"He was definitely here. Without him I couldn't have managed."

Airy wondered what had become of the unconscious doctor and nurse. If they remembered anything there would soon be trouble. "I'll be back in a minute." Airy opened the door a crack and peered out. In the hall all was quiet as though the entire staff had taken a break at the same time. Gunnar's doing, she was sure, but it wouldn't last long. She closed the door and turned to look toward the bed. "On second thought I think we should leave. Now."

It took an agonizing length of time to pack and get Fehin dressed and standing. She had him loop an arm around her shoulders before the two of them left the room and made their way slowly down the hall. Gunnar met them at the elevator, keeping watch as they slipped inside and pressed the button for the ground floor. When the doors slid open downstairs, the druid was waiting.

"Carla's parked by the emergency entrance. She'll take you to the motel. After that you're on your own." Gunnar pressed Fehin against his chest before backing away. "Take care of each other and remember why you're here," he said, his gaze going from one to the other. Airy watched his image grow fainter until there was nothing left of him.

By the time they reached the car Fehin could barely stand. Airy helped him into the backseat and then wondered what to say to Carla. Their last conversation had not gone well. But as she slid inside Carla turned toward her, a frown of worry on her face.

"I'm sorry I doubted you," the older woman said. "I should have known better after everything I've seen and heard. Will you forgive me?"

Airy smiled. "Without your help I wouldn't have known where he was. Of course, I forgive you."

Carla's hunched shoulders released. "That was Gunnar's doing. I was merely the conduit."

Later in the motel room Airy wondered if she'd done the right thing. Fehin was pale and sweaty, his eyes unfocused. He was so thin it was hard to look at him. "Lie down," she ordered, settling him under the covers. "I'm going for food."

At night Fehin had the shakes and there were several times he had a fever. His legs spasmed during the day and at night, and he had nearly constant diarrhea. When he threw up the first real meal Airy prepared, she realized that she had to be more careful—small amounts and easy to digest foods like yogurt and fruit and bread and butter--spiced tea with honey and milk. Soups. Herbs like ginger and peppermint made into tea. It seemed like a very bad case of flu, but when she looked it up on the Internet, she realized he was in withdrawal from the morphine. After she began the new regime, he kept the food down.

She'd moved them into another motel that had a room with a kitchenette and that's where she prepared the meals. Between them they still had some cash, but soon she would need to visit a bank.

Carla was gone—back to Milltown with encouragements for the two of them to come and live with her. Airy didn't say yes or no. She couldn't concentrate on anything beyond Fehin's recovery.

IT WAS a couple of months before Fehin was strong enough to leave the motel room for any length of time. Due to their hasty departure from the hospital and the circumstances surrounding it, Airy was careful to steer clear of that part of town. Instead, she and Fehin walked in the hills behind the motel, working their way under the trees and uphill to build his strength. But even that was a slow endeavor and several times she felt very discouraged. That's when she reminded herself that he'd almost died.

In early July her grandparents called to let her know that her parents were in Halston. "Where are you, dear? We've tried several times to reach you since school let out. The office told us you disappeared from campus and they've had no word. They told me to let you know that without summer school you won't move on."

Airy grimaced, slanting a look at Fehin who was sunk into a chair with a blanket over his legs. "I told you the last time I talked to you that I was searching for Fehin. Do you remember that? Well, I found him, and he's very sick. And since he's sick because of me, I have to help him through it."

There was a long silence and then Harold came on the phone. "Airy? What in the goddess's name are you up to? Where are you? I thought we told you to stay away from him."

Airy paused to take a deep breath. "You're wrong about him, Dad. Just because Brandubh is his father doesn't mean a damn thing about Fehin. If I hadn't listened to you this never would have happened. I have to go," she said, hitting the end call button. Airy sat down heavily in a chair and put her head in her hands. When she began to cry, she heard Fehin push out of the chair. A second later he was kneeling next to her.

"You shouldn't have to make a choice between me and your family."

She wiped her face on her sleeve and looked at him. "There's no choice here. They put me in this position because they don't trust me. That's why I can't have a relationship with them."

Fehin held her gaze for a full minute before heading to sit down. When Airy looked over at him he had his eyes closed, his head resting against the back of the chair as though he'd run a marathon.

~

"ONCE YOU'RE WELL AGAIN what shall we do?" she asked him during one of their walks. They had paused half way up a rock-strewn hill to rest. They had reached a new elevation today and were surrounded by pines and aspen for the first time. Summer had come and gone and now the hardwoods were turning color again. And during those months they'd both turned seventeen, their birthdays going by unnoticed.

Wind whispered through the golden aspen leaves, the round leaves shaking oddly. The bark and the leaves had anti-inflammatory properties that she could have used had she known they were here. He was beyond that now, getting stronger every day.

There was something melancholy about this time of year, she thought, listening to the geese calling as they headed south. Everything was shifting and going to sleep or migrating to warmer climes. Where would they be when it began to snow? She missed her home, her brother and MacCuill, and her friends. She would miss her parents if she weren't still so mad at them. And there was always Milltown to consider. With Carla's help they could get back into school if that's what they decided.

"I haven't thought about it, Airy. My brain feels fuzzy, as though I've been under water for a long time."

"I'm not surprised," she said, grabbing his hand. "I wish someone would just come and tell us what we're supposed to be doing. I've had no visions and no insights about this supposed bridge. What does it mean?"

Fehin shook his head, his breath coming in gasps. "This is enough for me," he said. "If I keep going, I'll sleep all day tomorrow."

THE NEXT MORNING after breakfast Airy took off alone, heading to the library. She did this nearly every day while Fehin rested. Here with the dusty leather smell of books and the whispers that came from them, she let her mind float free, asking for help to find what she needed. This had served her well when Fehin had first come out of the hospital—medicinal foods and herbal cures had appeared as though summoned, books she checked out, writing down the recipes before returning them.

She had some knowledge about this already and spent time researching Stinging Nettle, Burdock and Bell Pollen, all things that could help him build stamina. And luckily this small town had a good health food store with clerks who knew their business. The only hard part about it was the hordes of beggars hanging around outside the store. Sometimes she ended up giving them the food she'd just purchased, heading back inside for more. Other times she gave them money.

In the library this particular morning she found an old leather-bound book called *The Bridge* and excitedly pulled it off the shelf. But when she thumbed through it, she saw that it was about a certain bridge at a certain time in history and the importance it played in the war. She slid it back and then ran her fingers along the spines, letting her eyes close. When her hand came to a stop, she blinked her eyes open, staring at the title that lay beneath her fingers. *Mystical Bridges Through Time*. She pulled it out and opened it.

Bridges are connections, she read. *These connections can be between lands, or between places either real or in our imagination, or even between peoples. They allow us to cross great divides and speak in a language that is beyond our normal understanding. What is a bridge if not a mystical landscape? Without them we are unable to connect our thoughts or make the leaps of faith that lead to great inventions and discoveries. To build a bridge you have to know what it is you want to connect. A metaphysical bridge is made of mist and fog.*

Airy lifted her eyes from the page. "To build a bridge you have to know what it is you want to connect," she repeated softly. What was it that she and Fehin were meant to connect? Corra hadn't elaborated, but something inside her knew the answer. If only she could reach that internal place.

Whispers followed her back to the motel, the book clutched in her hand. The tree branches leaned toward her, the bright leaves giving off a pungent odor as they let go and swirled, landing at her feet. Among the whispers she heard a higher sound, a chirping that carried with it a warning. Her mind recoiled even though she couldn't understand what or who was speaking. Was it the birds? Or maybe it was all the little bugs and grubs who were now poised on the edge of their life span. When the cold arrived, they would die. Only one message came through loud and clear. *This is up to you and Fehin.*

"Did you say that?" she asked sharply, stopping in front of the oak she was walking by. But all was silent now, as though that one sentence said it all. Her ring caught her eye and when she glanced down it was radiating, as if a light had been turned on inside it, but when she took it off to take a closer look, it was once again the normal luminescent pearly gray.

This stone had been handed down through multiple generations. Finna, her Scottish grandmother had regaled her with stories of how its surface had contained a map when Finna first traveled through Otherworld. Finna had been pregnant with Airy's mother at the time. Later Maeve had worn the stone as a necklace, and although Airy didn't know the details, she knew the moonstone had assisted her mother in some way during her fight to save the Otherworld.

When her mother had it set into a ring and presented it to Airy just before her sixteenth birthday, she hadn't mentioned any magical properties or even hinted at the possibility. From what Airy had been told the stone had completed its task long ago.

THIRTY

Fehin waited for Airy to return, watching for her through the picture window. From this second story room he had a good view up and down the street. He was becoming restless and bored, signs that he was on the mend. The daily walks had strengthened him and he was ready to leave this motel—for good. But where to go was a problem. He and Airy hadn't discussed the future and he knew she had avoided certain topics until he regained his strength. And even though he was physically stronger there was something working inside him that required attention—something he didn't want to look at. The idea of getting on with his life and whatever destiny they shared had no meaning now.

He spied her before she lifted her gaze, the halo of bright hair standing out against the gray day. It was nearly the color of the leaves on the sugar maples. He watched her move along the sidewalk, his heart feeling a small jolt of longing. It had been three months since he'd left the hospital and they'd been together for all of it, but there was a distance between them that he couldn't make sense of. It was as though his brush with death had changed him in ways he was only now discovering. All he knew was that he couldn't afford to open himself up to her the way he had in the past. He rubbed his eyes and sighed, feeling a lot older than his seventeen years.

Her gaze met his before she climbed the stairs, her smile and wave warming him. He opened the door and waited, trying not to shiver from the cold air. Colorado was not a good place to spend the winter.

She walked inside and took off her heavy wool coat. "Wow, it's cold today. I hate to think how cold it will be in a month!"

"That's something I want to talk to you about. I'm ready to get out of here."

Airy looked up from where she was taking off her boots. "Where do you want to go?"

Fehin shook his head. "I haven't gotten that far. But the cold isn't good for me, I know that."

Airy turned back to her unlaced boots, slipping them off and then moving toward the loveseat. She sat down and curled her long legs under her. "So, somewhere warm," she said. "Oh, I found a very interesting book. I think it might answer some of our questions." She stood to get her pack, digging inside.

Fehin took the book she held out. "Looks intriguing," he said, reading the title. "You think the bridge thing is important?"

She headed back to the couch. "Don't you?"

"I don't know. No one mentioned it before I came to Milltown."

"If we're leaving soon, I should go to the bank." Airy looked thoughtful for a moment and then turned to regard him where he stood next to the window. "I wish I knew how to drive. We could get a car."

"We don't want the problems that come with a car. Buses and trains are fine for now. And Airy, I think we need to make a plan."

"Do you want to go back to school? I'm afraid what might happen to my money if I decide not to. After that last conversation they could have cut me off." Her gaze met his. "Carla said we could live with her, but why would we if we aren't enrolled in school?"

Fehin watched the wind moving through the tree branches and the cascading colors as the leaves spun and floated downward. A storm was brewing. He shook his head. "School won't help us right now. We got what we needed from it. And with your parents and grandparents against our relationship, it would only hinder whatever we're supposed to be doing."

Airy grimaced. "I seriously hate them all right now."

"Don't say that, Airy. They love you. They just don't understand."

"Of all people, my parents *should* understand, Fehin. They've completely closed their minds. To be honest, it really isn't like them."

"Maybe there's magic at work."

"You mean your brother?"

Fehin turned to look at her, wishing things were the way they had been before the incident with Wolf. He missed the way he'd felt about her then. Now it was like an invisible wall stood between them. "Possibly. We've been out of circulation for quite a while. We need to find out any news about him— where he is. Maybe Gunnar knows."

And that thought led his mind to Thule. He was suddenly aware that a large part of him wanted to go home and forget all about Airy and whatever destiny they shared. He didn't trust her like he had before. What had happened between them had not yet been repaired. Until it was, he didn't have the will to continue.

"What's wrong? What are you thinking about?"

He looked up, a flush coming into his cheeks. "I miss home," he admitted.

"Well, I don't," she said, unfolding her legs and heading into the kitchen. "I'll make us something to eat and then maybe we can talk about our next move?"

"Sounds fine to me," Fehin said, turning away to stare out the window again. The wind had subsided and in its place fat white flakes were floating out of the sky. He had to get out of here soon.

While they were eating the soup Airy prepared there was a soft whoosh of air and a second later Gunnar was standing in the middle of the room. Beside him Kafir looked stunned and dazed. When he saw Fehin he leapt forward and folded the boy into his arms. "Odin's ghost, boy, I didn't know how much I missed you! Thank all the gods you're all right! Your mother has been so worried!"

Fehin embraced the man who'd been like a father to him, Kafir's warmth taking away some of the cold that never seemed to go away. "This is Airy," he said, after they pulled apart, gesturing toward where she stood by the couch.

"Airy," Kafir repeated, regarding her with a warm smile. "I guess I have you to thank for my son's return to health."

Airy seemed embarrassed, a nervous smile making its way tentatively across her lips. "I was also the cause of his illness," she admitted, looking down.

"From what I hear you were bullied into it."

Kafir turned to Fehin. "Your mother wants to see you, Fehin. You being ill has been very hard on her."

"I shouldn't have told her," Gunnar said, speaking for the first time.

Fehin glanced toward the druid. "She would have known anyway."

Gunnar's mouth quirked. He nodded. "I often forget about Gertrude's psychic abilities."

When Fehin saw his mother in his mind's eyes, his heart felt squeezed. He had a feeling that the men's abrupt appearance signaled something they weren't saying. "I'm coming home with you," he announced.

"But Fehin..." Airy said, moving toward him. "We have our..."

Fehin put his hand up. "All of that can wait. Maybe you should come along too." Fehin glanced toward the druid who was leaning against the wall with his arms folded. "Is that possible?" he asked him.

Gunnar slid his eyes sideways and then shrugged. "Not the best idea

I've heard, but I suppose it's possible."

Airy looked worried and uncertain. "This doesn't seem...."

"Doesn't seem what?" Fehin asked, irritated. "I almost died, Airy. I have a right to go and see my mother."

"I didn't say you shouldn't. But now that you're feeling better, we..."

Fehin ignored her and went into the kitchen area. He fiddled around with the coffee pot, listening to the silence coming from the living room. He had a bad feeling in the pit of his stomach. "Does anyone want coffee?" he finally asked.

"No thanks," Kafir answered. "If I don't leave soon, I'll be old before my time."

"Will you come back for us, Gunnar?" Fehin asked, turning.

"You can meet me in San Diego," he said. "*Skidbladnir* will be waiting."

"But when?"

"Just get there as soon as you can." The druid took hold of Kafir's shoulder and they both disappeared.

Fehin watched the spot where they'd been and then turned to see Airy staring at him. "What?" he asked, belligerent.

Airy shook her head and turned away, heading into the bathroom. He'd invited her along. What was the problem?

THIRTY-ONE

"I don't think this is a good idea," Airy said, trying to get Fehin to look at her. He seemed remote and had been for weeks. He was different since the illness. She didn't know him anymore.

"And what would you suggest? I'm worried. Something's not right back there."

"Is that it or are you projecting because you want to go home so badly? What if we can't return? I feel like we're supposed to be doing this, whatever it is, sooner rather than later. Have you noticed how bad things are? There are more and more people on the streets every day."

"Have you even bothered to open the book Gunnar gave me? It's all explained in there. Why don't you go out in the snow and commune with the trees--maybe they'll tell you what to do."

Airy stared at him. "That was mean and uncalled for, Fehin. I don't have to read a book to know what's going on. All I have to do is open my eyes. Do you even like me anymore?"

When Fehin's eyes met hers, she saw a deep anguish and

sadness. He seemed to be struggling with something, but if he didn't tell her what it was, she couldn't help him.

"I'm sorry," he said, turning away again. "I have to get out of here soon. The cold is seeping into my bones. It's making me crazy."

"No cold weather on Thule?" Airy said, trying to lighten the mood.

"I made Thule temperate all year long. It's a wonderful place. You'll see."

If I go, Airy thought to herself. But her options were limited. She would either have to stick with Fehin, wait for him to come back, or do this bridge thing on her own. Either that or go back to school. "I think the bridge is us. We have to forge a connection between humans and nature—people hardly notice what's around them anymore, not that I blame them, and the government keeps passing laws that take away more and more of the wild places. The family farms are gone, replaced with those companies that poison everything to grow their crops. The trees and plants and bugs and animals are suffering because no one cares."

Fehin turned from his perusal of the falling snow. "What government? You mean the corporations? And how do you propose to do that? Start a cult?"

"I don't even know what a cult is."

Fehin made a derisive sound. "It's a group of people who believe something and go to great lengths to protect it and get others to believe. It's usually religious. We'd be the cult leaders. We could call ourselves the nature lovers."

"That sounds good," Airy said, not realizing that Fehin was being facetious.

"Airy, we'd have followers, weirdos who trek around with us and expect us to know what we're doing. We'd have to feed them and take care of them."

"I don't mind the idea of followers. We need to get people interested in our cause. Maybe some of the people who are out of work would come with us."

Fehin shook his head and sighed. "I don't think this is what Corra meant by a bridge. It has to be more metaphysical than what you're proposing. You need to quiet your over-active mind and meditate on it."

"Why are you treating me like a child?" Airy stared him down, her hands on her hips. "You've been acting strange. What is your problem?"

"Sometimes you act like a child, Airy. My problem is..." Fehin turned away and rubbed his hand across his face. "My problem is," he started again, "that I don't fully trust you and without that, we can't do anything."

Airy's face went hot. "How long have you felt this way?"

"Since we've been here. I didn't know what was bothering me, but now...now I know. Something in me has closed down. That's why I have to go home."

"I'm not going with you," she said, her eyes filling. "I can't believe you've been faking all this time, letting me take care of you and acting like we were working together on our mission. You are a real jerk." Airy went to pull on her boots and then got her coat out of the little closet. She opened the door and slammed it behind her, trying to muffle her sobs.

Nearly blinded by the thick snow coming down Airy blundered down the sidewalk away from the motel. She didn't know where she was going, only that she had to get as far from Fehin as she could. Her heart actually hurt. All this time she thought he loved her. They'd even said as much when he was still in the hospital. How could he pretend all this time, letting her fix his meals, plump up his pillows and cheer him when he was depressed? She felt humiliated, furious and betrayed by the one person she thought she could count on.

∾

WOLF WATCHED THE GIRL LEAVE, waiting to see what would happen next. He knew all about the druid and Kafir, had known the minute they appeared. After they left, he'd heard the shouts, had seen the tears on her face as she hurried away. When Fehin came into view at the top of the stairs carrying his backpack, Wolf smiled. His plan was working.

∾

WHEN AIRY LOOKED up she found herself in front of the library. A blast of hot air hit her when she opened the doors, warming her with a sense of familiarity. The librarian sat behind the desk as she always did, peering curiously at Airy over her half glasses. But she didn't say anything and Airy continued past her and into the stacks. Thank goodness there was hardly anyone here, she thought as tears continued to run down her face.

With the shorter days it was nearly dark by the time she left the historic brick building. She felt able to face Fehin despite the pain of his betrayal. Maybe her parents had been right all along—he was not what he seemed. Her insides hurt as though she'd been punched in the stomach.

When she reached the motel, the lights were off making her wonder if Fehin had fallen asleep. She slowly climbed the stairs, her feet growing heavier the further up she went. At the door she fit her electronic key into the slot and opened it. "Fehin?" she called, switching on a light. She moved into the bedroom and flipped the switch.

He was gone, along with all of his things. And on further examination she discovered he'd taken most of the cash she'd recently withdrawn from her account. "You bastard!" she screamed and then covered her mouth. If her parents had cut her off what in hell would she do? If Fehin had been there at that moment she would have put her hands around his neck and squeezed the breath out of him.

THIRTY-TWO

After using a sizable amount of Airy's cash to buy a bus ticket to San Diego, Fehin wrapped his jacket close and curled up on a bench outside the station to spend the night. He felt bad about taking Airy's money but what could he do? He had no money in his account and until he found a job he was without cash. Every cent he'd had, had gone into the trip to Colorado and then the hospital bills after he got sick. No one had mentioned it, but he was fairly certain that a lot of his care had been gratis, the doctors and nurses taking pity on him. And as far as taking Airy's money—her parents would never let her starve.

On the long bus ride, he fell asleep, his head lolling onto the shoulder of the heavy-set guy sitting next to him. He knew this because he woke several times and tried to lean the other way. The man didn't seem to mind. Fehin's sleep was deep and strange, filled with imagery he didn't want to see. Wolf was there lurking, and Airy, hurt and unconscious. If only he could turn the clock back to before all of that happened, he thought waking suddenly. He still loved her, but without trust it didn't matter much. Any time spent with her family would undermine how she felt for him. And the thought of her making a choice between them and him made his stomach hurt. He couldn't imagine cutting himself off from his mother or Kafir, no matter how bad things got.

By the time the bus reached San Diego he was stiff and out of sorts. He reached for his pack and then left the bus, heading inside to ask how to reach the Port of San Diego. The air was warm here and it helped his mood to feel it on his skin, to see the sun and the blue sky after so much cold and gray.

With the few dollars he had left he caught a taxi to the Port and then wandered around trying to figure out how to find *Skidbladnir* in the mass of boats and noise and commotion. After an hour of searching, he wondered if she was here at all, but just as he headed away, he caught a glimpse of a red sail and turned to see her sailing directly toward him. His heart lifted at the sight of her. But when he faced the druid, it was a different story.

"I have come to tell you that it is not your destiny to go to the future. Your path lies here in this world. Whether you choose to follow it is up to you, but I will not assist you in this folly. I would have tolerated it if Airy had come along, but you alone doesn't fit the story."

"What story are you talking about?"

"The one where you and the girl share a future. I am not clear on what your mission is, but I know you're supposed to be together."

"I don't feel like that anymore," Fehin answered. "She seems too young, and besides that I don't trust her."

Gunnar stared at him, his eyes narrowing. "Too young? Where did you get that idea? Do you think what she did for you in the hospital was childish, Fehin? She's braved the system to care for you, using her own money to buy you special food, finding herbal remedies and putting up with your depression. What more do you want from her?"

Fehin hung his head, shame making his face flush. He'd treated her as though she'd done something terrible when she'd done nothing but take care of him. Without her he'd probably be dead. But as that thought went through his mind he wondered if being dead might be better all around. He was tired of feeling empty, tired of not caring about anything and tired of the negative thoughts that constantly plagued him. "I have this hollow feeling, Gunnar. In here," he pointed to his chest. "I don't have the will to go forward."

"Fehin, it takes time to heal. Your body may be better, but your psyche hasn't caught up. You nearly died, and from what I observed you welcomed your death. Are you happy to be alive?"

Fehin thought about the question and couldn't come up with an answer.

"Spend time alone. Do what feels right. If that includes the girl, then go find her. But only if you can be kind and see her for who she is."

"How do *you* know who she is?"

Gunnar pressed his lips together and shook his head. "Don't be an idiot," he said before turning toward the boat.

"But what about my mother? Is there something happening you aren't telling me?"

Gunnar turned. "As long as she knows you're all right she'll be fine. And I'll tell her you are—would you try and make that the truth?" Gunnar raised his hand in a good-bye salute just before he slipped into the throng and disappeared.

THIRTY-THREE

Airy gazed around the motel suite wondering why she hadn't noticed how shabby everything was. And now with Fehin gone it was utterly bleak. She flung herself on the couch, letting grief take over, her hiccupping sobs reminding her of when she was small and her mother would come and soothe her hurt. But there was no one to soothe her now, and even the thought of her parents made her cry harder. If she were home right now MacCuill would comfort her, she thought, imagining his arms around her, the scratchy feel of his robe against her cheek.

When there were no tears left she went into the bathroom and looked at herself in the mirror. Her eyes were red and puffy, her face swollen. This thing with Fehin had turned her into a sniveling little girl. No wonder he said what he did. She splashed water on her face, angry with him and with herself. She was seventeen now. It was time to grow up.

The news on the TV said they were expecting a foot of snow out of this storm. She fell asleep to the sound of wind whistling around her door and windows.

In Airy's dream she was walking through a blizzard. She

was barefoot and freezing cold and the trees were trying to send her a message, but because of her chattering teeth she couldn't hear them. A face loomed out of the shadows--Wolf, and he was smiling. Waking suddenly, she was surprised to see her door wide-open, snow drifting along the carpet. She jumped up to close it and then mopped up the snow with the extra towels in the bathroom. When she saw the footprint, she let out a scream. It was a boot print way bigger than Fehin's foot and it was right next to her bed. Whoever had opened that door had stood next to her bed while she slept. She shivered violently, pressing her fingers into her eyes to stop the tears. She moved to the door and turned the extra lock, latching it securely.

In the kitchen making tea she wondered why she hadn't awakened. She had assumed the dream had to do with Fehin being gone. Even when he was at his sickest, she felt protected with him around. But that footprint was real, which meant that someone large had been looking down on her while she slept. It had to be Wolf. When she brought the cup to her lips her hand shook so badly that she spilled hot liquid on her leg.

The rest of the night was spent worrying about Wolf breaking her door down. She tried hard not to, but the tears came as she recalled the joy she felt every morning when she woke to see Fehin's smiling face. In her mind's eye he ran his fingers through his mussed hair, smoothing it and pushing it back off his face—a morning ritual that she'd grown accustomed to watching. His sleepy moss-colored eyes always followed her as she rose from the bed, his husky, 'good morning' brightening her day. Somehow these simple gestures made her feel wanted and loved. They had never moved past the few kisses they'd shared, but she'd sensed that what they felt for each other would be expressed in a deeper way when it was time. How could she have been so wrong about him? What would she say the next time she spoke with her parents? The idea of admitting that they'd been right all along, filled her with dismay.

In the morning Airy felt exhausted, her thoughts muddled and confused. Some part of her had hoped that Fehin would come back, but in the cold morning light she knew this wasn't going to happen. She wondered if he was on his way home. Would she ever see him again? But then anger replaced these softer thoughts and she stormed around the room to collect her things, throwing her clothes roughly into the bag. She hated him right now.

Outside wind began to rage and a minute later sleet pelted the windows so hard she thought they might break. When she looked out, a shadowy figure lurked at the bottom of the stairs, but when she moved to get a better view, there was no one there. *My mind's playing tricks on me,* she thought, but the fear had lodged inside her stomach, making her feel weak.

By the time she finished packing her mind had calmed. When she opened the door, the sun was peeking through the bare branches. Snow had drifted around her door and there was a pile of sleet melting on the window ledge. For a moment she wondered if Fehin had been right about her moods and what they could bring, but then she laughed it off, carefully making her way down the stairs and toward the office to check out.

Caught up in her thoughts she didn't notice the dark-haired figure watching her from under the trees at the side of the motel.

AIRY FOUND an ATM and withdrew more money, cursing Fehin for stealing hers. She wasn't sure if this was the last of it or if her parents would continue to support her. If she called them right now and told them what was happening, she was positive they would deposit money into her account immediately. They would dearly love to hear about Fehin's recent obnoxious behavior.

She shook her head trying to imagine getting a job. It the amount of homeless was any indication, there weren't enough jobs to go around. She walked the short distance to the bus station and bought a ticket for Milltown. At least there she had Storm and Carla to count on. It wasn't a direct ride and would take a couple of days to get there. Flying would have been easier, but the idea of it scared her too much. And besides she didn't have near enough money for it.

On the bus she wondered why she kept having a prickling sensation on the back of her neck. Was this some new ability she hadn't figured out? She turned once to see if someone was watching her, but everyone in the seats behind looked perfectly normal. There was only one guy with his hoodie up whose face wasn't exposed. She turned back and tried to concentrate on the future and what to do, but after groping her way blindly through her tangled thoughts she settled on a nap instead.

BY THE TIME the bus rolled into Milltown, Airy was certain she was being stalked. The prickling feeling had grown stronger during the trip and several times when the bus stopped and she got off, she'd felt as though someone was tailing her. But whenever she turned there was no one there. It was eerie and disturbing.

She hailed a taxi and gave the driver Carla's address and then settled back for the ride.

"Where's Fehin?" Carla asked after they'd greeted one another.

"He's gone home."

"Gone home? I thought you were together."

Airy sighed, following the older woman into the house. "So did I."

"Airy, you look exhausted. Why don't you go take a shower and I'll fix us something to eat. And then you can tell me all about it."

Airy carried her bag into the bathroom and pulled out some clean underwear and another sweater. These jeans would have to do since she had no others.

As the steaming water poured over her, she thought about why she was here. It hadn't been her intention to foist herself on Carla. She wondered, for the millionth time, why she couldn't figure things out for herself.

In the living room dressed in clean clothes she felt somewhat better. The apartment was cozy and warm and Carla's familiar face was comforting.

After Carla brought out a plate of sandwiches and placed them on the table she turned to Airy. "I don't want to pry into your life," she said, "but last I knew you and Fehin were working on a plan. Can you tell me what happened?"

Airy picked up a half of the chicken salad sandwich and took a bite. "He doesn't love me. He told me something had closed down in him. I think it's because of the illness, but I don't know—he said that's why he had to go home."

"I got a message not too long ago from Gertrude via the Internet. God knows how she manages it, but every once in a while, I get an e-mail from her." Carla smiled. "In this one she told me Fehin decided to remain here. She said he'd been having doubts, but that Gunnar set him straight."

"How do you get messages from the future?"

Carla shook her head and threw her hands up in the air. "I have no idea, but I think it's something to do with the druid.

Maybe she tells him what she wants to say and then when he's in this timeline he writes me an e-mail?"

"Gunnar has e-mail?" Airy laughed. "That is so weird."

Carla chuckled. "It is kind of strange, I agree. Unfortunately, I can't send messages back. I miss Gertrude so much." Carla took a bite of a sandwich, her gaze going into the distance.

When the door opened a few minutes later, revealing a young blonde-haired girl, Carla jumped up to greet her, hugging her close before asking, "How did it go?"

"Oh, fine," she said, her attention going to Airy. "Who are you?" she asked.

"Airy this is my daughter, Fanciful."

"Fan," the girl corrected. "Hi Airy. Are you related to Mom's weird friend, Gertrude?"

"No, I'm..."

"Airy is Fehin's friend," Carla interrupted. "They both go to the college in Milltown."

Fan looked her over, twirling one blond braid. She seemed about ten, the same age as Airy's brother. Carla hadn't said a word about her. And where was her father? There was nothing in the bathroom to indicate another person lived here.

Carla seemed nervous, glancing from one to the other. "Fan, do you have homework?" she finally asked.

"Some. Should I do it before dinner?"

"That would be a good idea. Airy and I have some things to discuss. I'm heating up lasagna."

Fan smiled. "Yum. See you later, Airy," she said, skipping away. A second later there was the sound of a door closing.

"I didn't know you had a daughter."

"She stays with her father half the time. We're divorced."

"Oh." Airy wasn't sure what to say to that—was it good or bad that they were divorced?

"It was amicable," she added, noticing Airy's expression. "We're great friends. But Airy, you have to be careful around her. She doesn't know anything about the other worlds."

"I won't say anything."

"Now where were we? Oh yes, I was telling you what I heard from Gertrude. I bet you Fehin's on his way to Milltown right now. What about school? Are you going back?"

"I'm not sure."

"The semester is just about over. The holidays are coming. But you could start after the New Year. The idea of you wandering around the city disturbs me. You have no idea what goes on in the streets these days. Luckily, I have a job, but there are so many who are without a home and unable to get work. I do what I can but mostly it seems somewhat futile."

"I don't understand. Can't you elect good people so the government takes care of the poor?"

"There are no more elections. The congress is appointed now and big business does the appointing. Their bottom line is always money."

Airy frowned. "I hope I'm not supposed to fix this."

"You and Fehin talked about a bridge. Maybe the bridge is to change the system. I worry about my daughter and what this world will be like when she grows up."

Airy stared into the distance. She thought of Otherworld and how easy life was. But because of her parents' narrow-mindedness she had no desire to go back.

Dinner was awkward with Carla filling the silences with idle chatter. She seemed nervous that Airy would betray something. Airy wondered why she cared so much, but chalked it up to being an overly protective mother. When dinner was over Airy helped clean up the kitchen and then gathered her pack.

"Where do you think you're going?" Carla asked.

"Motel?"

"No." Carla shook her head. "You're staying here tonight. Tomorrow I can help you make a plan. You have a lost look about you."

Airy laughed. "I do feel at loose ends. I'll just stay one night if that's okay." She glanced around and saw that Fan had gone back to her room. "I came here with the idea of a destiny that included Fehin, and now..."

"You don't know where he is or even if the two of you will be able to mend what's broken. I understand, sweetheart. I do think school would be safe and give you something to focus on until he finds his way back to you. From what Gunnar told Gertrude, Fehin's in a very dark place— 'a dark night of the soul' place, if you know what I mean."

Airy frowned. "But why? He's alive. Wouldn't he be grateful for that?"

"He's going through something, Airy. You have to give him time. If he loved you before I'm sure he still does. But he needs to discover this on his own. Don't give up on him--he's a very special boy."

THIRTY-FOUR

Fehin hung around the beaches of San Diego until the police rousted him. There were many like him the day the police arrived with guns and tasers. They ended up in jail for a night before the police let them out. The sun and the sound of the ocean had healed some of the hollowness, but the pain lingered the longer he stayed in this country. He wondered if this dark state of mind came from him or others. He'd never been very good at blocking his mind, but this—this was what he'd call a full-blown depression. He should have forced Gunnar to take him back to Thule.

He wasn't ready to see Airy, knew that he couldn't give her anything until he felt whole again, if he ever did. Someone he spoke with on the beach, a kid with dreadlocks who carried a surfboard, asked him if he'd been in the military and then mentioned some condition called PTSD. He suggested that Fehin find a shrink. Fehin had to ask what that was and then told the guy he didn't have enough money for such a thing.

In truth he had no money at all and ended up on street corners begging with all the rest of them. The small change people gave him kept him alive. It was months later that he got a job in a nursery, working under the table for five dollars an hour. He was good with plants and did well until the owner accused him of stealing. He hadn't, but he knew who had. He let the man fire him instead of telling the truth, since the employee who'd taken the money was in dire need. Fehin would never have turned him in.

Making a living was just about impossible, even for the people who were well educated. He'd read about the days when someone could start a small business and have it succeed. But now there was no support for small business and no niche in which they could flourish, aside from the restaurants, and even those were becoming more and more automated. People had nowhere to work, no place to live and no money. When the police came along, he and the rest of them scuttled into the shadows like rats.

More months went by as he tried to stay afloat. He hardly noticed the holidays as he slunk into his hidey-holes with the other indigents. He'd begun to take some drugs since they were passed around the streets like candy. They did seem to put him out of his misery for a while. In January he contracted a fever that lasted a month before he could shake it. In February he jumped a boxcar and headed cross-country, jumping off some-where in Texas. He found the homeless camps and settled in, making a few dollars by begging. But the drug community that hovered along the edges of these places finally sucked him in, devouring him whole. By the time he resurfaced it was June. Airy's face had begun to appear in his mind. He had to kick his habit.

It was late August when he hitched a ride with a trucker headed east.

∾

WHEN FEHIN ROLLED into Milltown on the produce truck in mid-October he wondered if he should have come back. Whatever was bothering him had not gone away. And after experiencing this country first hand, it was hard for him to think positively about anything. There were many kind people out there and many who were angry about their lives, and some who were both. There was something wrong with a system that only benefited the wealthy. Why hadn't his mother told him how horrible this place was? But then he remembered that this change had come about after she was gone. He had a feeling she wouldn't have encouraged him to come here had she known.

Due to his indecision, the trip back had taken a lot longer than he'd planned: one day he was on the road hitching a ride and the next he was looking for part-time work to keep him afloat for another week or two. But his burning need to see Airy won out in the end. She was all he'd thought about for months. Hopefully his instincts were right and she was here and willing to accept him back into her life. As far as their destiny, it was difficult to consider, especially since his magic was broken and hadn't returned. Even with magic he couldn't imagine tackling the problems he saw all around him. Young kids were on the streets strung out on drugs and a life of prostitution, and no once seemed to care. He'd attempted to help a few of these kids whose parents were either dead or in jail, but without having any resources of his own, it was hard to change their minds about anything. And with the track marks up and down his arms he could hardly set himself up as an example.

He thanked the Hispanic man and pushed the door open, lifting his pack onto his back.

"Vaya con Dios," the man said, lifting his hand.

Fehin felt tears well before he smiled and nodded, watching the truck pull away from the curb—the kindness of people in a world like this was always a surprise. He took off walking and then ran a hand over his scruffy chin. He hadn't had a bath for a couple of weeks—he knew what he must look like. Walking past a coffee store brought the aroma of what had become a favorite drink of his, but when he reached into his pocket there were only a few dollars left. Not enough.

When Fehin walked onto campus he felt a deep foreboding, as though Wolf was lurking around the next corner. He hoped this was just part of the past and how hurt he'd felt the last time he was here, but he kept alert as he headed toward the administration building. Classes were in full swing, the chatter of students reminding him of his months here. And then he realized he'd turned eighteen some time recently. There had been no celebration.

In the office he asked for Airy.

"Airy Fitzhugh? And who are you?" the woman asked, looking him over with disapproval.

"I'm an old friend," he answered. "Is she still here?"

The woman checked the computer. "She's registered but she's not in the dorms. She's staying off campus."

"Do you have an address?"

The woman shook her head. "I'm sorry. I can't give you that."

Fehin left and headed across the quad. If Airy wasn't living in the dorms, where would she be? And then he thought of Carla—she must be living with Carla.

"Fehin? Is that you?"

He turned to see the pirate staring at him. Her style was the same, but something had softened in her. "I'm afraid so," he answered.

"You look so different. What happened to you?"

"Life, I guess. I was looking for Airy but I heard she's not living on campus."

"She's staying with a woman--Carla, I think her name is. She lives down by the harbor."

Fehin remembered his one trip to Milltown back when he was seven. If he could find the harbor, he could find her house. "Which way is the harbor?"

"Are you planning to walk? It's like ten miles from here."

Fehin reached into his pocket and pulled out his three dollars. "Don't suppose a cab will take me for this."

Storm reached into her backpack. "I..."

Fehin waved his hand and shook his head. "The walk will do me good."

Storm frowned. "You look like something the cat dragged in, Fehin. Walking is the last thing you need. Now food, and sleep, those might..."

"Good to see you, pirate, I'll be on my way now."

"Pirate? Did you say pirate?"

Fehin grinned. "I did."

"That's so funny. My boyfriend calls me that."

Fehin chuckled. "Great minds think alike. Have you seen Airy? How is she?"

"I don't see her much. She's auditing a couple of classes. She seems depressed, if you really want to know."

"So, no boyfriends?"

Storm scoffed. "Her heart belongs to you."

THIRTY-FIVE

When Airy heard the doorbell ring she had the weirdest sensation in her stomach. She and Fan were in the living room playing a game of scrabble and Carla was in the kitchen cleaning up after their dinner.

"I'll get it," Carla said, moving to the door.

Airy heard her talking and then a deep voice answering. Her heart began to pound. She stood up as Carla closed the door behind a dark-haired man. He was bearded with hair to his shoulders and dressed in filthy jeans, high leather boots and a jacket that could have belonged to someone in the military. His gaze roamed the room coming to rest on her.

She stared into those dark eyes and something inside her turned over. "Fehin?"

He didn't move, his intense stare piercing into her soul. His gaze didn't waver as she made her way slowly toward him. It felt like she was moving through deep water, each step harder than the one before. She was terrified of this stranger with Fehin's eyes. He looked so much older, with eyes filled with sorrow.

When she finally reached him, he opened his arms and pulled her close. He smelled like sweat and dirty clothes and dust. It was an eternity before she could let go of him, afraid if she didn't stay close, he might disappear. She kept her fingers twined through his as she led him to the couch and watched him sink down in exhaustion.

Carla was in the kitchen and Airy heard her opening and closing the refrigerator. A few moments later she arrived with crackers and cheese and sliced meats. She placed the plate in front of Fehin and then sat in a chair.

Fan had been watching all this, her shyness keeping her away. But when Fehin beckoned she came over to sit next to him. "Are you Fan?" he asked.

She nodded and smiled.

"You told me what your name was before you were born."

Fan's eyes went wide. "I said that?"

"Not exactly *said*, more like imparted," Fehin answered.

Fan turned to Carla. "Mom?"

Carla smiled. "It's true Fan. I named you Fanciful because Fehin told me that's the name you picked."

Airy sat down on the other side of Fehin and held the plate out. "You look like you could use a decent meal," she said.

Carla laughed. "This is hardly a decent meal, but it will have to do for now. We'll have a real meal tomorrow. I have a feeling a hot bath and bed are in order for you."

Fehin put a piece of cheese in his mouth and nodded gratefully.

"You can sleep on the couch," Carla continued, heading off to find sheets and blankets.

"He's staying in my room," Airy said. "I couldn't sleep if he was out here."

Carla stopped and gazed at Airy. "Yes," she finally said.

"After all this time I wouldn't want to be separated from him either."

When Fehin emerged from the bathroom, Airy was sitting up in bed waiting for him. He'd shaved off the beard and looked more like his old self, but there was still something very different about him. On closer inspection she decided that he was taller, his frame larger, and even though he was very thin he had the look of a man rather than the boy of a year ago. His voice had even grown deeper. It hardly seemed possible that so much time had gone by.

"I don't have pajamas," he told her. "Should I wear my jeans?"

"Do what's comfortable," she said.

Fehin turned his back and let go of the towel around his waist, giving her a glimpse of his body. She could see each rib, each vertebra in his spine and the bony knobs at the top of his shoulders. His arms were muscular but lean, his shoulders wider. There were scars along his upper back and marks along the insides of his arms that she couldn't identify. He reached into his pack and pulled out a pair of boxers and pulled them on before turning toward the bed.

"What have you been doing all this time?" she asked him, moving over to give him room. "Do you realize it's been a year? To tell the truth I'd given up on you."

"Traveling mostly. I've seen a lot of the country. There's so much poverty, Airy. I met a young girl named Sitka—only six years old and she was living on the streets. Her parents are in jail."

"Why didn't some family member take her in?"

Fehin shook his head, his eyes dark. "There was no one else. She told me she ran away before they could put her in foster care."

Airy put a hand on his arm. "You've changed," she said, watching his eyes.

Fehin shrugged. "I don't have magic."

"What happened?"

He ran his fingers through his wet hair. "I don't know. It's just gone."

"Is that why you never answered when I sent telepathic messages?"

Fehin pressed his lips together and nodded. "I'm so tired," he said, sliding down under the covers.

When Airy snuggled close he put his arm around her. "I can't believe you're here," she whispered, but he was already asleep. She placed her head on his shoulder and closed her eyes.

IT WAS SOMETIME in the night that Airy woke, turning to see Fehin staring at her. "I missed you so much," he said, and then he began to sob.

She put her arms around him, holding him while he cried. When he seemed spent of grief. she kissed him.

"Airy, don't do that if you don't want..."

"I do want," she said.

He watched her for several long moments before he slid his hand under her T-shirt.

Airy trembled, her breath coming in short gasps.

"Should I stop?" he whispered.

"No," she said, pressing against him. And that was the end of talking for a very long while.

When she woke in the morning, she and Fehin were wrapped together, arms and legs entwined. He remained sound asleep as she carefully extricated herself. She pulled her T-shirt over her head and found her underpants and left the room, heading to the kitchen to make coffee. A glance at the clock on the wall in the living room told her she had missed her first class. Carla wasn't back yet from taking her daughter to school.

Airy thought of the sweetness of what they had done together—the step she'd always known would come. It hurt to begin with, but Fehin was so careful with her and so loving it made her cry. He'd wiped her tears away, his dark eyes full of longing. At the end of it they had both cried, holding on to each other like it was their last day on earth.

While she waited for the coffee to brew the door opened and Carla came in. "Good morning, Airy," she said taking off her jacket and hanging it in the closet. When she came into the kitchen, she leveled her gaze on Airy. "I think it's time to get you some birth control," she said.

Airy's face turned hot and she had to look away.

"I didn't mean to embarrass you. But it's obvious what's happened between you two. I'm just being practical."

Airy poured a cup of coffee with her back turned. "I don't understand how you knew."

"Look at yourself in the mirror," Carla said with a light laugh.

"Do you think it's wrong?"

"No, sweetheart, I don't think it's wrong. You're eighteen now, the age of emancipation. I'm surprised it didn't happen before this." She stared into the distance. "At least the system hasn't been able to eliminate Planned Parenthood." She turned back smiling. "It's free and they're very nice there."

Airy poured coffee into another cup and headed to the bedroom.

Fehin was awake and leaning against the headboard, his moss eyes trained on her. "Thanks," he said when she handed him the cup.

She slid in next to him, waiting for him to say something.

They both spoke at once, the words mingling in a jumble of emotions.

"Airy," he finally said, grabbing her hand. "I love you."

Airy's eyes welled as she watched him. "I feel the same. I didn't know how it would be. Was this your first time too?"

Fehin placed his cup on the bedside table. "No," he told her quietly.

"I didn't think so. Who...?"

"It happened several times. It didn't mean anything. I was living on the streets and..."

"Did you do drugs?"

Fehin's gaze slid away. "A few, but nothing major."

"I know all about drugs now. A lot of students are into them."

"I can't believe you don't have a boyfriend," he said, picking up his cup again and turning to look at her.

Airy stared wide-eyed. "I couldn't do that to you. And besides, everyone thinks I'm a freak." She shook her head trying hard not to cry. He'd been with other girls. "Promise me you won't keep things from me."

"Airy, I'm sorry for everything. I never meant to hurt you."

"I know that. I've known for a long time. I'm so glad you're here."

When Airy went into the bathroom to take a shower she took a look in the mirror. Her expression had changed, but she couldn't say how, and she had a rash around her mouth from all the kissing. No wonder Carla had said what she did. And thank goodness she did, because Airy wouldn't have thought of it herself.

Her mother had never mentioned birth control or much of anything regarding this part of life. Maybe she'd considered Airy too young for such a conversation. But that was over two years ago now.

~

IT WAS late morning by the time Airy and Fehin left the house. Carla had gone off to her job in the local bookstore, so Airy locked up, placing the key under the flowerpot. She decided to skip her classes for the day. Part of her never wanted to go back but she thought she'd talk it over with Fehin before making a final decision. Since her return to school her grandparents had been sending regular checks to her bank account. They knew that Fehin hadn't been around for over a year.

Fehin sat in the waiting room at Planned Parenthood while Airy had an examination and spoke with the nurse. She got what she needed and then the two of them headed along the sidewalk in the direction of the school.

"Let's get a coffee," Airy suggested as they walked by the local independent coffee shop. They had to push by several homeless people hanging around to get to the door.

"I never turn down coffee," Fehin said. "But I don't have any money," he whispered.

"My treat," she said, but Fehin had turned away to talk to a homeless man. Inside she ordered lattes, adding a few cheese buns and a couple of breakfast sandwiches to take out. Outside she headed toward Fehin and two other men who seemed lost in discussion. "Here's your coffee," she said coming up behind him. Fehin turned and took the cup. "And I brought some buns for your friends." Airy handed the bag to the closest man who took it, nodding perfunctorily. His eyes were dull and he wore a crazy patchwork of clothing and an army blanket around his shoulders. When Airy headed to the park across the street, Fehin finally moved out of their midst and came to join her.

"What was that all about?" she asked him once he was seated on the bench next to her.

He looked at her quizzically. "You need to read the book

Gunnar gave me. Those people illustrate perfectly what's wrong with the system. They have no housing, no money and no jobs and no way to get health care if they're sick. A lot of them have fought for this country and look what thanks they get. I told them I would do whatever I could to help. A stray dog gets more attention than they do."

Airy gazed at the little pond, the only thing left of the park. A plaque commemorating: SAVE THE PARK, had been embedded in a boulder right off the walkway. Airy knew that Carla had been instrumental in trying to keep this parcel of land away from developers. The pond and a few benches were all that was left of it, the rest given over to condos and fast-food restaurants. The other three benches held sleeping bags occupied by those who hadn't yet come under police scrutiny. "What can you do?"

Fehin grimaced. "If I had magic, I'd build them a village. Are you still talking to trees?"

Airy laughed. "Yes, and lots of other things too."

"Meanwhile I have nothing."

"Why do you think that is?"

"It could be depression. Maybe it'll come back now that we're together."

"I bet it will, Fehin. You need to be happy to have magic."

"Is that your professional opinion, Dr. Fitzhugh?"

Airy laughed. "It makes sense, doesn't it? Our minds are so powerful. We talked about that before—how so many people are unhappy here. I'm sure you saw a lot of that."

Fehin eyes darkened as he gazed into the distance. "Yeah, I did, but I also saw people who should have been unhappy but were full of joy. There's a lot of resilience in this country."

"Have you thought at all about our destiny?"

"Not much. I've been too preoccupied with staying alive. I have to get a job."

"What about your bank account?"

"It's empty." He swiveled toward her. "I'm sorry I took your money. I'm sorry I was such a jerk and I'm sorry I left, but I couldn't stay. I was lost, Airy, and I stayed lost for a very long time."

"And now?" she asked, turning toward him.

He shook his head. "I couldn't go on without seeing you. I'm just glad you accepted me after how I treated you."

"It took me a while but I finally figured it out. You had to be alone. I mean seriously, you almost died. Just picking up where we left off wasn't going to work. Do you think you're ready now?"

"I hope so," he said, touching her hair. "You have so much light in you, Airy."

Airy made a funny face. "Not sure what you mean, but I'll take it as a compliment."

"I didn't really see you before. I mean I did until I got sick, and then...well..." He shook his head. "Listen, if you have a class this afternoon, I'll go look for a job. I checked out the paper this morning and I have a couple of ideas."

"I want to go with you."

Fehin's mouth quirked. He picked up one of her curls and twisted it between his fingers while he watched her. "Afraid I'll run away?"

"Kind of. After what happened last night, I hoped we'd spend the day together."

Fehin rose and bent to kiss her. "I'll be back by five at the latest. Are you sure Carla doesn't mind me free-loading?"

"What does that mean?"

"It means taking advantage, not paying my way."

Airy shook her head. "You've spent one night there, Fehin. She'll tell you if she's unhappy about it."

"I'll see you later."

Airy watched him walk away, struck again by the profound changes in him. She didn't yet know this man, and yet she could barely stand to be parted. "Hurry back!" she yelled.

Airy left the bag of breakfast sandwiches on one of the occupied benches and headed toward campus. She knew very little about the lives of the homeless, hadn't had a conversation with one person about the ongoing problems. Mostly she was afraid of them and steered clear. It was only because one of her professors considered himself an activist and spoke often of rising up against the system, that she knew anything at all. After seeing Fehin with those men she realized how much he'd been involved in that life during the year he was gone. He was one of them. What if his magic never came back?

THIRTY-SIX

When he reached the edge of campus Fehin glanced over his shoulder to watch Airy. Her gait was deer-like, graceful and fluid, her hair a halo of gold/red as she hurried to her class. He hoped that what they'd done last night wasn't a mistake. He had to admit that after his experiences on the street she seemed very young. He didn't know if taking this step would help or hinder what lay ahead of them. But he couldn't have stopped himself if he tried. The only thing that would have ended it was if Airy had said no. He gave her the opportunity, but she'd welcomed him despite her obvious fear. And the experience with her was not like any he'd had so far—what happened between them was on a completely different level.

He sighed. If he didn't get his magic back it wouldn't matter one way or the other. He loved her, that much was clear, and she loved him. He didn't want to take away the sparkle of joy in her eyes or burden her with what he'd seen, and yet without doing so he wasn't sure he could impress upon her what was at risk. They had to find a way to build a bridge, whatever that meant. And right now, he was unable to come up with anything that made sense. Without his magic he was unable to contact Gunnar or send any kind of telepathic messages. He was stuck in the 'real world' and it was not one he liked.

"HOW MUCH EXPERIENCE HAVE YOU HAD?" the stocky middle-aged contractor asked. He had thick forearms and a belly to match, but he was definitely strong.

Fehin had no references. "Tell you what, if I don't pull my weight you don't have to pay me."

The man studied him for a moment, his hand going to his chin. "You have three days," he said. "Now grab a hard hat and follow me."

FEHIN WAS NOT USED to physical labor and was very tired by the end of the day. He left the construction site after promising to be back at eight o'clock sharp the following morning. He'd kept up with the work, but felt the man watching and assessing. He didn't want to lose this job. It paid well and was a project that would last several months. If he could stick it out, he might make enough to pay Carla for staying at her house and contribute to the household money.

On the way home he caught a glimpse of someone in the shadows who he was pretty sure was following him. His first thought was Wolf. He hadn't heard anything from his half-brother since Halston. But without his telepathic abilities he couldn't make contact with him—not unless his brother made himself known. A minute after that thought went through his mind, Wolf was standing in front of him.

"Here I am," he said.

Fehin kept on walking, trying to skirt around him, but Wolf

ran ahead, placing his bulky body directly in his path. "Why are you ignoring me?"

"Why do you think? All you've done is make my life miserable. What do you want from me?"

"You know what I want, but from what I've observed you don't have the power to give it to me. At least you have the girl now. Lucky you."

"No thanks to you. She almost died."

"That was a test which you failed miserably. Do you ever wonder why you no longer have magic?"

Fehin didn't answer, trying to move around him again, but Wolf blocked him. "Your mind is so open, Fehin. It absorbs every thought, every feeling. Don't you wonder why you've been in such a dark place?"

"Are you saying you're responsible?"

"Only partially." Wolf laughed. "This world is filled with darkness, or hadn't you noticed?" Wolf leaned toward him. "Seems you might have noticed while you were doing heroin and meth and crack and the rest of the shit you were into. Does your little girlfriend know about that?"

Fehin felt a prick of fear. He was off the drugs now, but it taken a supreme effort and many months to wean himself. How did Wolf know about his life on the street?

"I was there," Wolf answered, reading his mind. "You might not have seen me, but I was right along with you, feeding you thoughts and helping you find what you were looking for. I watched you fuck yourself up and writhe on the ground like an animal. And I saw the women you chose." He shook his head. "Does Airy know about them?" Wolf made a tusking sound with his tongue. "Whores and drug addicts. I'm surprised you didn't catch some dread disease."

Fehin tried to recall if he'd had any inkling of his brother's presence during those terrible months, but the memories were fuzzy and filled with drug-induced fog. Heroin was only one of the dangerous substances he'd become addicted to. "Are you saying you were the one procuring the drugs?"

"Maybe. I like those substances and how I feel when I'm on them. I can find them for you now, if you like."

"I wouldn't like," Fehin said, muscling by him. "Get the fuck away from me."

"You've changed, I'll grant you that. But dealing with me is not so easy."

"I don't have any magic to help you. What else could you possibly want?"

"I want what you have—a beautiful girlfriend, a nice place to live and a good job. Is that too much to ask?"

"What are you suggesting?"

"You get me a job and I'll leave you alone. If you don't help me, I can't be responsible for what I might do."

"Why in hell do you want a job?"

"I need money and so far, no one will hire me. They act like I'm some kind of circus freak."

"And so you are."

"Don't fuck with me Fehin. Imagine what I could do to Airy and then give me your answer."

Fehin stared at him. "I'll talk to Sam," he finally said.

"See you tomorrow at the construction site," Wolf said, leering at him.

Fehin hurried away, his thoughts scattering. The idea of Wolf working alongside him was completely insane. Damn it! He needed his magic. At least that way he could contact Gunnar. Now he had to worry about Airy finding out about his life on the streets. If she knew the truth she wouldn't understand—it would be the end of what they'd just begun. The light in her eyes would disappear, perhaps forever. He couldn't stand the thought of that. And if that bastard did anything to hurt her, he would find a way to kill him.

~

"JUST IN TIME," Carla said cheerily when he walked through the door.

"Where have you been?" Airy whispered. "You said you'd be back by five."

"Sorry," he whispered back. "Some things came up with Sam."

"Sam? Is he your new boss?"

Fehin nodded, heading into the kitchen to help with dinner.

~

"WHAT IS GOING ON WITH YOU?" Airy asked once they were in bed. "You were weird during dinner and now you've got your face in a book."

Fehin closed the book about the 21st century. He felt a burning need to come clean, but he couldn't. "Sorry, I'm just tired. It was a long day. You should read this book," he added, handing it to her.

Airy took it and placed it on the bed between them. "I understand you're tired, but the look in your eyes scares me."

"What look?"

"The last time I saw it was when Wolf was around. Is he here?"

Fehin sighed and got out of bed. He wanted to tell her so badly.

"He is, isn't he?" Airy jumped out of bed and came around to grab his arm. "Tell me the truth!"

Fehin wanted to say no, but he couldn't lie to her. "Yes, he's here."

"What are we going to do?"

"*You* aren't going to do anything. I'm going to find a way to kill him."

"Fehin! You can't be serious! You don't have magic and he's twice your size."

"He's blackmailing me into getting him a job at the construction site."

"Blackmail? What does he have on you?"

Fehin cursed himself for revealing this. "Let's just say I've done some things."

"What kind of things? Do you mean like murder?"

"No, nothing like that. It happened while I was living on the street. I don't want to talk about it."

Airy was facing him now, her eyes narrowed. "How does Wolf know?"

"Jesus, Airy. Can we drop it?"

Airy turned away and climbed into bed. She pulled her knees up and wrapped her arms around them. "I thought we said we wouldn't keep secrets from each other. I don't want to start the trust issues again."

Fehin sat down next to her. "It has nothing to do with you. It's in the past. Wolf was following me. I didn't know. I never saw him. He's responsible for a lot of the shit that was going on in my head at the time. He was feeding me dark thoughts."

"Fehin, I'm not a child. You can tell me what happened. Whatever it is I forgive you. If you keep this to yourself there's no hope for us."

She was right. Just because he'd lived on the streets and she hadn't, didn't mean she was incapable of understanding or forgiveness. They were connected and she could see right through his lies. He sighed heavily, leaned back against the headboard and closed his eyes. "You may decide you don't want to see me again," he began, keeping his eyes closed.

Airy's fingers touched his hand and then she twined them through his. "I can't think of anything that would make me feel like that—even if you'd murdered someone. Because I know if you did kill someone, it had to be for a very good reason. I know who you are, Fehin, even though you think I don't."

Fehin opened his eyes and took her face between his hands and kissed her softly on the mouth. "You wouldn't like the person I was during those months, Airy. I'll tell you, but don't say I didn't warn you."

THIRTY-SEVEN

Airy's heart was pounding and her hands had begun to sweat. She kept them folded together as she waited to hear the worst.

"I've done drugs, Airy, very bad ones—heroin, crack cocaine, meth, a bunch of hallucinogens. I'm lucky to be alive. In my defense losing my magic made me kind of crazy. The drugs helped, especially the hallucinogenic ones."

"So far I forgive you," she said, her gaze meeting his. There was pain there and it made her heart hurt to see it. "How did you get off them?"

Fehin let out a long breath. "It took nearly a year. I was a miserable mess. But I knew if I didn't, I'd be dead. After a point there's no coming back." He looked up, his eyes dark. "I saw a lot of people die."

Airy watched him, trying hard not to cry. The idea of him drugged out with no one to turn to made her feel sick inside.

"That's not the worst of it," he continued. "There were women," he went on, "Lots of them."

"Women you had sex with?"

"Yes, women I had sex with. There were prostitutes and

homeless women and drug addicts. We were all together, living on the street."

Airy began to cry. "Did you love any of them?"

Fehin didn't say anything for a long moment. Once she wiped her face he began again. "It's hard to feel much of anything when you're high. I liked them in my own way. We eased each other's pain." When she turned away, he grabbed her, forcing her to look at him. "I told you this would be painful."

Airy twisted out of his grasp and stood up. "What about me? Did you ever think of me?" She felt hot all over and could barely look at him. All she could see was Fehin wrapped around some other woman, kissing her, his hands on her body. She began to sob and ran for the bathroom, closing and locking the door behind her. She couldn't stop crying and only hoped that Carla wouldn't hear her.

A soft knock came sometime later and then Fehin said, "Airy? Please let me in."

Airy rinsed her eyes and unlocked the door. A second later it opened and Fehin entered. His face was covered in tears, his expression filled with sadness and regret. "I'm sorry. And in answer to your question, I thought about you every day. It was thinking about you that gave me the strength to get clean."

When he reached for her, she moved into his arms. "I didn't know it would be this hard," she mumbled, her face buried in his neck.

"Come on," he said, leading the way back to the bed. "Enough for now."

They both slept fitfully, waking several times in the night to continue the discussion. Airy learned the horror of his life in fits and starts, her mind recoiling at what he revealed. He'd been buried under something so dark that she honestly couldn't imagine it. He'd said it himself—he was lucky to be alive.

Around dawn they fell asleep for a couple of hours and when she woke again, she was lying in the circle of his arms. Looking down on his sleeping face she felt tenderness she'd never experienced before. She loved this man, and that's what he was, a man. She didn't feel like a woman yet, but she was on her way. When his eyes opened, he smiled and reached for her, pulling her against him.

"You're still here," he murmured. "I dreamed you left."

"I'm not going anywhere and neither are you," she said fiercely. "We have to do what we came here for."

When Fehin and Airy came into the kitchen later Carla was waiting for them. "Is everything all right?" she asked. "I couldn't help overhearing some shouting."

Airy turned to gaze at Fehin and then reached for his hand. "It is now."

Carla smiled and reached for the coffee pot. "I just brewed a new pot," she said, grabbing cups down from the shelf.

The three of them sat at the table, and after a furtive look at Fehin, Airy said, "Wolf is here in Milltown."

Carla looked like she'd seen a ghost. "How do you know?"

"Tell her, Fehin."

Fehin took a sip of his coffee and then related the events of the day before. "He expects me to get him a job, but now that I've bared my soul to Airy he doesn't have anything to hold over me."

"Bared your soul?" Carla glanced from one to the other.

Airy waved her hands in the air. "Long sad story, but the main thing is he can't blackmail us. I told Fehin we have to get on with what we came here to do." She smiled, turning toward Fehin. "Our destiny awaits, my prince."

Fehin bowed his head. "I am at your service, my queen."

"Wait a second," Carla interrupted. "Why is Airy a queen and you're a prince?"

They both laughed. "Okay," Fehin continued, "how about, 'I'm at your service, my princess'?"

"Or, 'our destiny awaits, my ancient king'."

"Ancient?" Fehin asked.

Carla let out a snort and rose from her chair. "Why don't you two figure out the semantics while I do the laundry?"

"Seriously, Carla," Airy said. "Fehin doesn't have magic and I'm at a loss as to where to start."

"Start at the beginning,"

When Carla headed toward her bedroom Fehin jumped up, his eyes wide. "What time is it?"

"Quarter till nine, why?"

"I was supposed to be at work at eight this morning. So much for having a job," he said, shaking his head. "I was on probation."

"This way you don't have to see Wolf," Airy reminded him. "Wasn't he planning to meet you there?"

Fehin raised his eyebrows. "You're right. Now I have to figure out how to kill the bastard."

"Quit saying that, Fehin. You're not going to kill your half-brother."

"Want to bet?"

THIRTY-EIGHT

"Do you have classes today?" Fehin asked as they left the house.

"Yes, but I think I'm done with the school thing. I was serious about getting on with our destiny."

"Building a bridge?"

"Coming up with a way across a chasm or abyss, either metaphysical or otherwise."

"That's good, Airy. Good start."

She laughed. "You like that? I have more. How about 'a symbol that links two disparate thoughts, worlds, ways of being, or even species'?"

Fehin grinned. "I think you're getting closer."

"So, what is it?"

"Let's get coffee and talk about it. I haven't had enough caffeine to discuss this deep a topic."

After Airy bought a latte for her and plain coffee for Fehin they settled into wrought iron chairs under an umbrella. It was a cold day and they sat hunched, warming their hands around the cups.

"For some reason this weather reminds me of your brother. I wouldn't be surprise if he showed up."

Fehin looked around and then turned his gaze on her. She noticed the softness in his mossy eyes, an expression he hadn't had until this morning. Unburdening his mind had definitely loosened something. But beneath his eyes were shadows that pointed to an unhealthy lifestyle and not enough rest. She reached for his hand and moved her chair closer. "I feel so different now," she said.

"Different...about me, about us?"

"About everything, Fehin. I feel closer to you than I ever have. And now that, well...you know...it's even more so."

Fehin smiled and squeezed her fingers. "I guess we had to go through our own special hell to get here."

"You more than me."

"I don't know about that. You had to deal with my illness and near death, me deserting you and not knowing if I was ever coming back. And now hearing about all the crazy shit I went through. I would say that was fairly hellish and painful. But the good thing is I got a first-hand view of the problems in this country."

Airy was just about to answer when a shadow came across the table and then a voice said, "Here you are. I wondered where I'd find you."

Airy let go of Fehin's hand and scrunched down in her chair.

"What are you doing here, Wolf?" Fehin asked.

"You weren't at the construction site. Sam is more than a little irritated. He hired me on, by the way."

"Good for you," Fehin said. "Now get the hell away from us."

Wolf put his attention on Airy, moving close. "I have a nasty little story to tell you," he began.

"I know everything," Airy answered, her eyes narrowing as she watched the monster version of Fehin. Her body had begun to tremble.

"You know all about the whores and the sex and the filthy disgusting life Fehin was into? The drugs that made him into an animal?"

"Yes, Wolf, I do. Nothing you can say will turn me against him. Now leave us alone so we can discuss our plans."

"Like how you two are going to save this world?" Wolf laughed. "Without magic my brother doesn't stand a chance. And anyway, this place is beyond redemption. Don't worry about it though, the coming nuclear war will blow it all to bits."

Fehin was suddenly on his feet, his fist landing in Wolf's middle and sending him sprawling. He grabbed Airy's hand. "Let's go."

They ended up in the woods behind campus, coming to a stop beneath the familiar pine tree, trying to catch their breath.

"I *am* going to kill him," Fehin announced.

And this time Airy didn't protest.

"HE'S PROBABLY RIGHT about the war," Airy said later as they were walking back to Carla's house. "There are wars all over the globe now. There's no end to it that I can see. More than half the countries have nuclear capability. My professor is worried."

"I didn't realize it was the entire world we needed to fix. That's going to be a hard one."

"You need your magic. Once you have that you could conjure another world."

Fehin laughed and then frowned. "Jesus, Airy. I don't have that kind of power. But you may be onto something. A metaphysical bridge could do the same thing, but not in such a physical manner." He shook his head and looked down. "I have to think on this for a while."

"Jesus was an avatar, right?"

Fehin looked over at her with a puzzled expression and then registered what she'd asked. "That's my take on it. Why?"

"Maybe we're avatars."

Fehin watched her, wondering why she'd brought this up. "We need to be dead and then come alive again to be avatars."

Airy stared into space for a moment, her eyebrows scrunched together. "If you conjure the world, what's my part?"

Fehin laughed. "Your mind is all over the place today. I don't know. Maybe it's up to you to convince them to go. You're the one who talks to trees."

"That'll be easy, especially since most of the people I've met think I'm a nutcase." Airy walked up the stairs ahead of him and fetched the key from under the flowerpot. "I'm glad Carla's not here," she murmured, opening the door.

Inside she grabbed Fehin's hand and tugged him with her into the bedroom. She closed the door and then pulled her T-shirt over her head. "Well?" she asked, unzipping her jeans.

Fehin took one look at her and undressed.

It was a while before they surfaced again, lying back against the pillows and attempting to re-enter the real world.

"What got into you?" Fehin asked, turning his head.

"All the talk of other women, wars and saving worlds, I suppose. Not to mention seeing you punch Wolf in the stomach."

Fehin nuzzled her neck. "You are not who I thought you were."

Airy pulled away to stare at him. "What do you mean?"

"For one thing, you're no little girl." He shook his head, grinning. "I love you," he said, serious.

"You didn't before?"

Fehin looked embarrassed for a moment. "I didn't know you could take it, Airy. I expected you to crumble after you heard what I did. You surprised me."

"We've both grown up."

"Yeah, I guess we have. Now all we need to do is get rid of Wolf, conjure a parallel universe and then move all the people and creatures from earth."

"No problem," Airy said, grinning. When she kissed him, he wrapped his arms around her and there was no more talking.

"Airy? Fehin? Are you here?"

Airy jumped up from the bed and pulled on her jeans. "I didn't think she'd be home so early."

Fehin looked at his phone. "It's nearly four in the afternoon."

"What?"

Fehin grinned and jiggled his eyebrows up and down.

"We're here!" she called out, trying to find her hastily removed T-shirt.

"Sorry, Carla," she said, pulling the bedroom door shut behind her. "We fell asleep."

Carla looked skeptical but didn't say anything. "How were your classes? I thought Fehin was starting his job this morning."

"He was supposed to be there at eight. He was on probation so he figured he was fired before he even started. And I skipped my classes. I'm quitting school."

Carla looked surprised. "Why is that?"

"Because we have a destiny and it doesn't include school. Wolf showed up while we were at the coffee shop. Fehin punched him in the stomach and knocked him down."

Carla's mouth dropped open. "I thought you said Wolf was enormous."

"He is." Airy went to the cabinet and opened it, pulling out a bag of chocolate chip cookies. "Fehin's a lot stronger than he looks."

"He looks quite strong to me," Carla said, taking the cookie Airy held out. "But I didn't think he would antagonize Wolf like that."

"Believe me, the antagonizing was all coming from Wolf. Fehin just had enough."

"I'm impressed," Carla said opening the refrigerator. "Would you two like to join me in a glass of wine? I'd love to hear your plan."

Airy glanced toward the closed bedroom door. "Fehin can't drink, Carla. He's an addict. And I don't drink alcohol."

Carla nodded. "Well, then, we can all have tea. How about that?"

"Sounds good. I'll go get him."

"I FORGOT TO TELL YOU," Airy said later, as she and Fehin were getting ready for bed. "I think I have a new power. I can feel what others are feeling and I can change their minds."

Fehin came out of the bathroom, a toothbrush in his hand. "How does that work?"

"I was talking to this girl at school. She's one of those people who don't care about anything but how they look—completely wrapped up in her own little world--you know the type. Well, anyway, I touched her on the arm for some reason and I said something about poisons in the environment and what was happening to the creatures, and she said, 'Wow, I didn't know that.' And there was a different look in her eyes."

"Could be she was primed for it."

"I don't think so."

"It sounds like a definite asset, but touching everybody in the world could prove difficult."

"Maybe it can happen without touching. Maybe it's from looking into someone's eyes."

"Still, Airy. Are you going to look into every single person's eyes on the planet to convince them to walk across a bridge?"

Airy frowned and turned away. "You're so negative. I thought it was pretty cool."

Fehin grabbed hold of her arm. "I didn't mean to be negative, just playing the devil's advocate. Before I lost my magic, I could deflect people's thoughts, but what you're talking about sounds even better because it might last more than a minute or two. I suggest we find this girl and see if something has changed in her life."

"I know her schedule because we shared two classes. Let's do it tomorrow." Airy glanced at him. "What about you? Can you do anything yet?"

His expression darkened. "If you're talking about magic, I check it every morning and every night and sometimes in between. So, no, I can't."

"I'm sorry," she said. "I wonder what's keeping your magic from coming back?"

Fehin shrugged. "Maybe I have to kill Wolf to get it back."

"Are you serious?"

Fehin pressed his lips together. "I don't know—just an idle thought. But I'll tell you, if he keeps this shit up, he's going down."

THIRTY-NINE

"There's someone lurking around down there," Carla told them the next morning when they came into the kitchen. "He got here early. Either that or he's been here all night. He doesn't look like a very savory character to me."

Fehin went to the window. "It's Wolf. I'll go see what he wants."

Airy grabbed his arm. "What are you doing? The last time we saw him you punched him. You think he's here to have a nice little chat?"

"I'm not afraid of him." And oddly, this was true.

"From what I've heard, you should be," Carla remarked.

Fehin glanced from Carla to Airy and then opened the door, pulling it shut behind him. "What are you doing here?" he called, heading down the stairs.

Wolf looked up and ran his thick deformed-looking fingers through his hair. "Sam asked me to get you back on board."

"Bullshit, Wolf. I know that isn't true."

Wolf smirked. "Maybe I just wanted to see you."

"That isn't true either." Fehin had to look up to meet Wolf's eyes, and what he saw there made a shiver run down his spine. He waited for Wolf's response.

"I have some news from Far Isle I thought you'd be interested in. Your mother's sick. Brandubh got a message to me."

"Really? How does that work, exactly?"

"Unlike you, I have my telepathic abilities."

"Thanks for the message. What do you really want from me?"

Wolf paused for a moment and then he smiled. "I want you and the girl to give up your idea of saving this place. I like it just the way it is. I've made inroads into several lucrative businesses."

"Okay, this I believe. Gambling and drugs, perhaps prostitution?"

Wolf looked surprised. "I thought you said you didn't have magic."

"Don't need magic to figure that out."

Wolf turned away. "Take care of the girl—she just might have an accident."

"You fucker!" Fehin lunged after him, grabbing him by the shoulder, but this time Wolf was prepared. He hit Fehin in the face knocking him back and bloodying his nose.

"You can't win, Fehin. It's either my world or yours. And without magic you're pretty much stuck. My powers are returning."

Fehin wiped his nose on his sleeve, turning to see Airy running down the stairs. She grabbed his hand. "Are you okay?"

"Fine," he mumbled, pushing her away. He followed her up the stairs and into the townhouse. When Carla tried to help, Fehin shook his head, heading alone into the bathroom. He cleaned himself up and checked his nose to make sure it wasn't broken. He was raw with anger, his entire body trembling with it. And the expression on his face in the mirror was not familiar. Something was happening to him and he had a feeling it was Wolf's doing. Wolf was infecting him with darkness and making Fehin into a monster.

When he came out again Carla and Airy were sitting at the table talking in low voices. They both looked up, their expressions questioning.

"He might not seem that dangerous, but Wolf could cause a lot of problems."

"He seems plenty dangerous to me," Carla said. "He's a brute and after what he did to Airy, I wouldn't put anything past him."

Fehin glanced at Airy. "You need to stay close to me at all times. That bastard just threatened you."

Airy's eyes went wide. "What did he say?"

"Just that you might have an accident. If what he said is true, that he's acquiring his missing powers, he could seriously thwart every single good thing we're trying to do."

"What does he want from you?"

"I think he wants to *be* me. I don't want to scare you, but he may want you for himself. And that really worries me."

Carla gasped. "You need to call the police."

"And tell them what? That my brother hit me in the nose?" Fehin shook his head. "I have to take care of this myself." Fehin thought about what Wolf said about his mother. Could it be true? Without magic there was no way to find out.

FEHIN and Airy were sitting together on a stone bench on campus. Fehin had just spent the better part of an hour explaining what Wolf had done in his world of the future—the reasons why Fehin had conjured the island. When he glanced at Airy her face was pale. He shouldn't have gone into so much gory detail, he thought, watching her. There was something working inside him that was seriously fucked up. He wanted to score some heroin and let all this shit go away for a while. He thought of the sweet oblivion, but then remembered coming down off it and the racking shakes and sickness. It was worth it.

"What if he does that here?" Airy asked, bringing his attention back.

"If he starts killing people the police will pick him up. He can't get away with mass murder. But I bet he could manage to rape and pillage and keep under their radar."

"What should we do?"

Fehin stood and grabbed her hand, pulling her up. "Right now, we're going to see what's happened with that friend of yours. Hannah? Is that her name?"

Airy smiled. "Her name's Allie. Here she comes," she added, pointing. "Hey, Allie!" she called out as the blonde girl came closer.

"Hi, Airy. Why weren't you in class?"

Fehin looked closely at her eyes. They were light blue and guileless.

"I dropped out. Allie, this is my boyfriend, Fehin."

"Nice to meet you, Fehin. Airy has told me some good things about you."

Fehin smiled. "I've heard good stuff about you too."

"Really?" Allie looked puzzled. "Well, good to see you. I have to go to my next class now."

Airy watched her disappear into a throng of students and then turned to Fehin. "What do you think?"

"Hard to know. She seemed perfectly nice."

"She wasn't like that before."

He shrugged. "Should we get some lunch?"

Airy looked away for a moment and when her eyes met his,

they were troubled. "Remember what you said about paying your own way? Carla and I talked about it the other day. She thinks you should get another job."

Fehin was instantly furious. "And what about you? Just because your parents are still filling your bank account with money means you don't have to work?"

"Well, I..."

"You *what*, Airy? Goddamn it, I thought we were doing something here. Fuck you," he added, walking away. He had an overwhelming desire to hit something or beat someone up, but instead he balled his hands into fists and tried to push the feeling down.

FORTY

"Slow down, Airy," Carla said, placing a hand on her shoulder. "It's hard to believe Fehin could act that way."

"I'm not making it up." A second later she was sobbing.

"This was over getting a job? He's the one that brought it up in the first place."

"I told him you and I talked about it. That's when he blew up. You should have seen the look on his face—I thought he was going to hit me. I've never seen him like that."

"Sit down, sweetheart. I'll make some tea. You need to calm down so we can talk about this rationally."

"Where's Fan?" Airy asked, looking around.

"She's at her Dad's house for a couple of weeks."

"A couple of weeks? Why so long?"

Carla moved to the stove and put the kettle on before turning to face Airy. "I thought it best with everything that's going on." She paused and started again. "You said Fehin was on drugs for a while. Do you think he's using now?"

"How would I know? He seemed the same until that day with Wolf."

"Drug withdrawal can cause these sorts of behaviors. And from what you said, he was into some nasty stuff. Honestly, I think it was the morphine that started him down this road."

Airy nodded, thinking back to the shakes he'd had after they left the hospital, his fevers, the depression. It must have set something up in his system—primed him for more drug use. "It's like our destiny is to go through one horrible thing after another. Maybe the bridge is between the two of us." Airy looked up and wiped her eyes with a napkin.

Carla frowned. "His magic has not returned, which must make him feel impotent, especially since yours is growing. Didn't you tell me about a girl that you influenced just by touching her?"

Airy took a tissue from the box on the table and blew her nose. "I hadn't thought of that."

"When he comes home, we have to confront him about the drugs. If he's using, we need to get him into rehab."

Fehin didn't come home that night nor the next or the one after that.

By the morning of the fourth day Airy was frantic, sure that Wolf had killed him.

"I'm calling the police," she told Carla, picking up her cell phone.

"I think that's a good idea."

After breakfast Airy announced that she was going to try and find him. She'd called the police but their response had been less than encouraging.

"Airy, if he's with other drug addicts it could be dangerous."

"Where would they hang out?"

"Wait for the police. That'll be the first place they look."

"They're not going to do anything. They were completely disinterested."

"I'll go with you."

Airy shook her head. "I'm going on my own." She grabbed a jacket and headed for the door. "If I'm not back by dinnertime let the police know that it's because of their ineptitude."

"Airy! I don't think this is a good idea!" Carla called out as she opened the door.

Airy closed the door, hurried down the steps and jogged toward the harbor. She'd seen a lot of homeless around there. It seemed a good place to start, especially since Fehin got along so well with them.

"Have you seen this man?" she asked the first person she came to. He had filthy dreads and was wearing ragged jeans and a shirt way too big for him. His eyes were clouded and she wondered if he'd even heard her, but when she held her phone out showing Fehin's picture, the guy at least looked at it.

"He might have been here. How badly do you want to know?"

Airy reached into her pack and pulled out five dollars. When she handed it over he perked up. "I saw this dude yesterday."

"What was he doing?"

"He was with some guy that looked like Frankenstein—the two of them were headed that way." He pointed south along the harbor.

Airy knew who Frankenstein was from her movie going days on campus. Sounded like Wolf to her. But why would they be together? She walked along the harbor, scanning the hidden places between buildings. There were groups of homeless, but none of them had Fehin in their midst. They ignored her as she moved by them.

When she reached the industrial section, she felt the familiar magnet-like pull in her abdomen. Fehin was close. And then she saw Wolf walking toward her. She hid behind a metal container.

"Think you can hide from me?" Wolf sneered, coming up behind her.

She let out a shriek and jumped away. "Don't hurt her," another familiar voice said. Fehin appeared behind his half-brother.

"Fehin!" She was about to go to him, but the expression on his face stopped her. He looked ragged and beat-up, a scraggly three-day growth adding to the impression. His eyes were molten with anger.

"You'll get out of here if you know what's good for you," he rasped. And then he and Wolf walked away together as if they were best friends.

Airy followed, trying to stay out of sight. She kept her thoughts neutral since Wolf was so adept at reading minds. When they disappeared inside a container, she stayed put waiting for them to reappear. It was fifteen minutes or so before they came out again and this time there was a very thin woman with them, and another guy who looked half-dead.

She followed them to a small tent set up behind a stack of pallets. They lifted the flap and crawled inside. It was a long time before Airy found the nerve to creep closer. She was a foot away but there was no sound coming from inside. After several minutes of this, she peeked through the opening. All four of them were sprawled on their backs with their eyes closed. They looked dead. Rubber tubing, needles and other drug parapher-nalia lay strewn around them. Airy's hand went to her mouth, stopping the scream that rose into her throat.

Fehin sat up, his unfocused gaze finding her. He put his fingers to his lips in a shush gesture before crawling toward her.

"Get out of here," he muttered, making a feeble attempt to push her away.

"Fehin, what's going on?"

"I'm doing research," he whispered.

"Please come with me," she said, grabbing hold of his shirt. But he pulled away and shook his head.

"Go home, Airy."

At that point Wolf opened his eyes and pushed himself up to his knees. A second later he lunged through the tent opening and threw her to the ground. "Such a pretty little thing," he said, his mouth working as he straddled her.

When Airy screamed Wolf pressed his hand over her mouth. With his other hand he worked at the zipper of her pants. He was so heavy she couldn't breathe.

Behind him Fehin suddenly came alive. "Get the fuck off her!" he shouted. He jumped on his brother's back, his nails raking across the larger man's neck and bringing blood to the surface.

When Airy saw the gun in Fehin's hand she let out a shriek. But it was too late, the blast deafening her. Wolf slumped sideways and she rolled out from under him. Her hands were shaking so badly she could barely re-zip her jeans. When she noticed the blood on her hands, on her shirt, on her jeans, she retched violently into the dirt.

The other woman and man had now risen to their knees, their expressions passive as they gathered the tubes and needles and other equipment while Fehin knelt beside Wolf feeling for a pulse.

"Is he dead?" she whispered.

He nodded. "Go," he muttered. "The cops will be all over this in a couple of minutes."

Airy stared at the gun still in Fehin's hand. "Where did you get that?"

Fehin looked down as though he'd never seen it before, and then hurled it across the asphalt. "I mean it Airy, you have to get out of here."

"I'm not going without you."

When sirens sounded in the distance the man and woman quickly exited and took off running.

"Airy, you have to go. NOW!"

Airy folded her trembling hands across her blood-soaked shirt and stared at him. The sirens were closer now and Fehin looked around wildly. "Okay," he finally said, pulling her to her feet. He grabbed hold of her hand and took off in the direction the others had gone. He stopped when they reached the container. "I'm staying here," he announced, watching her.

"Well, then I'm staying here too."

"Goddamn it, Airy."

When Fehin stared at her she stared back.

"I'm messed up. You don't want me around."

"I don't care," Airy said stubbornly. "If you don't want to go to jail, I suggest you come with me."

From their hiding place they could see several cops combing the area. "And if we don't go now, I'm going to be implicated in this too," she added.

Fehin shook his head and crept around the side of the container. "Follow me," he hissed, slinking away.

WHEN AIRY CAME into the kitchen the following morning Carla was waiting for her. "How is he?"

"He's still asleep. He had a really bad night."

"I'm not surprised. He's strung out.

"I agree he's a major mess. He spent most of the night throwing up."

"That stuff is poison."

"Do you think it was heroin?"

"From your description of what was lying around, I'd say yes. And how are you?" she asked, placing her hand on Airy's shoulder. "That was a very bad scene, Airy. I should never have let you go."

Airy tried to smile. "I'm better than I was yesterday. But I'm worried about Fehin. If the police find him, he'll be in jail for the rest of his life."

"We talked about all this last night. He's not in the system. Best thing to do is get him into one of those facilities. You should never have gone down there by yourself. Did you know I'm the one who called the cops? After you left, I panicked. My god, Airy you could have been raped or even killed!" Carla placed a hand on either side of Airy's face. "I have to go to work. Will you be all right on your own?"

"As long as he doesn't decide to run away."

"Make him some soup and try and talk to him. If you have a problem call me immediately. I don't want you getting hurt."

"I'm not afraid of him, Carla. I know he loves me."

"People hooked on drugs do strange things. Promise me you'll call."

Airy nodded and then handed Carla the bag of bloody clothing.

"Don't worry. I'll get rid of these," Carla assured her before heading to the door.

Airy watched her leave and then searched through the cupboards until she found a can of consommé. She used the electric can opener to open it and then poured the jellied liquid into a saucepan. While she was stirring, she heard the bedroom door open. Fehin looked ragged around the edges, with wild hair, his eyes shadowed and dark.

"I'm fixing you some soup," she said.

"I won't be here long enough to eat it," he mumbled, heading toward the door.

The spoon clattered to the floor. "Oh no you don't!" she yelled, running toward him. She caught up with him at the door and wrestled with him for a couple of minutes until he started laughing.

"You're stronger than I thought."

"Get your ass back in bed."

"Airy, language!"

"Shut up and go!" she yelled, pointing. "Or I can't be responsible for my actions."

Airy was shaking all over as she poured the warmed soup into a cup and walked toward the bedroom. When she opened the door Fehin was face down on the bed sound asleep. She placed the soup on the bedside table and smoothed his hair back. He was sweaty and felt feverish.

The afternoon and night before had been a blur. Once they reached the main road, she'd hailed a taxi and somehow managed to get both of them inside it before calling Carla on her cell phone. The driver had stolen glances at them in the rearview mirror, obviously terrified by the copious amounts of blood all over the two of them.

Carla was waiting for them when they arrived and it was Carla who paid the driver, adding a big tip to the bill, and then helped haul a nearly unconscious Fehin up the stairs and into the townhouse. Between the two of them they got him undressed and into bed. After that Airy ripped off her blood-soaked clothes and stood under the shower for a good half hour.

"Airy?"

"Yes, Fehin, I'm here."

"I'm sorry," he said, lifting his head. A second later he was snoring again.

Airy leaned against the headboard and closed her eyes, waking when she heard his voice.

"Is that soup still around here somewhere?" he asked, sitting up.

"It's right there." Airy pointed to the cup and watched him drain it.

He placed it on the table and turned to her. "We can't be together. I can't trust myself not to do this again. I thought I'd kicked it."

"Carla is checking into rehab places. Without me you'd be sitting in a jail cell right now."

Fehin's eyes were sunken and dull. "Wolf is finally dead," he muttered.

"Yes, he is, and I'm glad of it. Did he get you hooked again?"

"I can't blame it on him. I didn't have to go along with it. That's the thing about addicts." He looked over at her, bleak.

"That's crap," Airy said. "He was instrumental in this and I know he was doing something to your mind. I don't know how, but I'm sure of it. That day when you told me to fuck off? That's when I knew."

Fehin let out a long sigh. "I remember how I felt, as though I was about to explode. The heroin calmed all that down."

"I wonder how long Wolf was screwing with your mind. You said he was around you the last time it happened, right?"

Fehin raised his listless gaze to hers. "I didn't know it at the time."

"He was about to rape me."

Fehin blinked once and balled his hands into fists. "I know that. Why do you think I shot him?"

BY THE TIME Carla got home Fehin was sleeping again. Airy was waiting for her. "Fan's doing her homework," she told Carla once she'd hung up her coat. "If you want us out of here, I would understand."

Carla kicked her shoes off and headed to the refrigerator. She took out an opened bottle of white wine, poured herself a glass, took a sip and then moved to the couch in the living room, sitting down with her legs curled under her. "I've gone through some bad times in my life. I think I can handle this." She gazed at Airy who hadn't moved from her place by the door. "Why don't you come sit down," she said patting the seat next to her. "I talked to my friend and found a place for Fehin. It's a two-month program. They've had great results. But Fehin has to want this, Airy. Without his complete participation it won't do any good at all."

"Can I have a glass of wine?"

"I thought you said you didn't drink."

"Well, I've never had a drink, but it looks kind of good," she replied, eyeing the frosted glass.

"Help yourself."

Airy got a glass out of the cupboard and poured in the perfume-like liquid and took a long swallow. "It is good," she said, carrying it over to the couch.

"This is an Italian wine that I like. It's called Soave." Carla placed her glass on the coffee table and turned toward Airy. "We take him tomorrow. In the meantime, you need to have a long talk with him. Find out if he really wants to quit."

"He's miserable right now. I know he feels terrible about what he did. And he seems sick." Airy took another sip of wine, savoring it in her mouth before swallowing. It was making her feel slightly light-headed but in a good way.

"He's in withdrawal. They'll help him with that."

"Will I get addicted to this?" she asked, holding out the glass.

Carla laughed. "I don't think so. Wine isn't like heroin. But if you start drinking an entire bottle every night it could be cause for alarm."

Airy finished off her glass, took it into the kitchen and washed it out. "I'm going to check on him," she said, heading toward the bedroom.

"I'm making pasta for dinner. He might feel up to eating some."

Airy nodded, opened the bedroom door and closed it behind her.

Fehin was awake and sitting up. "I heard your plan for me," he said.

Airy was on her way to the bed but stopped when she heard his tone. "Then I guess you heard Carla say that you have to be into this for it to work. Do you want to quit?"

Fehin lifted his shoulders and let out a long sigh. "Of course, I want to quit."

"Well then, what's the problem?"

"I don't know if I can."

Airy moved the rest of the distance to the bed and sat down next to him. "That's the whole point, Fehin. You need support and help to quit. You may have to do some kind of outpatient program, like AA or something."

"Right now, I feel like shit."

Airy reached for his hand. "You went through this once before. You can do it again. I'm telling you, without Wolf around I know you're going to get through this way easier."

"I hope you're right." Fehin pulled his hand away and curled up on his side.

Airy watched him for a while and then went to take a shower. With water sluicing down her back she let the tears flow. No one would hear her sobs over the sound of the water.

FORTY-ONE

Fehin turned on his side and reached for his phone. It was close to eight a.m. and he was supposed to be in therapy. He jumped out of bed and pulled on his jeans, running his fingers through his hair. While buttoning his shirt he glanced toward the other bed where his roommate slept. It was empty and still made up. Maybe he'd been released. The two of them hadn't spoken much. The guy, whose name escaped him, was younger than he was and seemed to have a death wish. He'd managed to nearly blow off his hand while heating up some concoction he planned to shoot up. Fehin felt sorry for him.

He'd been here for over a month now. His days consisted of eating, therapy sessions and taking drugs that were supposed to help with the withdrawal. He felt more clear-headed than he had in a long time. Airy had not come to visit and he missed her. He didn't hold out much hope for their relationship.

He was late to group therapy and slipped in, trying to be invisible. "Glad you could join us," the counselor said.

These sessions consisted of each person baring his or her soul to the others. Sometimes there was crying, sometimes anger and sometimes it was just plain boring. Fehin hadn't said much so far since he didn't think it would be prudent to reveal that he came from 2468 to fulfill a destiny, and that he killed his sorcerer brother for nearly raping his girlfriend who was able to talk to trees. He chuckled to himself as these thoughts went through his head.

"Will you share this morning, Fehin?"

Fehin's cheeks grew hot. "Um...I have nothing to say."

"Can you tell us what led you to use?"

Fehin looked around at all the eyes trained on him. "I guess the first time it was because I needed to learn about life on the street."

"And how did that go for you?"

"I got off the stuff without any help from you," Fehin said defiantly.

The counselor blinked, but other than that there was no visible reaction to what Fehin had said.

"And this time?"

Fehin looked down, noticing that his shoelaces weren't tied. He bent over to tie them. "I don't know," he mumbled.

"You don't know why you started again?"

"That's right. I think it had to do..." Fehin trailed off, realizing he had nearly revealed that he had a brother. Not a good idea.

"Had to do with what?"

"Pressure from my girlfriend, from work, you know the drill," he lied.

The counselor watched him for a while without speaking and then turned to someone else.

At the end of the hour Fehin practically sprinted from the room.

Later, when the attendant came with his pills, he waved his hands, trying to distract him. When nothing happened, he took the pills and swallowed them obediently. *Shit,* he thought to himself. Is my magic ever coming back? That was the real reason he got into drugs to begin with. Those months after he left Airy in Colorado were the worst of his life. If his magic didn't return he couldn't be with her. It was too humiliating. Why was he part of a destiny when he couldn't do a damn thing to help?

AIRY WAS WAITING for him the day Fehin was released, her wide smile making his heart hurt. It had been over two months since he'd seen her. Christmas had come and gone, a sad affair here in the rehab center. When she hugged him, he hugged her back, but he knew he wouldn't be staying with her for long.

"I missed you!" she said in the taxi. "They told me not to come visit. I hope you realized I wasn't allowed."

"I knew," he said, turning toward her. Her wide eyes looked very green. He had a strange sensation in his lower abdomen, as though a magnet was pulling him toward her. "Are you doing that?"

"Doing what?"

"Never mind," he said, turning to stare out the window.

Airy reached for his hand. "How was it?"

"It was all right. I'm glad to be out of there, though."

"Carla's cooking a special dinner."

"She shouldn't have gone to any trouble. I'm only staying one night."

"What are you talking about?" Airy's clear-eyed gaze made his head hurt.

"I have to get a job, Airy. I can't hang around without my..." he glanced at the driver, "magic," he whispered. "What we were supposed to do depends on that. Since I don't have any I'm moving on."

Airy looked struck, her eyes wide. "Don't you love me?"

"I love you, but that's not enough."

"The hell it isn't," she said loudly, causing the driver to check them out in his rearview mirror. "You'll get it back. I know because I've had a bunch of premonitions."

Fehin scoffed. "You're having premonitions? With me in them?"

"Yes, with you in them," she hissed. "And you have your... abilities intact," she finished, glancing toward the front seat. "You can be such an asshole."

Fehin laughed so hard he had to double over. "Hearing you swear is totally weird. When did you start that?"

Airy sat up straight and folded her hands in her lap. "You bring it out in me," she said primly. And then she giggled.

FEHIN ROLLED over and took Airy in his arms. He kissed her and then moved his hands across the top of her T-shirt.

"Let me help you with that," she murmured, pulling it over her head. A second later there was soft warm skin under his fingers instead of rough cotton.

Her hands were on him, her breath in his ear. He responded to what she was doing. They were underwater, the murmur of her rhythmic breathing, the sound of his own breath, blue-green lights going off inside his skull. She smelled of sweat and flowers.

"FEHIN? Are you planning to get up today?" Airy was staring down at him with her hands on her hips.

He sat up. "What time is it?"

"Nearly noon."

Fehin shook the sleep from his head. "I think I need a major dose of caffeine."

"Coming right up, your highness." Airy flounced out of the room leaving the door open.

He heard her in the kitchen as he made his way to the bath-room. When he looked in the mirror, he was surprised to see how bright his eyes looked. He actually looked happy. He pulled on his jeans and went to join her.

"Why did you let me sleep so late?" he asked, accepting the cup she handed him.

"This is your first day back. I figured you needed your beauty rest." She poured a cup of coffee for herself, added cream and sat at the table next to him.

"I had the most amazing dream. We were...well, you know...you were touching me and I was..." Fehin shook his head smiling. "Anyway, it felt like we were underwater."

Airy's level gaze met his. "That wasn't a dream. You woke me up in the middle of the night. It felt like that to me too."

"We did it last night?"

"Yes, Fehin. Is that so shocking?"

"I was just surprised since we hadn't really talked, or..."

She stared at him. "Sometimes talking is overrated."

"Did you know I was asleep?"

Airy laughed. "You were pretty amazing for being asleep, Fehin."

FORTY-TWO

Carla glanced out the window. "There are cops out there. I suggest you two go into the bedroom."

It was March now, and they'd all relaxed about Wolf's death. This came as a surprise. Airy met Fehin's gaze. They hurried toward the bedroom.

"I told you I shouldn't have stayed here," Fehin whispered once they were in the room with the door closed. "If you get in trouble because of me, I'll..."

Airy put her hand over his mouth. "Stop talking," she hissed. She grabbed a glass from the bathroom counter, pressed it against the door and put her ear up to the other end.

Fehin stared at her, puzzled. "What are you doing?"

"Shut-up," she mouthed.

The murmur of voices went on for some time until she heard the sound of the front door closing. A few seconds after that Carla knocked on the bedroom door. "You can come out now."

"What did they say?" Airy asked, opening the door.

"You couldn't hear through the glass?" Fehin chuckled, following her into the living room.

Airy gave him a look. "It didn't work as well as it should have," she whispered.

Carla glanced at the two of them and then went to sit at the kitchen table. "They finally linked Wolf and Fehin, which led them to the construction site. I guess Wolf knew someone at the college? That's how they knew where to find you, Fehin. And you put this address on your application."

"Damn it!" Fehin said loudly. "I can't believe they didn't find me sooner."

"What did you tell them?" Airy asked, moving to a chair next to Carla.

"I said he'd been living here for a while but I hadn't seen him in several weeks."

Airy felt like all the air had been sucked out of her lungs. She leaned over to catch her breath.

"Airy, what's wrong?" Fehin was by her side in an instant, his hand on her back.

"She's hyperventilating," Carla said, unconcerned. "It'll pass in a moment. They could come back with a warrant to search the house since they don't have any other leads," she continued.

AIRY AND FEHIN had spent the last month going over the possible meanings of a bridge while they waited for Fehin's magic to return. They walked every day and went to the library on campus, researching the politics of the past ten years and trying to come up with an answer that made any sense.

Once a week Fehin went off to his Narcotics Anonymous meeting, coming back in a darker mood than when he left.

When Airy asked, he said it saddened him to see so many people struggling. Other than that, he refused to talk about it. She worried that he'd be tempted to use again, but when she asked him, he shook his head vehemently. "I'm not going down that road ever again. And if I do, you have my permission to kill me."

Fehin's magic was still absent, a glaring problem that obviously plagued him. Every day Airy asked him what to do and every day he said he didn't know. Airy's magic was stronger than ever, her connection to Fehin reaching mystical proportions. She felt linked to him all the time, even when they were apart, which wasn't often, and always knew what he was thinking and feeling. When he talked about getting work, she told him she didn't want him wandering around where the cops could find him. But in reality, she couldn't stand the idea of being parted for even an hour. After everything they'd been through, she just couldn't risk it.

"I THINK you should take my car and the camping gear and drive west."

"Neither one of us know how to drive," Airy said, glancing at Fehin.

"It's an automatic, about as simple as it gets. I'm sure you can manage if I explain a few things."

Fehin frowned. "But won't they come looking for us?"

"I suppose they could, but these sorts of deaths happen all the time. It could have been another drugged out addict who shot and killed Wolf. And they don't have the gun or the prints. Actually, I'm surprised they're still working the case."

"What about the other two people?" Airy asked, worried.

"Those two are totally out of it," Fehin said. "They're the ones who provide the drugs down there. They could be busted for that. Even if they said something, no one would believe them."

"They might be in jail already," Carla added. "Perhaps that's why the cops are still looking into it."

"Well, Fehin?" Airy said, taking hold of his hand. "Do you still think it's a good idea to head off without me?"

Fehin laughed mirthlessly. "That plan was gone a month ago."

"I'm glad to hear it," Carla said. "You two need to stick together. Whatever is going on has made it very clear that you belong together. Don't squander what's been given freely by the universe."

Airy laughed. "I like that. I wish we didn't have to leave, though. I'll really miss you."

Carla smiled. "I have a feeling this won't be forever. Our lives are too intertwined now to imagine never seeing you again. Why don't you go pack up your gear. When it gets dark, I'll take you down to the garage and show you how to operate the car."

When the front door opened, they all turned. "What's up?" Fan asked, staring from one to the other.

FORTY-THREE

A crescent moon was up by the time Fehin and Airy followed Carla down to the garage. Fan had gone to bed knowing they were leaving. All of them were crying by the time they closed the door to her bedroom.

"Okay. Stow your stuff and then one of you get behind the wheel."

Fehin threw his pack into the backseat and climbed in. "This is a pretty nice car to just give away," he said.

"It's a Range Rover, but it's nearly ten years old. I don't drive much and I have several years before Fan's old enough. I signed the title over to Airy, since she has a passport. It's in the glove compartment with the insurance card. If you get stopped for any reason, they'll ask for them. I'll keep paying the insurance. It isn't much. Here's the lever to set the seat where you want it and over here is the shift."

Fehin and Airy paid close attention as she went through the various pedals and levers and what they did. She explained everything on the dashboard.

She had them practice backing and moving forward,

braking and accelerating. And when it was over, they were cross-eyed with exhaustion.

"I know you're tired, but I think it best if you leave tonight. There will be less traffic on the road. One of you can sleep while the other one drives. I've put maps of the country in the glove box and there are also state maps. Airy, you have your cell phone?"

"I do, but once the bill comes, they'll cut it off."

"I'll pay it for you," Carla said. I wouldn't want you to be out there without a phone. I suggest you stop at a bank and withdraw all your money. If your grandparents call, I'll tell them you went camping."

"But..."

"No buts, Airy. You're like a daughter to me now."

When Carla reached to hug her, Airy burst into tears. "I can't believe we're leaving. I've been living with you for over a year now."

Carla laughed. "Remember how you said you'd stay one night?"

Airy tried to smile. "Thanks for everything, Carla. I'll keep in touch."

"You still have your computers, don't you?"

"I sold mine to buy drugs," Fehin admitted. "But Airy has hers."

"Just e-mail once in a while."

"What route should we take?" Airy asked.

"Take whatever one calls to you. And don't be surprised when Fehin has magic again. I see a change in him."

Fehin smiled and reached out to give her a hug. "I hardly know how to thank you," he said. "Without you, I'd..."

"Fehin, I met you when you were seven years old. I've always had faith in you. Sometimes we have to go through terrible things to find out what we're made of."

Fehin started the car as Airy got into the passenger seat. His eyebrows came together as he moved the gearshift into D1 and took his foot off the brake. He glanced at Airy before putting his foot on the gas. A moment later they were rolling down the street.

FORTY-FOUR

"Are you hungry?" Airy held out the bag of sandwiches Carla had supplied. They'd already reached the border between Massachusetts and New York and were heading south toward Route 40. Airy was navigating using a small flashlight she'd found in the glove box to read the map.

Fehin took the sandwich she handed him. "I'm not even tired," he said, glancing her way.

"Me neither. I love the night. There's something exciting about it."

Fehin grinned. "Maybe it's because we're making a new start. I feel better than I have for over a year."

"No more Wolf," she said.

Fehin swiveled to look at her. "I used to chant that when I was a little boy after they put him away."

"It just came to me. Sometimes I feel so connected it's like we're one person."

"Can you read my thoughts?"

"Sometimes, but it's more about feelings. I can feel you here." She placed her hand on her belly.

"Sure it's not just sex?"

"This is different and it's there all the time, not just when we're...you know."

Fehin laughed. "Are you afraid of the word? Sex sex sex."

"Stop it! I don't consider what we do sex."

"Really? What would you call it?"

"It's deeper, Fehin. I feel like we go somewhere else, like we're in another world. It isn't just physical."

He nodded thoughtfully. "I know what you mean. It's so much more than what I experienced when..." His voice drifted off and he glanced over at her with a worried expression.

"I don't care about that anymore." Airy stared out the window. "There's no place to camp around here. I was hoping we could camp. What is it with all these mud lots and sick looking cattle? And it stinks."

Fehin grimaced. "We have to get further west. Wait until you see Wyoming."

"You've been there?"

"I was all over the place."

"I hoped we'd discover it together."

"There's still a lot of wild out there where I didn't go. Why don't you get some rest? You'll need to drive pretty soon. "

When Fehin announced an hour later that he needed a break, Airy drove for a few hours. Her nervousness left her as the car moved smoothly down the nearly deserted road. It was sometime near dawn when they decided to stop. They both needed some sleep in a real bed instead of sitting up in a car. It wasn't hard to find a motel. They undressed and took a shower together, asleep as soon as their heads hit the pillows.

"WHERE ARE WE?" Airy bent over the map, frowning. They'd found a small diner close to the motel and we're having their first real meal since leaving Carla's. It was late afternoon and they planned to get on the road as soon as rush hour was over.

Fehin perused the map. "We're here," he said, pointing.

"Terra Haute? Doesn't that mean high ground?"

Fehin shrugged. "Maybe it's high in comparison to something else. Do you want to go see the Wabash River before we leave? I read about it in my history class. A bunch of battles were fought around it."

"I like that name. French again, right?"

"I think it originally came from an Indian word, but I don't remember."

AIRY EXAMINED the bare trees along the riverbank. They looked like naked people to her, their arms held out as they reached for the sky. Soon they would be dressed again and birds would build hidden nests under their leafy protection. The river moved soundlessly behind them, and when a heron flew noisily out of the bushes Airy jumped in surprise, watching it lift into the air. "Let's camp."

"You want to stay here overnight?"

Airy nodded heading toward where they'd parked the car to get the gear.

They set up the tent and made a fire, watching the flames grow smaller as night descended. "I love this," Airy said, reaching for Fehin's hand. "It reminds me of Otherworld. We even saw a heron. I thought they were all gone."

"I'm sure there's some wildlife left. It just isn't enough to keep the different species going. I think this was a rare occurrence meant for our eyes." He turned back to stare at the flames. "We have to know what's lost in order to find it again."

Airy turned to look at him. "That's kind of profound. This bridge thing is close to the surface of my mind. It's like if I just close my eyes, I'll see the solution."

"So close your eyes."

Airy made a derisive sound in the back of her throat. "It isn't that simple, and besides..."

"I know. I don't have magic," Fehin said, defeated.

Airy moved closer and put her hand on his cheek. "I didn't mean it like that."

Fehin pulled away and stood up. "Let's get some rest. We have a long way to go."

IT WAS the middle of the night when Airy woke to voices outside the tent. A moment later a flashlight beamed through the tent flap and a man's voice said. "What do you think you're doing?"

By this time Fehin was awake. He pushed Airy back and pulled on his jeans. A minute later she was alone in the tent.

"What is the problem?" she heard him ask.

"For one thing you're on private land. We got a call from the owner complaining about someone camping down here. They saw your campfire."

"I didn't know we couldn't stay here," Fehin replied.

"It's posted right by that gate you walked through. You didn't see the 'no trespassing' sign?"

"No, we didn't."

"You'd better show me some ID," one of the cops said. "And you and your girlfriend pack up. We'll meet you out by your car."

"You don't have ID," Airy whispered, once he was inside again.

"I know that," he hissed. "Maybe if you show him your passport he'll be satisfied."

"I don't think so, Fehin."

"What do you suggest?"

Airy stared into space. "Can you carry the camping gear? I'll take the computer and other stuff."

"You think we should just ditch Carla's car?"

"Do you have a better idea?"

"Shit," he said, shoving things quickly into his pack. "Move out and I'll take the tent down."

Airy stood by the river, her eyes trained on where they'd left the car. The two cops were there waiting, she could hear them talking.

A few minutes later Fehin joined her, laden down with all the camping gear as well as his pack. "Let's go."

They took off running, heading south along the riverbank. By the time they stopped again there were no roads in sight. "Do you think we lost them?" Airy asked, leaning over to catch her breath.

"I don't know, but I'll tell you I'm going to miss that damn car. This gear is heavy."

"I'm just glad you had the forethought to unpack the important stuff. We could be without my phone, my computer and all our food, not to mention my passport. The books, on the other hand, are heavy. Are you sure you want to lug them around?"

"I was afraid someone might break in and steal all our stuff. I guess I could part with the books, but I really like 'Zen and the Art of Motorcycle Maintenance' and the Carlos Castaneda ones about mysticism. And you still haven't read the one Gunnar gave me."

"I told you a long time ago that I don't need to read it to understand. That's not how I get my information. Besides, you've told me just about everything that's in it. What's the Zen one about?"

Fehin turned. "I found that book in a dumpster when I was living on the street. It helped me through a very bleak time. It's hard to explain what it's about, Airy. It's a philosophy of life and has to do with embracing it, I guess."

They walked along the edge of the river for about an hour before a road came into view. "Are you up for hitchhiking?" Fehin asked.

"What choice do we have?"

A COUPLE TOOK pity on them sometime before dawn and drove them as far as they were going, dropping them off along a narrow highway that led away from the main thoroughfare. Airy was exhausted, and when she glanced at Fehin his eyes looked sunken and red-rimmed. It was nearly noon and they hadn't slept or had anything to eat since the night before.

Airy sighed heavily and took her phone out, punching in numbers. When Carla answered she explained about being rousted in the middle of the night and why they'd done what they did. "We're somewhere in Illinois," Airy told her. "We left the car in Terra Haute."

"We're in Champaign," Fehin added, frowning at the map.

"Champaign, Illinois," Airy amended, looking at a sign along the highway. She put it on speaker so he could hear.

"Listen, Airy," Carla said, "I have a friend who lives not too far from Terra Haute. She can get it out of impound—I'll say it was stolen. She'll keep it at her house until you two pick it up."

Fehin shook his head and Airy took it off speaker. "What do you want to do?" she whispered.

"We're too far to go back now. Let's just push on."

"Push on to where?"

Fehin grinned and waved his hands in the air. A second later a tiny scene materialized in front of them. There were snow-capped mountains and valleys, tiny houses dotting the hillsides.

"Oh, my gods! You have magic again!" Airy pressed the phone to her ear. "Fehin's magic came back!" she shrieked.

"I knew it wouldn't be long. You don't think you need the car now? Is that it?"

"Fehin seems to think we're too far away. He doesn't want to go back."

There was a long silence and then Carla said, "Tell you what. My friend will pick it up and keep it at her house. That way if you need it, you can come back for it. I'll text you her address and phone."

"But don't you want it?"

"I bought a used mini."

"How's Fan?"

"She misses you. Give Fehin a hug for me, Airy. I miss you both so much. Be safe."

Airy put her phone away and danced around Fehin. "How long have you known?"

"Just happened," he said, pulling her close. "I told you I was feeling better." And then he kissed her.

"WHY ISN'T THERE any place to camp?" They had taken off the main road and headed into town to search for somewhere to pitch their tent, but all they found were RV parks with sites right next to each other and lots of people, kids and dogs. There were fences everywhere and very little grass.

"I can fix that," Fehin said. "But we need to find some green space where no one will happen along."

"Lead on, lord and master," Airy said, teasing.

Fehin laughed. "Follow me, milady."

He led into woods on the outskirts of town and told her to wait. "I want to surprise you."

Airy glanced around, making sure there were no signs that said 'no trespassing'." She took off the heavy pack and lowered it to the ground. Fehin having his powers back had changed things and she wasn't sure she liked it. He had suddenly taken charge of their lives. And he hadn't consulted her before he did so. She was staring into the distance toward a road a few miles away when he appeared next to her.

"Come along," he said, bowing and holding his arm out.

When she went ahead of him down a narrow path, she came upon a scene out of a storybook. In front of her was a small stone cottage. Smoke angled out of the chimney and she could smell bread baking. There were flowerboxes in the windows filled with red geraniums. "How...?

Fehin hurried ahead and opened the door, gesturing again as though she were a noblewoman and he was her servant.

Inside was one big room with a four-poster double bed covered in an old-fashioned quilt. A wide fireplace with an iron arm to hang pots stood catty-cornered with logs burning merrily. A loaf of crusty bread waited on the rustic wooden table and close to the far wall was a claw foot tub big enough for the two of them. Next to that was a real honest to goodness toilet, complete with water inside the bowl. "Is this real or will it disappear as soon as I've taken off all my clothes?" she asked, walking over to the tub.

"It should stay. I haven't ever done anything quite like this, but I figured if I could conjure an island, I could manage a small house. And this presented itself in a vision that included you, but we were definitely somewhere in the distant past. I added the tub and toilet since I thought it would be nice to have modern amenities to go along with our love nest." Fehin grinned. "In my vision you had longer hair and you were bigger on top." He laughed, holding his hands away from his chest to illustrate what he meant.

"You had a vision with me but I didn't look like me? What about you?"

Fehin shook his head. "You weren't that different—maybe just older and more filled out? Or maybe you were pregnant. I didn't see myself, but I felt like some incredible wizard or something. I know I was powerful."

"Pregnant?" Airy stared at him for a second or two before she tried out the faucets in the tub.

"Why don't you take a bath?" Fehin suggested. "I have something I need to do."

Airy turned the knobs, surprised when hot water gushed out. "Like what?" she asked, peeling off her jeans.

"I have to talk to Gunnar. It's been too long."

Airy stopped undressing. "In here?"

Fehin laughed. "I'm going outside. Don't worry, I won't bring him in."

Airy faced the tub and took off the rest of her clothes. "What if someone's walking through the woods and sees this house? Won't they wonder how it got here? Or did you put up some kind of invisibility shield?" There was no answer and when she turned, Fehin was gone.

Airy lowered into the steaming water, allowing herself to sink under the surface. The warmth loosened her sore muscles, untying the knots in her neck and back. She washed with the luxurious sweet-smelling soap she found resting in the wire basket hanging over the tub's curved porcelain edge.

When she'd had enough, she unplugged the stopper and stepped out, reaching for the thick towel hanging by a peg on the wall. Fehin had thought of everything.

She dried off and pulled on her nightshirt and went to the kitchen to cut herself a piece of bread. Fehin had not returned and she wondered what was keeping him. The idea of snuggling together under the quilt called to her.

As she munched on the bread, she suddenly registered Fehin's absence. She and Fehin were no longer connected.

FORTY-FIVE

"What have you done?" The druid's eyes were black with anger, a color Fehin had never seen in them.

"What are you talking about? I got my magic back today."

"I'm talking about Wolf. His death has caused pandemonium in the future. Loki has unleashed his wrath on everything, including Thule."

"Wolf was about to..."

"I don't care what he was about to do, Fehin. It was not your place to kill him. That pleasure was to be left to the gods. Do you remember me saying Wolf was part of it?"

"Yes, but I..."

"You will accompany me now."

Fehin turned toward the little house. "Airy's there, she..."

"You had a job to do here and so far, all you've managed is this?" Gunnar scoffed, staring at Fehin's creation. He took Fehin by the arm and in the next second layers upon layers of dense colors whirled by.

Fehin plugged his ears as a high-pitched sound screeched against them. When they landed, they were on a beach that looked scoured, driftwood and detritus covering it from one side to the other.

"This is what is left of Thule," Gunnar said.

Fehin felt a wave of shock. His beautiful island destroyed? There was not a person, a house, a tree or an animal left. A piercing pain entered his heart, nearly doubling him over. "My mother? Kafir?"

"They're safe for now. Loki has spared them. But until you rectify this mess there will be no rest from his anger."

"What can I do? Wolf is dead."

"You have to resurrect him."

Fehin stared at the druid. "How am I supposed to do that?"

Gunnar turned away, his narrowed gaze going out to sea. "You'll do it, Fehin. Because if you don't, everything you care about will be gone."

It was a long time later that Fehin finally came to grips with this new reality. After showing him the devastation, Gunnar took him back to Far Isle where he found his mother and Kafir, their faces wet with tears. It had happened suddenly, his mother told him, taking him in her arms.

"One minute we were planting and the next it was as though the winds of hell moved across the island. Gunnar saved the two of us, but I don't know what happened to the rest of them."

"Aki?"

Kafir shook his head.

"Why didn't someone warn me? No one ever said I wasn't allowed to kill that bastard. He made my life a living hell. He was about to hurt Airy."

"We didn't know anything about it," Kafir answered, taking hold of Fehin's shoulder. "Are you saying this is because of Wolf?"

"That's what Gunnar told me," Fehin answered, turning to

corroborate this with the druid. But Gunnar was gone. "What do I do now? I have no way to get back there. And Wolf's body is long gone, burned up in a crematorium, I'm sure. What about *Skidbladnir*?"

"Destroyed with the rest of it," Kafir said, his eyes glazed with tears. If Gunnar thinks it's possible. then he's the one to help you."

Fehin grimaced, his hands turning into fists. "Gunnar despises me. I'd be better off asking Loki."

Gertrude brightened. "That's a good idea, Fehin. Loki loves you."

Fehin turned to his mother. She looked older, as though the ordeal had sucked some of her life force away. He hugged her hard and then pulled back, holding her gaze. "I'll do whatever I can to re-create a home for you. I'm so sorry."

Gertrude grabbed his hand. "It isn't your fault, Fehin. You had another destiny. What's happened with that?"

"I left Airy alone without telling her where I was going. We haven't yet figured out what we're supposed to be doing—my magic just returned."

"You look so different—bigger, more grown up," his mother said, trying to smile. "You've been through so much," she continued, placing her hand on his cheek. "Gunnar said he'd lost touch with you, that he couldn't reach you through the ether."

Fehin stared at her. Gunnar, the man who moved through time, couldn't reach him? "Bullshit. He's a liar. He set me up. Wolf was on *Skidbladnir* when we entered Boston harbor."

"What?" Kafir's eyes went wide with shock.

"I probed his mind. Gunnar knew all about his little stowaway—told me Wolf was part of my destiny. Wolf nearly killed us, Kafir. The man was a monster. Why in Loki's name would I have to resurrect him?"

Kafir frowned and gazed into the distance. "Gunnar's playing games. He's done it before."

"Why? What does he want from me?"

Kafir shook his head. "It could be anything. Go see Loki, maybe he'll have an answer."

Before leaving, Fehin waved his hands in the air, producing a small house for the two of them. It was very much like where he'd left Airy, he thought, hopelessness settling into him. She must be frantic by now. "This will have to do until we can round up survivors and start anew. Wait here until I get back," he added, jogging toward the forest.

"IT WAS NOT I nor was it Odin who caused this chaos. As for Gunnar, I've never liked that meddling druid."

"What he told me isn't true?"

The god scrunched his eyebrows. "Of course, it isn't true. I wouldn't destroy Thule. Wolf's death will not be mourned by me nor any other gods or goddesses."

Fehin gazed around the throne room where he'd been ushered by the guards. Everything was the same as it had always been and the familiarity of the pale marble columns, the bright jewels embedded in the ceiling, the sumptuous red and gold cushions on the floor and the enormous logs burning in the wide stone fireplace were somehow comforting.

He turned his attention back to Loki. "What do you think happened to Thule?"

Loki's bushy eyebrows came together. "Did you say you lost your magic?"

"Yes."

"That could be why Thule was destroyed. As you know from my dealings with your mother, the past affects the future.

As to Wolf, I will have to consult the Norns, but as I said, I can only see his death as positive. What I wonder is, who released him from Svartalfheim?"

"He never said. Would Gunnar have that kind of power?"

"Perhaps," Loki said, pushing a hand through his wild hair. "I will travel to Asgard and find out the truth. In the meantime, Aki is at your disposal."

Something heavy lifted from Fehin's heart. "He's alive?"

"He and his mate and their offspring arrived here before it began. He must have known what was coming."

FORTY-SIX

Airy woke shivering and wet. The cabin was gone with no hint it had ever been there. Apparently, it had been drizzling for quite a while since her nightshirt was soaked through. At least the two packs were beside her, but how she could carry both of them and all the camping gear she didn't know. She remembered climbing into the comfortable bed and pulling the covers over her. When she fell into a fitful sleep, she was sure he'd reappear with some fantastical story to tell her. And then they would make love and everything would be fine. But it was morning now, and this...she looked around...this was not good. She quickly pulled off her nightshirt and found dry clothes.

As she dressed her dream came back to her. A medieval life it seemed from the surroundings that were very similar to the house that was now gone. Fehin was different, more filled out and older. She thought of the moment when her hand went to her belly that pressed against her thin nightdress, and the image of different Fehin standing in the doorway staring at her. Was he the father?

When her cell phone rang, she jumped, her first thought

going to Fehin. But Fehin no longer had a phone. It was Carla. After Airy explained the situation there was a long pause.

"Take a bus back to Terra Haute," Carla finally instructed. "I spoke with Susan and she's picking the car up from impound this morning."

"What if they don't let her have it?"

"I've told the police she's coming, and proven to them that it belongs to me."

"And the title?"

"It isn't signed, is it?"

"I never looked at it, so I guess not."

"Good. This absence you mentioned, do you think Fehin is still in our world?"

"If he were here, I'd know. I'm pretty sure Gunnar took him to the future, which means something terrible must have happened. Fehin would never leave me like that."

"Please heed what I said, Airy. The idea of you hitchhiking by yourself gives me the heebie jeebies."

Airy didn't question what that term meant; the words made her feel like bugs were crawling all over her. "I'll do it, but I need to find a bus station."

"Your smartphone has GPS—just type in Greyhound in Champaign, Illinois. It'll give you walking instructions. Will you call to let me know what happens?"

"If my phone hasn't run out of battery by then."

Once the call was over Airy felt more alone than ever. Without Fehin the bridge was a moot point. She moved further under the trees and typed in Greyhound and Champaign, Ill. The information she received said it would take her a half hour to walk there. Dragging all this stuff along would probably take even longer than that. Sighing, she arranged one pack on her back and dragged all the rest of it behind her as she trudged toward town.

On the bus Airy placed her hands on her middle. Fehin's absence was an aching void, a wound that hurt every time she took a breath. She closed her eyes, her heart reaching out, searching through the ether. Where was he? Her ring finger hurt and when she looked down, the moonstone was burning hot and full of light, glowing like a little moon. When she took it off and held it in her hand, she could feel a buzz of energy. *I love you, Fehin. Please let me know where you are.* She closed her eyes and must have dozed off because she began to dream.

Airy was standing on dry dirt outside a massive dark stone castle. A hill rose up behind it and in the far distance she could see snow-capped mountain peaks. Behind her was a dense forest of strange deformed-looking trees. The sky wasn't blue or gray, nor was there any sign of sun. It was hard to tell what kind of weather to expect. Strange bellowing sounds that reminded her of dinosaur movies she'd seen were coming from the open space surrounding the castle, but a high wall kept her from seeing what it was. There was nothing to indicate where she might be other than the strange storybook quality of the scene.

Perhaps this was a dream that had taken her into one of the stories she'd read when she was younger. Or maybe she was dreaming about someplace in Otherworld where she'd never been. There were lots of castles there that housed gods and goddesses. She pinched herself on the arm and let out a yelp.

When she turned back from her perusal of the forest, she noticed a figure exiting the twenty-foot-high heavy wooden doors leading into the fortress. Whoever it was seemed vaguely familiar as he moved in her direction. For a moment she was unable to move. And then she began to run.

FORTY-SEVEN

Loki's castle, 2470

Fehin saw her but couldn't believe his eyes. Airy here? It made no sense and yet she was running toward him. Before he had time to puzzle it out, she was in his arms.

He pulled her against him, feeling her heart beating and the sound of her breath. She was definitely real.

"Is this the future?" she whispered.

"This is the future," Fehin answered, grabbing her hand to keep her from disappearing. "How did you get here?"

Airy smiled. "Never underestimate the power of love."

Fehin stared at her. How she got here was a mystery they could discuss later. With her sudden appearance his worry and sadness lifted. He had the sudden sense that everything would work out. Their gaze met and clung, telepathic messages moving back and forth between them.

She picked up his hand. "Something happened to Thule."

Fehin's eyes filled with tears.

Airy's mouth dropped open. "Your parents?"

"They're fine, but everyone else..."

"My gods, Fehin. I'm so sorry."

"Having you here changes everything. Shut your eyes," he said. "I have a surprise."

"A bigger surprise than being in 2470?"

"You'll see." He led her along the edge of the bailey, stopping in front of a very high gate. "Okay, you can open them now."

Airy's eyes went wide. "Dragons?" she shrieked, "You never said there were dragons!"

"Didn't I? The one coming toward us is Aki. Don't be afraid, he belongs to me. The others are Loki's."

"They're beautiful."

Aki made a soft bellow as he approached, heading directly to her.

When Airy reached through the fence he blew out softly sending puffs of white smoke into the air and then his nose touched her hand. She turned to Fehin. "Does he fly?"

Fehin opened the gate and headed inside the pen. When Airy hesitated he grabbed her hand. "I know they're big, but they won't hurt you. See the one over by the fence with the baby? That's Aki's mate and their offspring." Fehin walked across the pen and bent down to stroke the small one beside her. Aki let out a bellow and left Airy, crossing the pen in two strides. Fehin looked up. "I told you it wouldn't be so bad without me here," he told the dragon, turning back to admire the baby's iridescent scales.

"Aki says the baby's name is Lir," Airy called from the gate. "And his mate's name is Saral."

Fehin turned. "You can talk to him? I thought I was the only one."

Airy smiled. "It's part of my magic and my connection to you."

"Do you want to take a ride?"

Airy looked surprised. "You can't break up this family."

Fehin laughed. "Aki's mine, Airy, family or not. He knows his place."

"That isn't very kind."

"He doesn't mind, do you?" Fehin asked, rubbing his hand across Aki's wide nose. The dragon released a puff of smoke and moved his head from side to side. Fehin turned back to Airy. "I'll give you a boost up."

Fehin helped her and climbed on behind, wrapping his arms around her waist. "Ready?"

Airy turned her head. "What do I hold on to?"

"See those knobs where his neck starts? Grab one of those. I've got you," he added, snugging her against his body.

When Aki ran across the pen and lifted into the air Airy let out a shriek. A moment later they were soaring over the forest.

"This land is known as Far isle and the town of Fell is below us," Fehin yelled in her ear. Aki flew over the beach and out to sea. "That's what's left of Thule," he called as they headed toward the island covered with flattened trees and detritus.

He could feel her shaking as she gazed down, and when he put a hand on her cheek, he felt tears. And then he was crying too, his head against the back of her neck as he sobbed.

The dragon circled and headed back, veering north toward the rest of Far Isle. "This is Tolam, one of the villages Wolf demolished," Fehin called out, pointing down. A few rustic houses appeared, clustered together. "I'm glad to see it's still inhabited," he said as Aki dove closer. They flew over a swampy area and then over a mountain range covered in snow before turning south again.

Fehin called out words in a foreign tongue before Aki flew toward the beach. A few moments later they were on the ground. Airy slid off, her legs crumbling beneath her.

"I'm sorry, Airy," Fehin said, helping her up. Her face was white and she was shivering. He took his sweater off and handed it to her. "Put this on."

She pulled it over her head and folded her arms across her chest, trying to stop trembling. "I wasn't scared. But seeing your island like that after how you described it was so awful. I can imagine how lovely it was since it's so beautiful here," she added, looking around.

Fehin followed her gaze to the dark forest behind them, the expanse of sugar-colored sand, and the sea, dark and mysterious. Above them the strange overcast had cleared, allowing the sun to burst forth in all its glory. The air was already warmer. He put his arms around her, burying his face in her neck. His tears had begun again. "I don't know how it happened," he whispered. "But I do know that Gunnar has turned into a royal asshole."

FORTY-EIGHT

Fell, 2470

Airy scanned up and down the beach, before turning to the dark forest behind them. The trees looked tropical and ancient. "Where are we?"

"This was the town of Fell, before Wolf, that is."

"Fell. Is this where you lived before Thule?"

Fehin nodded. "And before that I lived in Loki's castle. My mother and Kafir are down the beach," he said, pointing. "Do you feel up to meeting them?"

"Of course." Airy wasn't sure if this was true or not. The shock of being here, taking a ride on a dragon, and the odd quality of light, made her feel quite peculiar. And seeing Thule ruined made her feel sick inside. She had already met Kafir, but Gertrude was another matter altogether. From what Fehin had told her, his mother was a strong woman who spoke her mind.

"If you're noticing light-headedness or a feeling that you aren't quite here, it's because of the time dilation. It'll go away soon."

"Glad to hear that. Honestly, Fehin, I have no idea how this happened. I thought I was dreaming."

"Where were you?"

"I was on a bus heading to Champaign to pick up the car."

"Hmm. Did you do anything special, think something, say anything?"

"I was thinking about you and fiddling with my ring. That's all."

"Your ring?" Fehin bent to examine the moonstone. "What was going on with it?"

Airy took it off and handed it to him. "It was glowing and vibrating."

Fehin turned the ring over in his hands. "My mother told me some stories about a moonstone. Did someone in your family ever use it for magic?"

"They all did. I told you that. My mother was the last one. But when she had it made into a ring for me, she said..."

"She said it wasn't magic anymore?"

Airy nodded.

Fehin handed the ring back. "There's magic in it. I can feel it. It may be how you ended up here."

Airy slipped the ring back on her finger. "I'm very glad I have it then."

"If this ring moves you through time we have to figure out if I can go with you."

"It might have just been the one time—a special circumstance."

"I don't think so, Airy. If the ring has magic, the ring has magic. It doesn't come and go."

"Then why hasn't it worked before this?"

"Maybe it has to be in combination with something else."

"Like love? Because that's what I was feeling when it

happened." When Airy glanced down the beach two people were walking toward them. "Is that your mom?"

Fehin took hold of Airy's hand and headed to meet them.

Once they'd been introduced Fehin's mother stared at Airy for a full minute before her expression softened. "You look so much like your great-grandmother, Catriona."

Airy, overwhelmed by the recent revelations about her ring, was surprised by the words. "I heard stories about her, but she died before I was born. I never saw a picture."

Before Gertrude could answer Kafir took Airy in his arms. "It's wonderful that you're here. Couldn't be better timing," he added, slanting a glance at Fehin.

Gertrude moved closer, placing a hand on Airy's forearm. "I knew your mother and father in another life," she said with a nervous smile. "They didn't much like me back then. And Catriona, your great-grandmother, let's just say she hated me, for lack of a better word." Gertrude let out a laugh.

"I'm not on very good terms with them myself," Airy answered, smiling. A second later she was pressed against Gertrude's ample chest and she knew she'd been accepted.

Fehin stared at Airy with wide eyes. "We're related," he said, worried. "Catriona was my father's twin sister."

Airy glanced toward Gertrude who was frowning. "That is correct. I guess you've gone beyond the friend stage at this point?"

Airy turned beet red and Fehin had to look away.

"The relationship isn't close enough to cause a problem. You aren't pregnant, are you?" she asked, staring pointedly at Airy.

"No!"

Gertrude seemed to relax. "Now that you know, would you consider stopping what you've started?"

Fehin shook his head. "I don't think I could."

"Me neither," Airy agreed.

"Okay, it's settled then. Now, Airy, tell me how you got here?"

"We think the ring moved her through the ether," Fehin answered. "And if that's true, maybe I can go back with her."

When Airy held out her hand Gertrude bent to examine the moonstone. "I remember this stone. Maeve wore it as a necklace."

"Airy's mother told her the stone's power is gone."

Gertrude smiled. "I guess she didn't realize. I hope you two can stay for a while."

When Airy glanced toward Fehin he looked surprised. "I thought my destiny was important to you," he said, leveling a look at his mother.

"Things have changed since then, sweetheart. Thule is gone and you and Airy are here together. Maybe this is your destiny."

Fehin hesitated for a moment. When he spoke again his tone was deadly serious. "There is no doubt in my mind that Airy and I have a job to do in the past. I didn't want to tell you, but corporations run everything now."

"What?" Gertrude's eyes widened. "No more elections?"

Fehin shook his head. "You wouldn't believe how many homeless there are."

"That sounds like an impossible situation. The problems here would be simpler to fix," she said with a hopeful expression.

"I'll do whatever I can to resurrect Thule. Have you found any survivors?"

Kafir shook his head. "We lost all our friends, Fehin. Resurrecting the island is the least of our worries."

Fehin's eyes turned dark, his narrowed gaze going from one to the other. "What exactly do you want from me?"

Airy put a hand on his arm. "What's wrong with you? Your parents are trying to explain how they feel. They've lost everything, Fehin."

Fehin turned, his expression bleak. "It's my fault Thule is gone and all those people are dead!"

Gertrude put her hand on his arm. "Why would you say that?"

Fehin looked down. "I lost my magic because I was doing drugs."

Kafir stared at him. "And what does that have to do with it?"

Fehin looked away, his eyes filled with tears. "My magic is what kept it going, Kafir. Loki told me."

Kafir shook his head. "No, Fehin. That island was completely independent of you. There has to be another explanation for what caused that storm."

"Do you think Gunnar did it?" Fehin shook his head. "Why would he hurt all those people?"

"Why would he tell you that killing Wolf was a bad thing?" Airy asked him.

"Loki's on his way to commune with the other gods. I hope he'll have an answer."

"You should talk to Gunnar," Airy said. "He's the only one who can clear this up."

As if on cue the druid arrived. "Don't you know it's impolite to talk about someone behind their back?" He glared at them with his arms folded.

No one said a word until Airy finally asked, "Can you please explain why you brought Fehin here, what happened to Thule and why it was a bad thing to kill Wolf?"

Gunnar raised his eyebrows in surprise. "And how do *you* come to be here?" he asked.

"My being here has nothing to do with you," Airy

answered. As soon as the words were out of her mouth, she realized her mistake. This druid could more than likely strike her dead on the spot.

Gunnar seemed unnerved for a moment. "You do realize I'm privy to things I cannot share?"

"Why not?" Airy asked him.

"I travel through time, Airy. This means I've seen the future as well as the past."

"Is that the best excuse you can come up with for not answering my questions?" Out of the corner of her eye Airy saw Fehin's mouth quirk and then he made a funny sound as though trying to stop his laugh. A second later he turned away and coughed.

Gunnar let out an exasperated sigh. "I brought Fehin here because he's needed at the moment. Thule is gone and his parents are without a home. As to why Thule was destroyed, that is yet to be revealed."

"So no longer Loki's fault?" Airy made a disgusted sound in the back of her throat. "And what about Wolf who would have raped me if Fehin hadn't shot him? Tell me how that was a bad thing?"

Gunnar ran a hand over his face and stared into the distance. "Do you understand the concept of yin and yang, light and dark, good and evil, balance?"

"Of course, I do, but that doesn't explain allowing a force for evil to go unchecked, does it?"

"Killing is never the answer," the druid said, turning his full gaze on her. "It might seem so in the moment, but ultimately it does more harm than good. Everything in this world exists for a reason. You should know that since you communicate with plants and animals."

Airy glanced at Fehin before turning her attention back to the druid. "But what if he raped me?"

"Fehin could have stopped him without killing him."

"How do you know? And why is Wolf's life so important?"

"He was never able to redeem himself."

Fehin snapped alive. "Like he would have!" he yelled out, glaring at the druid. "The guy is without a conscience. I've spent enough time with him to know."

Gunnar didn't react. "The point is he didn't get the chance."

"Gunnar," Kafir asked, "were you responsible for setting this entire thing up? Did you release Wolf and take him with you on that boat?"

Gunnar shook his head. "I discovered him during the trip. By then it was too late to do anything about it."

"Who released him from Svartalfheim?" Gertrude asked.

"That's the question, isn't it?" Gunnar said. "We may never find out. But I do think it's possible to start over."

"What?" Fehin asked. "Do you mean go back in time?"

"I do. And this time, don't kill him."

LATER, when Airy and Fehin were alone, he took hold of her shoulder. "You surprise me every day."

"What are you talking about?"

"That scene back there with Gunnar--you stood up to him like I've never been able to."

"You grew up with him, Fehin. He's like a father figure to you. If he'd been MacCuill I never would have spoken to him like that."

Fehin stared at her. "Remember what I said about the light you carry? It's so strong, Airy. It's like you have a halo around you."

"Oh, so now I'm an angel?" Airy scoffed.

"That's not what I mean. You have a glow. You're very

rarely down. When was the last time you were depressed? You are the light to my dark."

"You're not always dark," she said, placing a hand on his cheek. "You've been way happier these past few days."

"I know, but what I'm saying is we balance each other perfectly."

"Is this the first time you realized that?" Airy laughed and shook her head. "Maybe it's because we're related. I'll race you to the log down there," she called out, taking off.

"No fair, you have a head start!" he yelled, taking off after her.

They landed in a heap in a sand dune, both of them laughing. "If we had a baby, would it have two heads?" Airy asked.

Fehin pulled her close, nuzzling her neck. "Only if it was twins. They do run in my family, and apparently, in yours too."

"This is kind of weird, Fehin."

"Tell me about it. But on the bright side, maybe your parents would accept me if they knew we shared a common relative."

Airy stared into the distance. "Or maybe they already figured this out and it's the reason they're against our being together."

FORTY-NINE

The next few days were peaceful and untroubled aside from Airy and Fehin diagraming their family tree to decide if it was a problem. Neither one of them could stop thinking about it. They also swam in the ocean, walked along the beach and lay naked in the sand, letting the healing rays of the sun burn away their worry and doubts. In the evening they spent time with Kafir and Gertrude, catching fish and cooking them over a fire and talking late into the night.

The day they were due to leave, Fehin and Airy returned Aki to the castle. But when Airy asked to meet Loki, Fehin said no. He told her that now was not the time, especially after what they'd learned from Gunnar. Loki was not one to change his mind about things, and any more conflict with the druid would surely make matters even worse. Fehin tended to believe Loki over Gunnar, since the druid seemed to change his story to suit whoever was listening. Gods weren't normally in the habit of lying. Why should they? They were all powerful beings.

They said their good-byes to Gertrude and Kafir with the knowledge that the sailor and Fehin's mother wouldn't have any memory of this meeting once Airy and Fehin went into the past. Airy was sad to think the connection she and Gertrude had forged would be forgotten. But on a lighter note, Thule would be back to its former self and all the residents alive and well. That seemed to cheer them, although Airy noticed tears in Gertrude's eyes once she and Fehin turned to go.

A taciturn Gunnar transported them to the docks in Milltown and left without saying good-bye. Fehin said it was because the druid was overcome with emotion, but Airy thought he was just being rude. "I agree with your former assessment that he's a royal asshole," she said in her prim way, making Fehin laugh.

Once they were headed to the scene of the near rape, she became terrified, wondering if Fehin could stop his brother without shooting him. Would she need to be raped in order to save Wolf's life? But this time around, Fehin was on top of him before Wolf pushed her backward, laying into him with a force Airy had never seen him display. He hit Wolf so hard that he actually knocked him out before he grabbed Airy by the hand and hurried away.

"Wow," she whispered. "I didn't know you had it in you. And you're high, aren't you?"

"High with another consciousness. The drugs can't touch me."

"Do you have to go into rehab again?" she asked him once they stopped to catch their breath.

"I don't know. I don't think so."

"What do we do now?"

Fehin grinned. "Now that Wolf isn't dead, we don't have to worry about the police. And I have my magic back. Don't you think it's time to talk about our destiny? Maybe we should concentrate on the bridge for a change."

"Does this mean Thule is okay?"

He nodded. "We just changed the future, Airy."

Airy looked skeptical. "I think we should consult Gunnar."

Fehin grimaced. "We were just with him."

"I know, but he's the only one who can explain. What if we're supposed to be re-doing everything exactly as before?"

"Wolf being alive changes everything. From here on we're starting over." Fehin grabbed her hand. "We don't need to consult Gunnar every time we have a doubt. Let's head west. There's a special place in Wyoming where I want to go."

"Without saying good-bye to Carla? And we don't have any transportation."

"We already said good-bye. As to transportation, we have your ring."

Airy stared at him for a long moment. "What about clothes?"

"You still have money, right? We can buy clothes on the way."

"Uh oh," Airy said looking back. "Here comes Wolf, and he doesn't look happy."

"Do your thing, Airy," Fehin hissed, taking hold of her arm.

Airy had a moment of panic wondering if she could recreate the one time she'd moved through the ether. Would she be able to take Fehin with her? Frantic, she watched Wolf blundering toward them. She took a deep breath and concentrated on her love for Fehin as she pressed her fingers around the ring. A second later the scene blurred into white fog.

"WHERE'D YOU TAKE US?" Fehin asked, looking around. They were standing on a bluff overlooking a valley filled with what looked like the remnants of old castles.

"I don't know. All I thought was west."

"This looks like the wild west where they made a lot of cowboy movies. Do you still have your phone?"

Airy reached into her pack and handed it over.

Fehin fiddled around for a while and showed her the screen. "We're in northern Arizona, close to monument valley." He grinned. "I like this mode of travel. Saves time and money."

"Why are we here? Is this something to do with the bridge or is our destiny to keep going back in time to fix what we mess up?"

"We fixed it, Airy. We haven't messed up anything else that I know of. As to the bridge, I've had some insights."

"I'd love to hear them."

Fehin turned to scan the valley and didn't seem to hear her for a moment. "You know what's weird? I don't feel Wolf in my mind anymore. I guess what I had to do was defeat him in some way. I didn't need to kill him at all."

"That's because we went back in time and you were different."

"You might be right. The drugs didn't affect me the same way."

"It was like you didn't have them in your system. I still don't get why there weren't two sets of us."

Fehin raised his eyebrows. "I'm sure Gunnar had a lot to with that."

"He got rid of our older selves and replaced them with us?"

Fehin chuckled. "The drug-free thing would indicate that. I'm still disgusted with him, but I'm not questioning him anymore."

"I'd watch what you say. He tends to hover around in the ether listening in on conversations." Airy shaded her eyes to look up at the endless expanse of blue. "I've never seen a land-scape like this. It's so open. And the color of the sky is amazing."

"The red hills down there are unbelievable," Fehin said, pointing into the distance. "I read about this place. The Anasazi lived here 1500 years ago."

"Where's the closest town? I need to buy a pair of sunglasses."

"By normal means or...?"

"I think we should hitchhike. I wouldn't want to appear out of thin air."

Fehin laughed.

They hitched a ride with a Native American man headed into Kayenta, sharing the back of his truck with a cage of chickens, two large but friendly mongrel dogs and several burlap sacks filled with feed. In town they found a Motel 6, checked in and went to find sunglasses.

EARLY THE NEXT morning Fehin woke her. "I want to explore those rock formations down in the valley."

Airy yawned and rubbed her eyes. "What do you hope to find?"

"There's a brochure on the table about cliff dwellings. I'm hoping they left some energy behind."

"1500 years later? I doubt it, Fehin. What about the insights you mentioned yesterday?"

Fehin smiled. "The bridge is us, Airy. We're the bridge."

"We decided that a long time ago, but it doesn't help anything."

"If we follow our hearts, we'll discover what it means."

"Follow our hearts down to monument valley?" Airy laughed. "You mean your heart."

"You're the one who brought us here. Why do you think we ended up here?"

"I don't know," Airy said, exasperated.

"We have to stop thinking and try and feel. You told me it was love that allowed you to travel to the future. That's what I think the bridge is all about."

"A bridge to love?" Airy scoffed. When she moved to get out of bed Fehin grabbed her.

"I don't know if it's a bridge *to* love. It might be a bridge *of* love."

"That might be true, but it doesn't explain how to do it."

"Why are you being so logical all of a sudden? Our destiny isn't about logic and neither is this." Fehin pulled her close and kissed her. When he released her she said, "More, please."

Fehin smiled and kissed her again and this time he didn't stop there.

THE RESTAURANT TABLE in front of them was laden with eggs and toast and pancakes. "So, we have to go to monument valley and explore the cliff dwellings before we can decide what the bridge is?" Airy asked, stabbing a pancake with her fork. She brought it to her mouth and stuffed it in.

"Will you stop thinking? Just be quiet for a while and let this place seep into you."

Airy felt a jolt of irritation. She finished the rest of her breakfast without saying another word, watching Fehin read the brochure he'd taken from the motel room.

"If I specify a place, do you think you can take us there?" he asked a few minutes later.

"I have no idea."

Fehin pointed to a place on the map provided inside the brochure. "I want to go here."

"Now?"

Fehin thought for a moment. "I want to spend the night there. That way, when we arrive no one will see us."

"Just the ghosts of the Anasazi," Airy said sarcastically.

Fehin glared at her. "I hope so," he answered.

Airy finished her tea, trying to sort through her muddled thoughts. Why was she so irritable? She felt as close to Fehin as she always had, in some ways even closer. She wasn't worried anymore about their blood ties and he was happier now than he'd ever been. And then she got it. This bridge was supposed to be a joint effort, which meant that their combined abilities would come into play. It wasn't that she didn't like it here, but to her it didn't feel right—it wasn't the place where they would fulfill their destiny.

"Fehin," she said, looking over at him, "What about Wyoming?"

Fehin glanced up from his perusal of the brochure. "I read about an ancient medicine wheel. It's in Bighorn national forest."

Airy immediately got goose bumps up and down her arms. "That's it. That's the place."

Fehin stared at her. "You feel it?"

Airy nodded, rubbing her arms. "I know you want to explore, but I think the medicine wheel is where we're supposed to be."

Fehin lowered his gaze. He didn't say anything for so long Airy wondered if he'd forgotten the conversation. When he finally looked up she noticed a different expression in his eyes.

"I have to admit I can feel it too," he said, rubbing his arms. "Maybe that's why you've been so weird. Sorry for pushing the monument valley thing. Not sure why your ring brought us here, though."

"I might have had a picture in my mind—I can't remember now. Or maybe we were supposed to come to this joint realization. It just seemed strange that I wasn't excited about being here. But I still have no idea what we're supposed to do when we get there."

Fehin grabbed her hand excitedly. "We'll figure it out."

"We need camping gear since I left ours on the bus heading to Terra Haute, and I need some warmer clothes. I think I'd like to travel by bus again."

"Are you sure? It's a long way from here."

"The trip will give us time to talk. And the scenery is spectacular."

Shopping took up the morning hours, and in the afternoon, they hopped on a tour of monument valley. Early the next morning they boarded the first bus of many that would take them to Wyoming.

FIFTY

The campfire had burned low and Airy was cold. She huddled close to Fehin, trying hard not to shiver.

"Get in the sleeping bag."

"But I like the fire. I love sitting out here under the stars." She looked up. "It's amazing to think how many galaxies are out there."

Fehin rose from the log and went over to the cheap two-man tent they'd purchased in Kayenta. When he came back, he wrapped her sleeping bag around her shoulders.

"Thanks."

They were camping in Bald Mountain campground not far from the medicine wheel. The hike up the mountain would be arduous since the medicine wheel was at the very top, at 10,000 feet.

"I've never seen this many stars."

"No ambient light here. I would have thought the sky in Otherworld would be similar."

"Too many trees. This is wide open."

On the way on the bus, they'd talked about rituals they could do, ancient ceremonies that might help them realize their goals. They'd discussed purchasing drums or flutes or even buying an Indian peace pipe. Fehin had read a lot about Native American culture and brought up ceremonies that included peyote, ones that had to do with fasting, and several that required chanting and dancing. They discarded the peyote one right away because of Fehin's addiction problems, and then eliminated the fasting one because it required several days of no food. For some reason they both felt that the first of April was when it needed to happen. As far as chanting and dancing, neither one knew what that meant.

Airy brought up ceremonies her grandmother and great-grandmother had participated in, naming a few of the gods and goddesses involved. In the end they scrapped all of them, agreeing that it was up to them to come up with something entirely their own.

Fehin poked at the embers, sending up a stream of sparks. From where they sat, he could see several other campfires. It was very quiet with an atmosphere of respect, as though the other campers were here for the same reason Fehin and Airy were. And yet he knew that couldn't be true.

"What do we want to achieve?" Airy asked suddenly.

"Achieve? All I can think about is bringing love to heal the earth. What about you?"

"I'm still caught up in the bridge thing. It has to connect something with something. What are we trying to connect?"

"People with the earth?"

Airy nodded. "Human beings have placed themselves outside the web of life. They think they're separate and act as though they can control the rest of it when in reality, they're ripping it apart. And think about all the poor and homeless we've seen. They feel completely powerless in this society."

She turned and made a face. "I can't imagine having the power to pull this off."

Fehin put his arm around her shoulders. "Why don't we wait until we're there? Maybe the medicine wheel will tell us how to proceed. After all, it's a sacred site. This may have nothing to do with power."

Airy stared into the shadows. "Somehow we have to reweave people back into the web."

Fehin nodded. "That's a good way of putting it. I hope the natives aren't having ceremonies tomorrow. I asked the ranger, but you never know."

"Why here, Fehin?"

Fehin shrugged. "I think it's because of what you said—the web of life thing. In native cultures they don't talk about connection because everything's already connected. This is a sacred pre-Columbian site and the tribes have been using it continuously for fasting ceremonies, vision quests, and a bunch of other rituals. I'm sure the energy up there is amazing."

"It called to both of us, so it has to be right, doesn't it?"

"Are you doubting this?"

Airy turned, her eyes reflecting the firelight. "Just nervous, I guess. You know our money is nearly gone."

"Have you checked your bank account lately?"

"No, but once they figure out what I'm doing, they..."

"Remember, Airy, we're in the past now. Maybe they aren't angry anymore."

Airy scoffed. "How they feel about you hasn't changed. And my phone is nearly dead and I don't have a charger."

"Why do we need a phone?"

"Carla asked me to keep in touch."

"That was before we came back. Carla may be pissed now that we took off without saying good-bye."

Airy's eyes went wide. "I don't want her to be mad at us!

The last thing she knew I was heading to find you—she must be worried sick. We should have gone back, Fehin."

Fehin's brow furrowed. "I feel bad now that you put it like that, but it's too late to do anything. Why don't you call?"

"It's after midnight back there."

WHEN THE PHONE rang the next morning Airy came instantly awake. She reached for it, her worried gaze going to Fehin who was now awake too.

"Airy? Where are you?"

Carla sounded frantic. "Carla, I'm so sorry. I'm fine. Fehin's fine. We've had quite an adventure. I would have called sooner but once you hear what happened you'll understand."

She was still talking when Fehin pulled on his jeans and left the tent to make the fire.

Airy joined him twenty minutes later. "My phone is now officially dead. But at least I had time to explain everything to Carla. She was kind of skeptical at first, but I'm pretty sure she believed me."

"Did you tell her about the future and the moonstone?"

Airy nodded. "And then I told her the second go-round and why we had to do it."

Fehin grimaced. "I hope it wasn't wrong to reveal this."

"You mean like her knowing might mess up the time-line continuum?"

Fehin chuckled. "You've seen too many sci-fi movies. No, I just meant it would be kind of weird to have someone tell you your future."

"Her future won't be the same. Everything's different now."

"You're right." He poured ground coffee into a small

saucepan of water and placed it on a rack over the fire. "Coffee will be ready soon, milady."

Airy turned, exasperated. "Will you stop that?"

Fehin grinned. "I don't know where it's coming from. It's like I'm channeling someone."

"I hope you're not the reincarnated king of somewhere, like my dad."

Fehin looked down. "Maybe it's coming from one of the books I read while I was in rehab about King Arthur and the Knights of the Round Table."

"Camelot? I love that story!"

"It's not just a story—it's true."

"How do you know?"

Fehin shrugged. "I just do. It's part of my magic."

Airy glanced down at her ring. "If it's true we could go there."

Fehin laughed. "One thing at a time, Airy. First we have to save *this* world." He poured hot coffee into the collapsible metal mug and handed it to her.

Airy took a sip. "When should we head up the mountain?"

"Tomorrow is April Fool's day. Today we eat, hike and scout things out. I'm glad we have another full day to let this place soak in."

"Do you want to go up there and check things out?"

Fehin shook his head. "It makes more sense to me to come upon it for the first time on the first of April. What do you think?"

"I agree. Otherwise, we'll start making plans and having all sorts of expectations."

FIFTY-ONE

"It's time to go," Fehin whispered, shaking Airy's shoulder.

Airy opened her eyes. "How long did we sleep?"

"Five hours or so. I thought dawn would be the best time. We can watch the sunrise from up there and there won't be any people."

"Dawn has good energy," Airy agreed, looking for her clothes. She pulled on jeans, a shirt and a sweater and her thick socks and hiking boots. When she opened the tent flap it was pitch black. "How do we find the trail?"

"I scoped it out yesterday when you were napping."

"Do we need to bring anything?"

Fehin shook his head. "You have your ring?"

"I never take it off. Why?"

"I don't know—it just came to me that it might be part of all this."

"I'm excited," Airy said, following him out of the tent. "But it's strange not having a plan."

"That's the best part," Fehin said, turning to look at her.

"We should go as quickly as possible. Who knows when the tourists will arrive?"

The silence was unnerving as they headed toward the trail up the mountain. There were tents scattered here and there, but all the occupants were still sound asleep. Airy's boots were wet with dew by the time they reached the Medicine Wheel trailhead.

By now the sky had turned a pale shade of gray and the tall pines loomed out of the darkness like sentinels. The stars that had been so bright an hour before, were disappearing one by one. Airy stopped for a second and closed her eyes. "They like what we're doing," she whispered, but Fehin was too far ahead to hear her. She hurried after him.

Her breath was a cloud of white as they climbed. There were no more trees now, only rocks and scrub grass. Fehin didn't look back as he moved steadily upward. They had not spoken for a good half hour. Her thoughts were muddled, wondering what they would find at the top and how they would decide what to do. When she looked down her ring was beginning to glow, becoming brighter the further up she went. She wanted to tell Fehin, wanted his easy laugh and assurance that this was a good thing, but she didn't have the breath or the energy to call out.

It seemed like hours before she could see ahead to where the ground leveled out. There were streaks of orange and rose in the sky now, mixed in with the gray. How long till dawn? They had to be up there and engaged in whatever they were doing before the sun rose. Adrenalin shot through her body giving her the stamina to catch up to Fehin. She grabbed his arm. "Are we almost there?"

"You know as much as I do. What's wrong? You look like you've seen a ghost."

"It's almost dawn."

"Yeah. So?"

"We have to do it before dawn."

"Who says?"

"Well, I...I...." Airy stuttered.

Fehin took hold of her hand and threaded his fingers through hers. "We're nearly there."

They walked together the rest of the way, his warmth calming her as they climbed up the last rock-strewn ridge. And then they were standing on the top with a 360* view. Below them the valley stretched into mist-filled distance, fog filling in the gaps between the lineup of smaller hills and ravines. The sky was a dome of pale blue-gray and at the eastern edge it looked as though a huge paintbrush had slashed across it, turning the clouds rose and the horizon deeper shades of orange and gold. "Holy crap!" Fehin said, his eyes going wide. "This is incredible!"

Airy rubbed her arms. "I have chills all over my body." She pulled her gaze away from the horizon and stared at the enormous circle, taking in the vastness of it and the imbedded rocks that had been in the same place for hundreds of years. Those who had visited had left behind bits of cloth, feathers, plants, shells, and stones stacked into Cairns.

"Do you feel that?" Fehin asked, holding his arms out.

As Airy felt energy bubble up inside her she began to dance in a circle, grabbing Fehin's hand as she skipped by. "I can see the web! It's all around us!"

She pulled him with her, heading to the center. They twirled together, going faster and faster as the sky lightened around them. "I see colors," Airy called out. "We're caught in the web and it's full of colors!"

Fehin glanced down at her hand. "Your ring, Airy—look at your ring!"

The moonstone hummed, sending out rays of brightness in

every direction. "Take it off! Put it on the ground!" Fehin grabbed her finger and tugged.

Airy began to laugh hysterically. "I'll do it." She pulled the moonstone off and placed it where it wished to be. Colors of every hue spiraled upward from its surface. Airy grabbed Fehin's hands again, her eyes meeting his. "I love you," she said, her gaze liquid. "I love you, I love you, I love you!" Her voice grew stronger with each utterance. And then Fehin began, his tone deep and resonant. "I love you, Airy. I love you, I love you!"

They spun together lost in the rainbow that came from her ring, and as they moved, they lifted into the air, pulsing in rhythm to their continued chant. A web reached outward, into the heavens and beyond, intricate golden threads weaving together seamlessly.

"Can you see it?" she asked at one point. "Can you see the web?"

Fehin nodded, smiling as he briefly moved his eyes from hers. A second later he met her gaze and it felt as though he *was* her, or was it the other way around? They had become a spinning ball of white light. "Look!" he yelled out.

Energy moved from them in waves. As it expanded, bridges grew within the pulsating colors. They were woven, gossamer, webs within webs, strong but delicate, and there were four of them, one for each of the four directions. The bridges of mist and fog moved outward in ever expanding distances until they narrowed into nothingness. Airy held tightly to Fehin's hands as they spun and spun and spun. They had dissolved into a blur now, but each one could feel the other as though they were one being.

The sun slowly rose in the East, its rays joining the rainbows coming from the stone. And with the sun came a feeling of limitlessness. They felt it outside themselves and inside themselves—boundless, infinite, and never-ending possibility. Their minds were one now and so they reveled in each other, exploring and touching deeply.

Very slowly the stone took back its colors and Airy and Fehin returned to the earth. They stood facing one another, their eyes locked together before moving close until they were pressed as tightly as they could possibly get. Their hearts beat in time as though they had one heart between them. And when they kissed time stopped for those moments of pure bliss.

When Airy and Fehin came out of their trance and pulled apart they heard applause. Around them were people, lots of them, and their smiling faces looked beatific in the morning light. They clapped and clapped and then they all locked arms and began to chant 'I love you', as though they were part of what had happened here. And they were.

FIFTY-TWO

When Airy and Fehin came down off the mountain nearly one hundred people followed them. Somehow the news had spread, bringing more and more hikers to the medicine wheel to participate in the ceremony. In the campsite they were treated like royalty, given gifts of food, jewelry and other trinkets. They refused these offerings, trying to explain what they hoped had happened.

"What do you feel?" Fehin asked them, standing on a stump.

"It's like being reborn!" a woman yelled.

"It's like the world has turned on its axis!" another one called out.

Airy took hold of his hand, looking up. "What I feel is so much love I can barely contain it." Tears coursed down her cheeks.

"Me too," someone agreed. "My chest feels about to burst." And then there were a lot of tears and many hugs all around.

"Now we have to figure out how to keep it," Fehin said, his eyes roaming the crowd.

A natural born speaker, Airy thought to herself watching him. "Just remember that it's all about love," she called out.

A cheer went up and then Fehin jumped down from the stump and took Airy in his arms. "God, I love you," he whispered.

"Is that the old man in the sky god or do you mean one of our gods?"

"I mean all the energy of this vast universe—that's the god I evoke. And 'she' sparkles inside each one of us. Maybe I should call her mother earth or Gaia." Fehin placed his hands on either side of her face. "I saw you, Airy. I know you as well as I know myself."

Airy smiled. "I saw you too, Fehin. Our relationship is infinite like the stars. We've been together many times before. You and I are the bridge between our two families. Brandubh was the dark part and Catriona the light."

Fehin smiled. "I see the past like two lines of light fading into the distance. All our relatives moving along, and then the intersection that brought the two of us into being." He grabbed her hand. "What now, my goddess?"

"Now we eat and we sleep, and then we travel to other parts of this country and see what's happened."

THEY STAYED FOR TWO DAYS, partying with the people who had been on the mountain with them. It was a celebration that they all needed. But on the third day Airy woke Fehin, telling him it was time to go.

"My little voice is insistent," she said. "I have to find out if what we think happened really did."

Fehin sat up and pulled on his shirt. "I could stay here

forever basking in this energy we created, but I bow to your little voice."

When they emerged from the tent and began dismantling things, several people asked where they were headed. "Parts unknown," Fehin answered, grinning.

"Can we come along?" a woman asked.

Fehin looked over at Airy and then shrugged. "Sure. Why not?"

They were at least seventy of them who ended up on the highway together. A few stuck their thumbs out and were immediately picked up. They had decided beforehand to head into the nearest big city, which was Lovell, Wyoming. After Lovell, Fehin and Airy planned to travel in an easterly direction until they reached Milltown.

It was amazing how quickly they were all picked up, people climbing into the backs of pick-ups and cars, as well as larger delivery trucks and even semis. The truck driver who stopped for Airy and Fehin seemed almost giddy with happiness. He told them that something had changed, but he didn't know exactly how to put it into words. All he knew was that heaviness had lifted from his shoulders. His wife, who had left him a month earlier, had called to say she was coming back. He knew in his heart that his life was about to get a lot better.

But what had really happened? Were their lives better or was it a passing atmosphere that would drift away after a few days?

FIFTY-THREE

Airy scanned the streets of Lovell looking for their new friends. The entire town had a party atmosphere as though it was a holiday. People from the shops were on the streets drinking coffee and talking with friends. Even the homeless seemed happy. The April weather was warm and pleasant, the sun pleasing on her skin. She took off her jacket and tied it around her waist, holding her head back and arms out. "What a beautiful day!"

"What's happened?" Fehin asked a man pushing a basket of belongings.

"I don't really know except people have been stoppin' me on the street and handin' me money for the past few hours." He pulled out several twenties from his pocket. "I haven't seen this much all at once since 1992."

"Are you a veteran?"

He pushed filthy fingers through his long hair. "I am, but the government, such as it is, ain't been helpin'. Maybe this is the start of somethin' different."

"I hope so," Fehin said, his gaze going to Airy.

"The book said corporations are in charge," Airy whispered. "How can what we did have an effect on that?"

"The book, you say? I thought you didn't read the book." Fehin jiggled his eyebrows, grinning. He reached into his pack and brought it out, leafing through the pages at the end. "Shall I read it, your highness, or do you want to do the honors?"

"Go ahead," Airy smirked, looking over his shoulder.

On April fool's day a massive shift took place around the world. No one could explain the change in policies that seemed to appear overnight. Instead of their usual greed, corporations began to care for the people, making sure the homeless had shelter, that workers had jobs, that veterans had benefits. Normal people with money began handing it around as though making up for all their years of hoarding. The populace in the U.S. and several other countries began peaceful demonstrations against the way governments were run, leading toward new systems that represented them rather than what had been going on for decades.

Fehin read this passage out loud, his eyes bright. "That's where it ends."

Airy grabbed the book. "There's print still moving across the page, Fehin." *Wars began to wind down as disputes were settled,* Airy read in a hushed whisper. *In some places in the Middle East there was peace for the first time ever.* She waited for more, but when it didn't come she handed it back to Fehin.

He pushed it into his pack, watching her. "Time to go back to Milltown and see Carla."

"Where do you two think you're going?" a woman asked, grabbing Airy by the shoulder as she and Fehin walked by.

Airy turned, her gaze meeting the brown eyes of one of the women on the mountain. She looked to be in her thirties, wearing a multi-colored skirt that came down to her calves.

Bracelets of silver tinkling bells circled her ankles, her toes adorned with silver rings. "We're heading east," Airy told her.

"I'm Sandra," she said. "You two are our heroes. You can't just leave us here. There's a lot of work to do."

Airy glanced at Fehin. "What do you think?"

"I don't want to be a celebrity," he said, his eyebrows pulling together.

"It's too late for that," Sandra said, laughing. "You must be aware that it takes more than a day or two to bring about a miracle."

Airy and Fehin spent the night in a park on the northern edge of town surrounded with everyone from the mountain. When it grew dark, wine, beer and guitars, drums and flutes were produced and people began to sing. Many of the street people joined in, their cracked and off-key voices mingling with the others. It didn't matter; the only thing that mattered was the sense that they were all in this together. Around midnight the police appeared, but instead of rousting them they sat down on the grass and sang along.

It was the wee hours of the morning before Fehin and Airy crawled into their tent. They fell asleep to music and the soft murmur of voices.

It was the next day before the shit began to hit the fan.

"I KNEW IT COULDN'T LAST," Airy said, reading the newspaper headlines on the fourth day of April. **Riots break out across country as corporations fight back against a rising tide of unrest.**

"There's always a backlash," Fehin said, reading over her shoulder. "Remember the idea of balance. Everything can't be all goodness and light."

"I understand that, but I was hoping this would last a few days longer!"

"There's tremendous resistance to change, Airy. History proves it over and over. Anything that happens too quickly won't stick. What we've begun is in its infancy."

"So do we have to stay until the baby grows up, or can we get on with our own lives?"

Fehin looked puzzled. "I thought our lives were all about this."

"The bridge is built, Fehin. I don't want to witness the trouble that comes from it. We did our job, didn't we?"

"We did, but I feel somewhat obligated to stick around and see where it all goes."

"I don't. We've gone through hell for the past couple of years. It's time to have a life."

"You have something in mind, don't you?"

Airy smiled. "I do, but before I tell you about it, I want to go and see Carla and Fan. We owe her. But how do we leave without all these people coming along?"

Fehin grinned. "Use your ring."

"And what about Wolf?"

"What about him? Maybe he's changed too." Fehin stared into the distance for a moment. "I can't reach him. Maybe he's gone."

"He's here," Airy said, turning away to gather her things together. "The reason you can't connect with him is because he isn't the same person."

Fehin tried to catch her eye and then gave up and turned to pack.

~

ONCE THEY HAD the packs and camping gear on their backs, Airy took off her ring and held it in her right hand. She twined the fingers of her left hand tightly through Fehin's. "I'm going to try and get us as close to Carla's as I can, but don't expect any miracles."

Fehin chuckled. "That's funny, Airy." But his words were lost in the rush of air as they spun away in a rainbow of colors.

~

THEY ENDED up on the steps outside Carla's townhouse a minute later.

"That's about as close as you could get," Fehin said, squeezing her hand.

Airy met his gaze with a quirky embarrassed smile and knocked on the door.

Carla smiled widely and hugged them both. "The news is crazy. What did you two do up there?" She ushered them inside and pointed toward the television where repeating footage showed the scene at the top of the mountain.

Airy watched the two of them spinning and lifting into the sky and turning into a ball of white light. "Wow! How did they film it?"

"Cell phones. They've shown several different versions now. It's all over YouTube." Carla turned to stare at them. "How did you get here so fast?"

Airy held out her ring. "It's a time-traveling device."

Carla took the heavy ring in her hand and turned it over. Her expression was skeptical as she handed it back. "I guess I shouldn't doubt anything after what's happened."

The television was now showing people marching in the streets carrying placards that read: **April Miracle!** The scene changed to another city where the homeless were marching along with others. The expressions on their faces were peaceful and full of joy. "We saw a newspaper headline in Lovell that had a different story," Airy said, watching it all.

Carla turned. "Yes, there's been some unrest here and there. But over-all it's a sea change, Airy. Fan will be back tomorrow. She'll be so happy to see you."

∽

IT WAS the next night that things changed on the news channels. Fan returned in late afternoon and the four of them had eaten dinner before Carla switched on the set. At first Airy thought it couldn't be true, but as the pictures flashed across the screen of screaming people throwing rocks at windows, looting and clashes with police, she grew more and more dismayed. "What's happening?"

"It's bringing out the crazies," Carla said. "I'm glad you're here. I wouldn't want you two involved in that. Did you know you have some followers out there?" She pointed toward the door. "Not sure how they found you. I noticed them when Fan got home."

When Airy and Fehin rose from the couch, Carla said, "Bring them inside. They can sleep on the couch and the floor."

Airy moved through the door first, stepping over bodies inside sleeping bags. An older woman with silver dreadlocks stood at the bottom of the steps.

"I'm Kit," she said, holding out her hand. "You two are miraculous. I've been living on the streets for more than five years and this the first time I've felt hope of any kind."

"There's weird stuff going on," Airy whispered. "A lot of violence."

"Really?" Kit's eyes widened. "On the news?"

Airy nodded. "Do you want to see?"

"Sure, if you don't think your friend will mind."

Airy took her into the house, leaving Fehin to find those who might want to sleep inside. Many had been deprived for a very long time and weren't in good health.

Airy turned on the set and sat on the couch next to Carla and Fan while Kit lowered onto the floor. The news came on showing scene after scene of violence and police dragging people away in handcuffs. The newscaster droned on about a populace out of control and the lies that had spread across the country about a miracle. According to him what had happened was all a hoax.

The door opened and Fehin appeared with several ragged-looking people behind him. "What's going on?" he asked, taking in their expressions.

"Someone is trying to undermine what happened," Kit told him. She waved at the television. "This is all bullshit."

Where do you want us?" an emaciated young girl asked, looking from one person to the other. Another man and two women came in behind her carrying sleeping bags.

"Any place on the floor is fine," Carla answered, showing them where to go. "And once we all go to bed the couch is available."

Kit watched the screen. "This is old footage. It could be from the seventies. If you look closely, you can see how people are dressed. And look at the cops—they don't wear uniforms like that anymore."

Carla moved closer to the T.V. "I think you're right," she said, glancing at Kit. "I remember some of this."

Airy and Fehin turned and stared at each other. "Wolf," they said at the same time.

"Who's Wolf?" Kit asked.

FIFTY-FOUR

Fehin and Airy woke at the exact same moment the next morning. Their eyes met and they both knew what the other was thinking.

"We don't even have to talk out loud anymore, do we?" Fehin asked, moving so that he could place his lips on hers.

Airy pressed into him, savoring the moment. But it was less than a minute later that she pulled out of his embrace. "We have to find out what happened before we lay all the blame on Wolf," she said, swinging her legs off the bed.

Fehin pulled on his jeans. "I've been trying to reach him since last night, but so far I've had no luck. I'm almost positive he has powers. Otherwise, he wouldn't be able to block me out."

Carla was cleaning up when they came into the kitchen. "Where is everyone?" Airy asked, pouring a cup of coffee for Fehin and herself.

"They ate breakfast and took the rest of what I cooked out to share with the others. Kit asked for you two."

"Sorry about all the cooking and food outlay," Airy said carefully, watching Carla throw away an empty egg carton.

Carla shrugged. "It feels good to contribute. I've been holed up here like a recluse since you two left and I feel like I haven't done anything to remedy the situation."

"You've done tons, Carla. Fehin's rehab, giving us your car..."

"What car?"

Airy realized abruptly that all of that happened in the other timeline. "I guess that was before," she said.

Carla paled. "You told me about this on the phone, but it still makes me feel very strange that I have no memory of what went on."

"I'm sorry I said anything," Airy replied, looking over at Fehin.

Carla tried to smile. "Let's concentrate on this reality and what you two accomplished."

"Now we have to deal with the repercussions," Fehin said darkly.

Carla grimaced. "I would suggest a trip down to the local news station where that footage originated."

"How do you know it originated there?"

"I don't, but I recognize that newscaster. He lives here. Do you still think Wolf had something to do with it?"

Fehin and Airy's eyes met. "Yes," they both said.

Carla laughed. "You two are like Siamese twins now. I'll drive you down after you have breakfast."

"WHO AUTHORIZED THE FAKE FOOTAGE, BOB?" Carla demanded, standing in front of the newscaster with her hands on her hips.

"I got a call from the head of Light and Oil. He sent it over."

"You must have known it was old. Why did you go along with it?"

"Because he told me if I didn't, I'd lose my job."

"What's the address?"

Bob stared at her, his gaze slanting toward Airy and Fehin. "He's not someone to mess with, Carla. He's a billionaire and he didn't get there by being nice."

"We'll take our chances," Carla said, winking at Fehin.

Outside the broadcasting studio Carla led the way back to her Range Rover. "How do you feel about confronting this bastard?" she asked once they were all inside the car.

"I'm in," Fehin said, his gaze sliding toward Airy.

"Me too. He can't hurt us."

The building that housed Light and Oil was a glass-fronted high-rise. A guard stopped them at the door. "You can't go in there without authorization."

Fehin waved his hands and walked by the dazed guard. He opened the heavy glass door and ushered Carla and Airy ahead of him toward where another uniformed guard sat behind a desk. Fehin glanced at the list of businesses on the wall above the desk and pointed out the name Bob had mentioned.

Carla nodded. "We're here to see Mr. Crandall," she told the guard.

He picked up a phone. "And who are you?" he asked.

"Tell him I'm Carla, a friend of Bob Freeman's."

The guard pressed in numbers and spoke quietly. A moment later he shook his head. "Mr. Crandall says he doesn't know you."

"Ask again," Fehin said, waving his hands.

A few minutes later they were in the elevator moving upward. When the doors opened on the seventieth floor, Mr.

Crandall was waiting for them. He was balding with a slight paunch and dressed impeccably in tweed slacks, shiny Italian loafers and a dark blue linen button down shirt. His gold cufflinks glittered in the light from the art nouveau sconces on the walls. But with all his fancy clothes his eyes were what singled him out. They were dark, and held not one ounce of kindness or empathy. In a word they were cruel.

"To what do I owe this pleasure?" he asked in a decidedly unfriendly tone.

"Are you the one that authorized the footage of riots from the seventies?" Carla asked, staring at him defiantly.

"Who are you people?"

"We're the ones who are fighting for truth and justice," Fehin said. And then he smiled.

Mr. Crandall's pompous expression crumbled as his gaze met Fehin's. "There's someone you might want to meet before you shut me down," he said, pointing down the hallway. "He lives in apartment seventy-two."

Fehin's gaze narrowed. "Wolf," he muttered. He headed off, Airy and Carla hurrying behind him.

When Fehin knocked he looked completely calm, but Airy felt his frayed nerves as though they were her own. She was terrified, her mind filled with horrible scenarios about what Wolf was up to.

Carla stood apart, her gaze going from one to the other. "Should I be here?" she finally asked.

Fehin turned. "I won't let him hurt you." A second later the door opened.

"What the hell are you doing here?" Wolf asked, staring at Fehin.

He was dressed in a dark suit, his hair slicked back and oiled. His nails were manicured and he had the air of someone who has the world by the tail. The view into his living room revealed black furniture and a lot of glass and steel. Abstract monochromatic oils adorned the white walls. He'd definitely come up in the world.

"You've been undermining what Airy and I accomplished," Fehin said, pushing past him into the hallway.

Wolf looked stunned for a moment watching the two women walk by. "I was only saving what's mine. You were on the way to ruining it. Look, I'm expecting a guest any minute and I'd like you to be out of here before she arrives."

"No can do," Fehin said, staring at him. "Sorry, Wolf, but the bottom just fell out of your investments in prostitution, drugs and all the rest of it."

"I don't think so," Wolf snarled, his eyes going dark. He closed the door behind him, his bulk filling the narrow hall. His expression hardened. "Not if I have anything to do with it. You do realize I have my powers now."

"I figured as much."

"You can't go against me, Fehin. I will always win." He sneered, glancing at Airy and Carla. "And why did you bring them along? You must know I'll kill them first." He laughed. "And I'll enjoy every minute of it," he added, his gaze moving across Airy and Carla as though deciding the best method of murder.

"Look at me," Fehin said sharply, drawing Wolf's attention. Fehin had an expression on his face Airy had never seen before. He seemed to be concentrating and at the same time holding his brother's gaze. For his part, Wolf seemed nearly hypnotized, all his focus on his brother.

"Who let you out of Svartalfheim?"

Wolf laughed, breaking the connection. "Are you still on that? Not that it's any of your business, but the man's name is Pryderi."

"Pryderi?" Airy stared at Fehin. "He's the goddess Rhiannon's son, a demi-god. My mother told me about the horrible stuff he's pulled over the years."

"That's right," Wolf agreed. "His powers put Rhiannon's to shame. She's never been able to control him."

Fehin's expression darkened. He stared into the distance and muttered some words no one could hear. It was only a few seconds later that the door flew open and a hurricane force wind whirled and tore through the hallway, pulling at their clothing and making a high-pitched whistling sound. "What the hell?" Wolf yelled, moving to close it.

But before he reached it, a voice boomed, "Time to face your next exile. And this one will not be so kind."

A pale face appeared and then the rest of the body materialized. A sparkling long black dress made of some fine material clung to her curves, her head nearly touching the nine-foot ceiling. She was fearsome but also beautiful in a dangerous sort of way, especially for one so old. Her hair was all white, long and wild like a witch. But this was no simple witch.

Her dark eyes pierced downward, focusing on Wolf and pinning him like a bug. "If you do not recognize me, son of sorcerers, I will introduce myself. I am Skuld!" The room reverberated with her words. By this time Carla had paled and moved to the door.

Airy heard Fehin in her mind. *I brought her here.* She reached for his hand.

By this time Wolf was cowering against the wall. "Don't make me go back there," he whined like a little boy.

Skuld laughed, her lips turning up to reveal strong white teeth. "I have no intention of taking you back to Svartalfheim." Her eyes narrowed as she reached out, her claw-like hand taking hold of Wolf's upper arm. Wolf let out a piercing shriek and tried to pull away, but she hung onto him. "I am taking you to Helheim where you will be as dead. You will never see the world again. Your father and his consort will be lost to you as will everything you have worked so hard to bring forth." She smiled wickedly and turned toward Airy and Fehin. "I am in your debt," she said, nodding her head once in acknowledgment.

Wolf's expression contorted into one of abject fear, his mouth opening in a scream. But before the sound could come into being, the two of them disappeared. At the same time Carla slumped to the floor.

"Carla? Are you all right?" Airy asked, kneeling next to her.

The older woman's eyelids fluttered for a moment and then opened. "Is she gone?" she whispered.

"They're both gone," Airy assured her, helping her up.

As they moved into the hallway, a fleshy sallow skinned woman arrived, her overly plucked eyebrows rising in surprise. "Where's Wolf?" she asked, her hand going to straighten her wind-blown, heavily bleached hair. Her tight polyester blouse had popped a button, revealing a tired-looking chemise. The word floozy appeared in Airy's mind, although she had no idea what it meant or where she'd heard it.

"He had an emergency appointment," Fehin told her. "I wouldn't expect him back anytime soon."

She stared at the three of them suspiciously and entered the apartment. Apparently, she didn't believe Fehin because they could hear her calling, "Wolfy? Where are you, Wolfy?", as she headed into the living room.

They stopped by Mr. Crandall's apartment/office on the way out to tell him that Wolf was no longer on this earth. The man visibly paled, his hand going to his throat.

"You killed him?"

"He isn't dead, but he may as well be," Fehin answered. "I don't know how much you know about him, but Wolf is not of this world. And the Norn who meted out his punishment isn't either."

Mr. Crandall looked like he might be sick. "Norn?"

Fehin nodded. "Norns are supernatural beings who control the destinies of gods and men. This one comes from a place in the future, and that's where she's taken our friend from room 72. Rest assured, you will never see him again."

Mr. Crandall's mouth opened, but when he began to protest, Airy interrupted.

"And I would suggest you stop your efforts to undermine what we did on that mountain."

His eyes widened. "What *you* did? That's impossible! Have you seen the footage? It's completely faked. Don't know exactly how, but photo shop can do wonders these days."

Airy placed her hand on his arm for a moment and when she removed it Mr. Crandall's expression had gone from anger and disbelief to one of wonder and happiness.

He reached out to shake both their hands. "I'll be sure to include this meeting in the next newscast I'm involved in. You two have changed the face of the planet and I'll do everything in my power to help the cause."

"Make sure you keep it this way," Fehin told him before glancing at Airy. He reached for her hand and nodded to Carla before the three of them headed toward the elevators.

FIFTY-FIVE

Fan was waiting by the door when Carla, Fehin and Airy entered the townhouse. "Where have you been? The people out there have been coming in and out, using the shower and all sorts of stuff. I didn't know how to stop them!"

Carla grabbed her daughter and hugged her close. "I'm sorry we left you alone with this, Fan. You did the right thing. They deserve our help. But right now, I need something to calm my nerves." Carla went to the cabinet over the sink and took down a bottle of dark liquid. "This was the scariest experience I've ever had, including the time I washed overboard on a rafting trip." She laughed weakly, her hands trembling as she poured brandy into a shot glass. She held the bottle up. "Anyone else?"

Airy looked at Fehin who shook his head. "No thanks," she answered.

Fan sat on the couch next to Fehin. "What happened to you guys?"

"You don't want to know," he said. And then he reached over and playfully messed up her short hair, making her laugh.

After Fan and Carla left to do some shopping, Fehin pulled the book out of his pack and opened it to where he'd left the bookmark. "Look at this."

The factions driving the unrest and disinformation surrounding the April fool's day miracle disappeared a few days after they began. Sadly, when the hordes of followers searched for the two young people responsible for what happened that fateful day on the Medicine Wheel Mountain in Wyoming, they were never able to locate them.

"I'd say it's time for us to leave," Airy said, looking up. She closed the book and handed it back.

Fehin stuffed it into his pack. "Are you ready to share where we're going?"

Airy giggled and moved toward him. She put her lips to his ear.

"What about your parents? My parents? Are we going to say goodbye?"

"I'll leave a note for Carla, but as far as my parents go, they can do without me. They never apologized or even hinted that they might be wrong about you. If this was about our being related, they could have been honest." She shook her head. "When the time's right I'm sure I'll see them again."

Fehin stared into the distance. "As long as we have the moonstone, we can visit the future whenever we want, right?"

Airy nodded. "I'm pretty sure we can go to any time we want."

When Carla and Fan returned an hour later there was no sign of Airy or Fehin or any of their belongings. A note lay in the middle of the kitchen table.

Fehin and I have gone walkabout. We both love you and Fan so much. Thank you for everything!

Fin